The Last Snowman

By Kathleen Gilles Seidel

From Lyrical Press e-books

Standing Tall series

The Fourth Summer
The Last Snowfall

The Last Snowfall

Kathleen Gilles Seidel

LYRICAL PRESS
Kensington Publishing Corp.
www.kensingtonbooks.com

LYRICAL PRESS BOOKS are published by

Kensington Publishing Corp.
119 West 40th Street
New York, NY 10018

Copyright © 2019 by Kathleen Gilles Seidel

First Electronic Edition: May 2019
ISBN-13: 978-1-5161-0734-6 (ebook)
ISBN-10: 1-5161-0734-9 (ebook)

First Print Edition: May 2019
ISBN-13: 978-1-5161-0737-7
ISBN-10: 1-5161-0737-3

Printed in the United States of America

To Louis

From your Bubbe

Chapter 1

Richard and Margaret Forrest, known to their friends as Rick and Peggy, were even-tempered, intellectual people. Reading books, discussing meaning and significance or walking through the woods with even more books so they could identify the birds and the wildflowers, these were what they and two of their three children treasured. Their middle child, however, wanted to go to demolition sites and watch things get blown up. A little Tom Sawyer of a kid, Nate Forrest was happy to join the family in the woods, but *walk*? Who would want to walk when you could run?

His younger brother always finished his homework the night before it was due; his older sister seemed to do hers before it was even assigned. Nate did his at the breakfast table a day or so after it was due…if he did it at all.

This apple had fallen quite a ways from the family tree.

They lived in southeastern West Virginia, former coal-mining country, a place that offered few opportunities. Boys like Nate often ended up with crashed motorcycles, dishonorable discharges, and judgments against them for child support payments.

Nate was luckier than those boys. He was a Forrest of Forrest, a town named after his something-great-grandfather who had gotten his start by pitching a tent outside the entrance to the mine and selling dried beans and cast-iron skillets. Nate's own father was the superintendent of schools, and his mother taught first grade. They were sensible enough to know that there was no point in trying to change Nate.

Fortunately, his appetite for risk came with extraordinary physical aptitude. One of his teenage babysitters and her boyfriend looped a little safety harness around his chest when he was barely four and took him to the nearby slopes. He started out skiing, but quickly switched to snowboarding.

At first, he was a miniature meat torpedo, a kid who barreled down the mountain joyously unaware of his speed and the danger he posed to himself and others. His parents, who loved him dearly even if they didn't understand him, found formal instruction for him, and when they saw how hard he worked, they tried to give him all the opportunities they could.

He picked up his first sponsor at age twelve, and by the time he was twenty, he had X Games and FIS Alpine World Ski Championship medals of every color. With his strength and speed, Big Air was his specialty. He muscled his way through tricks, hitting record-setting heights.

Riding like that was risky. Risk-takers get injured, often badly, occasionally enough to end a career. After Nate's last injury, the doctors had warned about spinal fractures, wheelchairs, and paralysis. His usually fearless mother had looked frightened. This was why, on a Sunday afternoon in late March, at age twenty-nine, he was back in his hometown.

He couldn't remember when he had been here last. He had been—not surprising—in the hospital when his grandfather had died and couldn't make it out for the funeral.

A lot had changed in the town over the past decade. The high school had closed. The dentist shut his office. The once-daily newspaper was publishing twice a week. After his grandfather's death, the Forrest family couldn't find anyone to take over the once-thriving hardware store. The beautiful stone building with *Forrest Dry Goods* chiseled into the stone over the door sat empty. The liquor store had expanded, although that wasn't necessarily a good sign. There was a major new construction project east of town, but it was outside the city limits. And Nate's parents had moved away.

He had been seventeen when his father's contract as superintendent had not been renewed. The school board offered him a teaching position. People assumed that if he didn't want to go back to the classroom, he would work in the hardware store. But once Rick and Peggy had sent their daughter off to college, they had gathered up their younger son and did the American thing—they went west, buying a failing winter-sports resort on Oregon's Mount Hood, renaming it *Endless Snow* because Mount Hood was the one place in the United States that had snow year-round.

The family tree had hopped closer to the apple.

The town had been shocked. It had never occurred to anyone, not even the school board, that demoting Rick would cause the family to leave.

After twelve years of very hard work, Endless Snow was a success. Just as the hardware store had been, the resort was a family operation.

Nate's siblings had joined the business as soon as they finished college. Now their spouses worked there as well.

Nate had done his part. He was the face of Endless Snow. He was featured on every web page, on every piece of marketing material. He hosted happy hours whenever he was there. He handed out medals to the kids at the end of the weeklong training camps. He was the brand.

He wasn't a household name across America; only one snowboarder, Shaun White, had ever achieved that. Within the snowboarding world, however, Nate Forrest and his records for height and speed were a big deal.

But now he was on the other side of the country, sitting at the kitchen table of one of his mother's friends, listening her talk about people he hadn't thought of in fifty million years if he had even heard of them at all.

He learned that the McFarlands had so many tomatoes last summer that they ended up leaving them in a box outside the liquor store for the construction workers to take…that the last winter had been dry and warm, and people were worried about scale on their bushes…that the Lutheran congregation had gotten so small that it was having to share a pastor with a church in the next town over. And the high school closing! What a shame that was.

The school systems around here had been so strapped for money that several years ago they'd consolidated into a county-wide system with only one high school. "The county seat is only twenty miles away," Nate pointed out. That didn't seem too far to do the Friday Night Lights thing.

"It's not the same." Mrs. Pritchard sighed. "There were always bake sales and car washes going on. You remember how the marching band would get out of class to play in the elementary school Halloween parade? That was so much fun. The little kids loved it, but the new school won't let the band come this far in the middle of the day. If only your father hadn't left…he could have saved the high school."

"I can't say, ma'am."

He was relieved when his phone chirped. He had warned Mrs. Pritchard that he was being picked up, so she broke off in mid-sentence and waved him to stand up.

"You know a storm's coming," she cautioned. "You boys need to be careful."

"We'll be fine."

Indeed, the sky outside was low and charcoal-colored; the air was thickening. When Nate had made his flight reservation this morning, he saw that the airlines had suspended all change fees in and out of the West Virginia airports because of an impending "weather event." He wasn't worried. Snow had always been his friend. While the rest of the county was dreading the storm, he was eagerly waiting to be picked up by another longtime friend, Pete Willston. As kids, they had had plenty of adventures together. Nate wasn't going to let their being grown-ups get in the way of that.

Pete was Nate's only friend outside the snowboarding world. They'd been in kindergarten together, and Pete, unlike everyone else Nate knew, had a normal life. He and his wife, Cheri, another kindergarten classmate, owned a garage in Frederick, Maryland, a rapidly growing suburb north of Washington, DC. He had come back to Forrest to work construction, something that made Nate wonder about how the garage was doing.

Nate was at the curb in front of Mrs. Pritchard's house when a midsized green pickup with Virginia plates pulled up. Nate reached the driver's side door just as Pete was getting out. They each had their right hand out, but the handshake quickly became a left-arm man hug. They were glad to see each other.

Pete was two or three inches shorter than Nate. Before he and Cheri had moved to Frederick, he had done four tours in Afghanistan, and his skin was still leathery from the harsh sun. He carried himself like an army veteran—seasoned, compact, and dense, with muscled posture and close-cropped hair.

The army had turned Pete into a wizard of a mechanic. If a part was supposed to move and wasn't, Pete could get it unstuck. If it was moving and wasn't supposed to, he could get it to behave. He could fix anything.

"This was some kind of sudden trip," he said to Nate.

That was true. Nate had decided to leave Oregon only this morning. "I was pissed at my family. They think I am too much of a wild man to have anything important to do with the business."

"And suddenly flying all the way across the country into a snowstorm is going to convince them of your maturity?"

Pete might have a point there. "I'm not seeing any snow," Nate said. "It looks like you're all upset about nothing."

"Let's hope. The system's moving slower than expected. So when it does get here, we'll be hammered because it's going to squat down and stay." Pete reached for Nate's backpack. Nate had spent too much time sitting around airports in wintry weather not to take his computer and a toothbrush everywhere. "We've got to go out to the job site to pick up Hex. There'll be time to show you around."

Hex was Pete's German shepherd. Nate had been visiting Frederick when Hex had been a fuzzy little puppy. Pete had wanted to name him Tool or Wrench, but Cheri wouldn't let him.

"So, what's up with your family?" Pete asked as he pulled away from the curb. "Why are you pissed at them?"

"It's my little brother. We were having this family meeting about long-range planning. I don't usually go to those, but I figured that since I am done competing, it was time."

"Are you really done with snowboarding?"

"With the serious part. I'm not supposed to leave the ground, which kind of makes it pointless. My last spill was a sparkler, and I don't think I'm cut out for life in a wheelchair."

"I wouldn't bet on that. You would have figured out something."

Nate laughed. "Like how to injure myself even if I were paralyzed from head to toe?"

"Something like that. But why are you mad at Cooper?"

"He went on and on about my value as a pretty face, how I represented the resort to the public."

"That's true, isn't it?"

"It sure as hell is." It had been a lot of work. "I don't even get parking tickets because that would reflect badly on the brand. I mean, seriously, am I the sort to have a clean driving record?"

"You would seem to err on the side of speed."

"It hasn't been easy, that's for sure, but I am squeaky-clean. Anyway, Cooper was saying that this was such an important contribution—which I know—but then ten minutes later, he was talking about how we needed to develop a more aggressive relationship with kids because dear Nate's value had a shelf life."

"He wouldn't have said that."

Pete liked Nate's brother. Once Nate got serious about his sport, he was gone for most of the year. Pete had played catch with Cooper, let him hang out in the locker room with the high school football team, and helped him with his little pinewood derby car. Sometimes Nate felt like Pete was more a part of his family than he was.

"Okay, those weren't exactly his words. He said that my Q Score would diminish with time. But he was clearly saying I was about to be a has-been."

"Isn't that inevitable?"

Now, this was the trouble with guy friends. Any pretty lady would have cooed and gone all goopy about how hard his fate was and how awful his brother was. Not Pete. "Sure, and I don't want to be one of these pathetic has-beens lurking around, trying to get something going for themselves again."

"I'm missing something here," Pete said bluntly. "You don't want to try to outlast your marketability, and Cooper wants to prepare for that day. It sounds like you're on the same page."

"I'm not saying I want to walk away from Endless Snow. I always assumed that I would take a more active role in the management, and Cooper shot that down. And my sister was right there with him. I am a piece of meat to them, out there risking my neck year after year for the resort. They think I'm some kind of hothead who can't be trusted around a balance sheet. Or probably even a bedsheet."

"What kind of role did you envision for yourself? Were they specific about why that wouldn't work?"

"Okay, so I hadn't gotten that far, and I probably should have thought things through a little more."

"That is useful in running a business," Pete said mildly.

Well, yes, it probably was.

Nate was done talking about this. He must be sounding like a big whiny-pants crybaby. What did he really have to complain about? He could walk and run without pain. He had plenty of money. So his family didn't treat him like a god? Oh, boo-hoo.

"Did my folks ever ask you to come out to Oregon to work at Endless Snow?" he asked...although that wasn't a complete change of subject.

Pete nodded. "As soon as I got out of the army. Absolutely, they did. And it was a good job. Head of engineering."

"Why didn't you take it?"

"Cheri didn't think she should be that far from her mom, since they only have each other. Then after your grandfather died, they asked if I wanted to take over the hardware store, but by then things were going well in Frederick."

Nate had not known any of this. Clearly his family trusted Pete more than they did him. That didn't make him any less pissed off at them.

"So, the garage's still doing well?"

"It is. Some of the people around us have really long commutes. It's hard on their cars and great for us. Cheri's got us looking into opening another location."

That wasn't the answer Nate had expected, but he was glad of it. He knew that Cheri, with her endless enthusiasm, had been the force behind Pete taking the risk to open a business. It was great that the gamble had paid off. "If the business is doing so well, why are you here?"

"I came out supposedly for a week or so as a favor to a guy whose cars we work on. But right away the company offered me this salaried position that had great benefits, and if Cheri's mom moved into the house, they'd let me pick up coverage for her. If I stay on until construction's finished, there's a big bonus, and we won't have to pay through the nose for money to open another garage. At least that's the plan."

Once the mines had closed, the area's best hope for economic growth was either tourism or a prison. But the state already had a correctional center in Beckley, and the feds had a minimum-security camp in Alderson. There had been several attempts to build a resort in the mountains east of town, but this time it seemed to be working. The investors had fifty million dollars for top-of-the-line snowmaking equipment, a luxury spa, a hotel complex, and pricey condominiums. Construction had been going on for nearly two years. That's why Nate had to stay with his mother's friend. Out-of-town construction crews were taking up all the rooms in a twenty-mile radius.

The resort was to be named Almost Heaven after the John Denver "Country Roads" song. The song began "Almost heaven, West Virginia" and then ignored geographical realities after that. The Blue Ridge Mountains were in Virginia and North Carolina, and the Shenandoah River skirted into West Virginia for only a small fraction of its run, but most West Virginians believed that the songwriters had nailed the "almost heaven" part.

A new bypass road led out to the Almost Heaven site. The county had gotten the construction company to help pay for it. Its four lanes skirted town and were keeping all the construction and interstate traffic from lumbering down Main Street.

"Parts of the site still look pretty bad," Pete warned, "as ugly as strip-mining. But these DC guys are all about resource efficiency and environmental responsibility. If you're going to build in the mountains, this is the way to do it."

Pete slowed as they came to the construction gate. The guard waved them on through to a big gravel-covered lot. Although it was Sunday, the lot was nearly half full. Clearly there was a Sunday shift. The front row was almost empty, all the spaces marked with white *Reserved* signs. Those spots must be for the bigwig types who didn't work on Sundays.

Nate was a little surprised when Pete steered into one of those spots. *Reserved for Head Equipment Manager*, its sign read.

"Is that you?" Nate asked.

"In my dreams," Pete grumbled. "The electricians hate their guy, so they are always coming to me. And the laborers...I keep telling them that they aren't equipment, I'm not their manager, but it doesn't seem to make a difference."

So, Pete's dream would have been to manage *only* the equipment. "But you are head equipment manager?"

"It means that I don't get overtime."

They tromped up a temporary path to the construction area. Pete was obviously fascinated by the green construction techniques, and he went on and on about the roof gardens, the active and passive solar features, and all kinds of other grown-up things. Clearly he could have stayed for hours, but it had already started to snow, and he wanted to take Nate to the other side of town to see the new residential construction sites too.

"It sounds like the new housing is near the high school," Nate said as they walked back to the parking lot.

"Not near. On. The developer bought the property from the schools and took everything down."

"Even the stadium?"

"Even that."

"Did the new school go up a league?"

"Jumped straight to Triple-A, and the coach, he's good."

What a difference that might have made in Pete's life.

Pete's parents had both come from mining families. Without mining work, his dad had tried to pick up odd jobs in good weather, but being this close to the mountains, the town had a lot of bad weather. Pete's mom had cleaned houses in a town where almost everyone cleaned their own. Nate's tactful parents called children like Pete "underserved." Everyone else called them poor.

Pete had been a remarkable football player, but Forrest High had played in the A league, the one for the smallest schools, and the coach hadn't known anything about college recruiting. Pete hadn't had a chance at college money.

As they came to the parking lot, a few snowflakes started to fall. Pete pulled out his phone and made a quick call. "You can send him out now."

At the edge of the parking lot was a one-story, vinyl-sided building with a fenced-in yard off to the side. The door was opened from the inside, and a handsome German shepherd appeared. He had a tan chest and head. Black saddle markings flowed across his back and hindquarters. He really was a good-looking dog.

"If that's Hex, he sure has changed." Nate had forgotten that they were going to pick him up.

"The company set up a kennel so people could drop off their dogs. You're supposed to sign them in and out, but if I am in a hurry, they'll let him out. They trust him."

Indeed, the dog, instead of charging through the parked cars as any dog Nate might have trained would have done, carefully trotted around the perimeter of the parking lot, avoiding the cars. He carried himself with confidence and dignity, as if he knew that his owner had a parking space in the executive row. His ears went up when he saw Nate. Nate put out the back of his hand for Hex to sniff, and in a moment or two Hex decided that Nate was an acceptable companion.

The shift was out, and workers were streaming into the lot. Car doors were slamming, and engines were starting, some grinding, some coughing, a few racing. Pete turned on his windshield wipers to clear the light snow and then pulled into a line of cars waiting to pass through the construction gates and head back down the mountain.

By the time they reached the bypass road, the snow was falling more heavily. The steep, rocky terrain had softened into low, rolling hills and more friendly soil. Little groves of beech trees clustered near the creek bed, and occasionally a grand old oak tree stood majestically in the middle of a sloping pasture. Not enough snow had fallen to hide the earth. The rough pasture grasses poked out of the thin coating, and the potato fields on the hillside were marked by ridges of stubbly brown separated by furrows of white.

Traffic on the bypass was heavy in both directions. Nate had never seen anything like it in Forrest. "Isn't this a lot for a Sunday?" he asked Pete.

"Sunday afternoon often gets bad. All the guys—and the women—who went home for the weekend are coming back just as the shift ends. And now everyone is trying to beat the snow. But as long as traffic keeps moving, it will ease up in fifteen minutes or so."

The road took a bit of an S-curve, and suddenly Pete had to put on the brakes. A hundred yards later they were at a dead stop. For as far as they could see ahead, cars sat on the road, their back windows dusted over with snow. "It's the DC drivers," Pete groused. "They can't drive in the snow. Let me go look at the median ditch, see if we can turn around."

Before he could get out of the truck, an SUV in front of them tried to make a U-turn and got stuck in the mud hiding under the fresh snow. The driver gunned his engine. His tires spun and sank deeper in the mud.

"Okay, we're not going to try that." Pete unzipped his parka and wormed his way out of it. Nate did the same. Apparently they were going to be here for a while.

Pete opened an app on his phone. If they got moving in forty-five minutes, he said, they would be fine. But those forty-five minutes were going to be crucial. The wind was already picking up, the snow would increase, and darkness was coming.

Pete's phone chirped. Pete looked at the screen and asked Nate if he minded Pete taking the call.

"Not a bit."

Pete mostly listened for a few minutes and then started to sound annoyed. "What did they think would happen... When has that ever worked?... Oh, for God's sake...tell them to...okay, okay, I'll take care of it." He disconnected the call and stuck the phone into the cup holder.

Clearly someone had screwed up, and Pete was expected to provide the solution.

It had now been thirty minutes since the traffic had stopped, and the snow was coming down hard. Without the wipers on, snow was coating the windshield, and the cab of the truck was growing darker. Hex shifted uncomfortably in the narrow space behind the seat. Pete's phone chirped again.

"Is it okay if I take Hex out for a minute?" Nate asked.

Pete nodded, already engrossed in the call. Nate put his coat back on. "Does he need a leash?"

"Hex?" Pete muffled the phone against his chest. "No, he's good, and we're outside the city limits. There's no leash law out here."

Hex scrambled out from behind the seats and trotted around the truck to check out things in the median strip. Nate followed him, glad to stretch his legs. The SUV wasn't the only vehicle that had tried to cross the ditch and had gotten stuck. The tow trucks would be busy tomorrow.

Everything that an hour ago would have been mud and dried grass was now fresh and white. The snow did that, made the world beautiful.

A man was walking down the line of cars, carrying a red gas can. The can was swinging so easily that it had to be empty.

Nate rapped on Pete's window. "Do you have any extra gas?"

Pete made a face. What kind of idiot goes out in a snowstorm with the fuel needle on empty? "It's in the back. You can give him a couple gallons."

Nate made a big waving gesture to the man and then dropped the tailgate of the pickup.

"I don't have much cash," the man said.

"Don't give it a thought." Cash was one thing Nate had plenty of.

Pete had two five-gallon gas cans next to a big plastic tub secured with a bungee cord. Curious, Nate opened the tub. Inside was everything you need if you got stranded: blankets, water, a tow chain, flares, flashlights, beef jerky, some dog food, and a slab of cheap chocolate. Nate's grandfather had always been prepared like this.

Pete had worked in the hardware store right up until he left for the army. Nate supposed that Pete had spent more time with Grandpa, had learned more from him, than Nate ever had.

I am not a part of this. I don't belong here. For all the time Nate had spent in wintry weather, he carried an AAA card, not his own tow chain.

The wind increased, the snow increased, the darkness kept coming. Traffic on the other side of the median was stalled too. Pete was getting impatient. "The bitch is, once we get moving, this is going to happen again. It's not like sitting here has taught people how to drive any better."

After eighty-seven minutes, the traffic started to move. The snow was coming down hard. "We're getting off," Pete said as he turned the engine back on, "or we will be here the rest of our lives."

He managed to get in the right lane in time to turn off onto the next county road. Nate couldn't figure out where they were.

"Don't you remember?" Pete said. "The back of the Byrd place is up ahead, and after that is the big burnt-out barn."

"That's still there? Isn't that where we—"

"Why don't we try to forget about that?" Pete interrupted. "I might have left one or two things off my job application."

They had been kids, maybe eleven or so, and it had been summer. They never had enough to do in the summer. So, the day after the barn had burnt, they had ridden their bikes out and started kicking around the ashes, because they were eleven-year-old boys without enough to do.

Nate had poked at one of the collapsed beams with a stick. Suddenly an orange ember glowed in the dark char. They fed it with a few pieces of dried glass, and they had a flame. The flame started to travel, to grow. And grow.

They were horrified. They didn't have a bucket; there was no water. They stamped on the flames, trying to shove dirt with their hands, and finally had to beat them out with their shirts.

The scorched shirts meant they had to tell their families what had happened. Nate's mother, furious and embarrassed, called the volunteer fire department to go out again. "Oh, Nate," his father asked, not for the first or the last time, "what were you thinking?" And Grandpa had put both boys to work breaking down boxes at the hardware store.

All these years later, no one had pulled down the rest of the barn. Pulling down a barn cost money, and people around here didn't have money.

The truck's headlights swept along the barbed-wire fences and the telephone poles. In the fields, the cornstalk stubble poked out of the snow. The farm pond at the Byrd place was a dark bull's-eye; the winter ice must have melted in an early thaw.

Visibility was poor. Pete was driving slowly. For a while there had been a pair of red taillights glinting through the snow ahead of them, but that vehicle had been going faster, and they couldn't see those lights anymore. A horn blared behind them, and Pete pulled close to the shoulder to let a minivan speed past.

The next warning was a deep, long blast from an air horn, and the cab of Pete's pickup grew suddenly bright from the headlights from a big rig. "I'm as close to the edge as I can get," Pete told the rearview mirror. "Just don't accelerate when—"

Metal screeched against metal. Nate jerked forward against his seat belt. The pickup spun, the road disappeared from the windshield, and they were sliding, going down. A gunshot exploded, something slapped hard into his chest and face. His ears started to ring. He was trapped against a big white balloon.

"What the hell was that?" The balloon was deflating with a hissing whine. He started coughing. The air was thick with something powdery and white.

Pete was coughing too. He was batting his airbag down, trying to twist in his seat to check on Hex. "That was a rig that accelerated when it was passing us. The back end of his trailer whipped out and hit us."

"What's this white crap?" It certainly wasn't snow.

"It's talc. They pack the airbags with talc so the folds don't get stuck."

Nate kicked his airbag under the dashboard and used his sleeve to wipe the grit off his face. This was a different adventure than he had been hoping for. Pete was getting out of the truck. Nate opened the passenger door and sank to his bootlaces in the snow. The pickup was angled into the ditch, its headlights sending a faint glow from inside a snowdrift.

Nate shuffled through the snow up to the road. Grainy white pellets whipped against his face. Pete was shining a flashlight on the rear of the pickup. Hex was next to him, a dark dog-shape amid the swirling snow.

The back tires of the pickup were on the shoulder, leaving the rear of the truck almost in traffic.

"How bad is it?" Nate asked. "Any chance we can get out without a tow?"

"Nope. That's why I drive a company truck. Stuff like this happens all the time."

"How long will it take for a tow?"

"Forever. And we aren't calling. The tow trucks need to be taking care of people who are in real trouble, not us."

Oh, right. Good old West Virginia self-reliance didn't rely on tow trucks. A fellow looked out for himself around here.

Hex suddenly let out a warning yip and shoved at Pete's thigh, forcing him to grab the pickup to keep from falling. Over the whine of the wind, Nate heard a rumble. The rumble grew louder. He stumbled and slid down one side of the pickup while Pete and Hex skidded down the other. Pete shone the flashlight on the road, alerting the oncoming hauler to their presence. Not slowing at all, it lumbered past with a blast from its air horn, missing the end of the pickup by only a foot or so.

Two near-death experiences within ten minutes…they hadn't managed that even when they had been a pair of teenage idiots.

"So, what was this about us not being in real trouble?" Nate made his way back to the road.

"Okay, I should have said 'people without resources.'" Pete dropped the tailgate. "We have resources. The usual advice is to stay with your vehicle, but we're too likely to be hit again. So, let's grab some stuff and hunker down in the burnt-out barn. It's not that cold. We will be fine until we can find someone to come get us."

And they would have beefy jerky, cheap chocolate, and bad memories. "There were lights on at the Byrd place. What about if we cut across the field and throw ourselves on old Mrs. Byrd's mercy? Is she still alive?"

"She was at Christmas."

Pete handed Nate the gas cans, telling him to put them in the ditch away from the truck. No point in making a collision even worse. Nate then reached into the truck and scooped up his backpack.

"Any chance we could get lost?" he asked while Pete was setting the flares. Standing in the bed of the pickup, they had been able to see Mrs. Byrd's lights, but they'd lose them once they started walking. "It'd be a shame to end up frozen in a haystack, two little orphans lost in a snowstorm."

"We aren't orphans, no one makes haystacks anymore, and we have a dog. We won't get lost."

"It feels like Cheri ought to be here." They might not have liked girls when they were eleven and starting barn fires, but soon enough they had discovered that their summer adventures were more fun if Cheri was with them.

"Easy for you to say," Pete answered. "You're not the one who would have to carry her if she was wearing the wrong shoes."

He had a point there. Not that Nate would mind bending his knee and having Cheri put a foot on his thigh to swing up on his back, but Pete was her husband.

They crossed the road, slip-slided down the other ditch, and set off across the pasture, letting Hex guide them. Their flashlights carved yellow tunnels of light through the snow. Except for the back of Pete's coat and an occasional glimpse of Hex's dark hindquarters, the world was white.

In a few minutes they reached the crest of the field. Along the ridge was a windbreak, the line of cedars planted to break the power of the wind. It was quieter within the protection of the trees, and the snow was less deep. They could walk side by side. At the end of the trees, they had to go back to trudging single file. Hex led them up a little swell. Mrs. Byrd's yard lights appeared, one suspended from an iron arm arching off the side of the hog barn, another on top of the old steel windmill.

The wind had scraped parts of the farmyard almost clear, driving the snow against the sides of the outbuildings in drifts as high as the latches. The faint tracings of one set of car tracks led to a brick outbuilding that must be used as a garage. The driver's footprints leading to the back door were now only little hollows in the powdery snow.

Hex led them to the back door. Nate knocked, using the side of his hand to get a deeper sound. The wind was loud enough that a person of any age might have trouble hearing a knock, and old Mrs. Byrd had been "old Mrs. Byrd" for long as he could remember.

An outdoor light came on. The curtain covering the window in the back door twitched. Nate ducked so that Mrs. Byrd could see Pete's more familiar face. The door opened.

This was not old Mrs. Byrd. This was *so* not old Mrs. Byrd.

Chapter 2

The woman who answered the door was about their age. She was holding the collar of a Siberian husky, keeping the dog close to her jean-clad thigh.

She wasn't beautiful-beautiful like the women with blond hair, breast implants, and a life goal of hooking up with professional athletes. She was better than that, with a natural wholesomeness to her even features and golden-brown freckles. Her hair, the color of shelled hickory nuts, was long and wavy, spilling over the shoulders of her flannel shirt. Strong cheekbones and a strong jaw were softened by full, curving lips. Even her dog, with a coppery coat and white face and paws, was a handsome creature.

"Pete, what a surprise. Come in." She was smiling, sounding pleased. "Get back, Tank." She let go of the dog's collar and shoved him with the side of her leg. "Give them some room." She knelt down in front of Pete's dog and scratched Hex behind his ears. "Hex, my man, you are one wet doggie, aren't you?"

Then she looked up. Her eyes were warm, a golden-hazel color.

"You must be Pete's friend Nate."

"I am indeed."

Coming home might have been an immature impulse, but it was looking like a good choice now. Pretty women were always a mood elevator…at least until they weren't.

They were in a bead board–sided mudroom. It had hooks on the walls and a big vinyl mat inside the door.

"I had no idea you lived here." Behind Nate's shoulder Pete sounded hesitant. He hadn't moved away from the door. He hadn't started to kick the snow from his boots, and he wasn't unzipping his coat. "I thought Mrs. Byrd…although I guess it makes sense…I'm sorry…"

What was going on? Nate looked at him curiously. All afternoon Pete had been confident and decisive, a model West Virginia guy. He had good tires and carried extra gas and beef jerky. People called him when no one else could figure things out. And here he was sounding as nervous as he had been the first time he had asked Cheri out on a real date.

"I've been living here with Dr. Byrd's mother ever since I came to town." The woman spoke easily. She wasn't showing any of Pete's awkwardness. "But she fell in January, broke her hip. She likes to think that she's going to come back from the nursing home, and she doesn't want to rent to strangers, so I'm still here."

"I guess that makes sense," Pete said again.

Not to Nate it didn't. He pulled off his glove and put out his hand. "I'm Nate Forrest," he said even though she already knew that. "Pete and I grew up together."

Her handshake was firm. "Lacey Berryville."

"Dr. Berryville," Pete put in.

"You're a physician?"

"No, a veterinarian." Her hair moved as she shook her head.

So it did make sense. Old Mrs. Byrd's husband had been the town veterinarian. His son had joined the practice. The senior Dr. Byrd had died while Nate's family was still living in Forrest, and the younger one became *the* Dr. Byrd. Lacey Berryville must be working with him. A place to live was probably one of her benefits.

Since Pete still wasn't saying anything, Nate explained the mishaps that had led them to this doorstep. "We were going to see if old Mrs. Byrd would let us wait here. I don't think she much liked the pair of us, but she was friends with our grandmothers."

"At least with Nate's grandmother." Pete finally spoke. "And I'm sorry. This shouldn't have happened." He still seemed awkward. "I was watching the weather, but then we had to sit on the bypass for more than an hour."

"You did seem like the last guy on earth to get caught in a storm." Her voice was warm. She knew Pete, she liked him. "But it can happen to anyone. In fact, it sounds as if it is happening to everyone tonight."

"So, I hope you don't mind if we hang out here while we try to scare up a tow."

Nate glanced at Pete again. Hadn't he said that they weren't going to try for a tow until morning?

"Of course," she answered. "You must be hungry. I actually cooked. I made chili."

The kitchen was what Nate would have expected of a farmhouse kitchen, large and inefficient, with metal cabinets and Formica counters. A good-sized dog crate was in one corner next to the metal feeding bowls. The table was set for one. The place mat and cloth napkin were blue, and the dishes were green and white. Next to them were a blank crossword puzzle and two sharpened pencils. A pair of candles was burning. Grated cheese and chopped onions were in little saucers. Nice touches from a woman in flannel shirt.

By now her dog, his light blue eyes glittering, was sitting in front of Nate. Nate had put out his hand for the dog to sniff, but the dog was ignoring the hand and sniffing closer to Nate's hip.

"He's hoping you have treats in your pocket," Lacey said. "Shove him away." She snapped an elastic band off her wrist, swept her hair back into a ponytail, and went to the sink to wash her hands. She wet them thoroughly before pumping some liquid soap into one palm. Her hands were nicely shaped, and they looked strong, a little broader than most women's hands. She began rubbing her palms together, the fingers interlaced, the soap lathering up between them. She started massaging her right palm against the back of her left hand, then switched.

Nate was fascinated. She was chatting lightly about the weather, paying no attention to what she was doing. Without looking at her hands, she started rotating one thumb in the other fist.

If she were obsessive-compulsive, she would have been watching what she was doing, but Lacey Berryville was doing this automatically. She was a health care professional whose training spilled over to the rest of her life.

Pete had taken his phone out of his pocket and stepped back into the mudroom. As Lacey was reheating more chili, he came back into the kitchen. He mumbled something about trying again in an hour or so.

All afternoon Nate had felt as if Pete were winning. He was clearly at the top of his game, while Nate had no idea what game he was supposed to be playing. But talking to a pretty woman—that was something Nate could do and do quite well.

When they sat down to eat, he asked if she did indeed work with Dr. Byrd.

"*For* would be the correct word." The county had been declared a veterinarian-shortage area. By working here for three years, she was getting a large chunk of her student loans forgiven.

"We have nearly the same debt as medical students," she said, "but a fraction of their earning power."

She had been here for two and a half of her three years, so she had seen the changes the construction had brought. Few of the men had brought their families, because they weren't planning to stay once the construction was finished. They didn't have the right skill set for working at the resort when it was completed. They lived like itinerants, filling the motels, renting rooms in people's homes.

"But at least, thanks to Pete, they can bring their dogs. That improves the quality of their lives."

"Are you talking about the kennel I saw out at the site?"

Although the motel in town allowed pets, guests couldn't leave the animals locked in their rooms all day. So the workers had been taking their dogs out to the site, chaining them to the fence, leaving food and water. It wasn't a great solution, and it nearly became a disaster when some bored high school kids thought it would be great fun to sneak through the gate and cut the dogs' collars.

"That sounds like the sort of thing I might have done," Nate said.

"Not to a dog," Pete responded. "Even you wouldn't have done that to someone's dog."

Nate shrugged. He had always gone a little crazy in the summers when he was away from the snow.

Fortunately the high school kids were stopped after two or three dogs, and no great damage was done, but the company had issued a prohibition against the animals.

And a couple of the best workers quit. It was hard enough for a guy to be here without his family. For some of them, a dog's companionship was the only thing that made life tolerable.

Pete had already been trying to get the company to put up a day kennel. Now that he could show that employee retention would improve, the company agreed, as long as a veterinarian signed off on each animal's health records and would act as liaison with the county's part-time animal control warden. Pete had approached Lacey. That was how they had gotten to know each other.

Dogs, kennels, retention rates on construction sites…Nate was sure that those were all fascinating topics, but he was interested in this woman.

"Now, Lacey, you are a veterinarian. What else? Where are you from?"

"We moved around a lot."

"Military brat?"

She laughed and shook her head. "Hardly."

She wasn't being very informative. "Are you going to tell me why you laughed? If you won't, I'll muscle it out of Pete."

"No, you won't," Pete said. "Even if I knew something, you couldn't get it out of me, but I don't know a thing."

"It's the idea of my parents being in the military," she explained. "They were both attached to the music industry. My father was a photographer, and my mother was a makeup artist for glam-rock, hair-metal bands. They met while on tour with one of the bands."

"That's not your usual veterinarian ancestry, is it?"

She smiled. "It was all before I was born, but they wanted to be the center of attention themselves. They thought they were too creative to have ancillary jobs. They didn't have any success with their own music or art, and they didn't know how to move forward after that. They eventually split up, and my mother became a yoga instructor. We moved around so much because she couldn't seem to find a studio that appreciated her."

Endless Snow had once hired a yoga instructor who had floundered through one year at the bottom rungs of the pro circuit. In her yoga classes, she tried so hard to make the guests believe that she had been important that it made them uncomfortable, and Nate's parents had had to let her go.

He wondered if Lacey's mother had been like that, always name-dropping, always trying to prove that, like Marlon Brando in that old movie, she could have been a contender.

Nate supposed that he had a leg up on those ladies. He had been a hell of a lot more than a contender. Did that make it better or worse?

Well, that wasn't something he was going to think about now.

They were done eating. Although Lacey waved for him to sit still, Nate cleared the table. As a kid, he and two other guys, Seth Street and Ben Healy, had trained together, chaperoned by Seth's mother. When they were on the road and she couldn't cook in the little camper they traveled in, she had looked for all-you-can-eat buffets, because the three of them ate so much. Then Mrs. Street had always insisted that they leave their table immaculate. She had promised the other two moms that she would make sure they learned to clean up their own messes.

Pete tried making some more calls, but he came back in the kitchen, shaking his head. "I'm sorry, Dr. B. I hate—"

"I thought we were done with the 'Dr.' thing," Lacey said.

He ignored her. "I hate to impose on you, but it doesn't feel right to make someone come get us, not when there are people with kids stuck in their cars. So, do you mind if we wait here until morning? We don't need beds or anything."

"You may not need them, but you're going to get them. There are three empty bedrooms upstairs." She held up her hand when Pete started to protest again. "Stop it. I'm going to win, you know I am, so come help me make up the beds."

Nate got up to follow the others out of the kitchen when he felt his phone vibrate. It was his mother. He murmured an excuse.

"Mom?"

"Nate, where are you? Are you okay? Marge Pritchard called me. She's worried sick. She says there's no visibility on the roads."

Nate winced. He should have checked in with Mrs. Pritchard. "I'm fine," he said. "I'm with Pete. We're at old Mrs. Byrd's place."

"You are? How is she doing?"

"Crappy, I assume." He explained that she had fallen and that Dr. Byrd's assistant was staying in the house.

His mother got sidetracked with some questions about Mrs. Byrd's fall, none of which he could answer, but eventually she circled back to her main point. "You need to call Marge right away. I gave her your cell phone number, but she didn't want to bother you."

"I will, but, Mom, I was with Pete. If we didn't kill ourselves in middle school, we aren't going to start now."

Mrs. Pritchard was relieved to hear from him, and then, even though she had been right to be alarmed and he had been a jerk for not thinking to call her, she apologized endlessly for worrying.

He had to go through the living room to get upstairs. The room reminded him of his grandparents' house, except there was a fireplace where Grandma and Grandpa had kept a piano. He could hear some movement overhead. He supposed that Lacey and Pete were doing the sheets and towels thing. He picked up his backpack and headed up the stairs.

And for a moment—a very unpleasant moment—he stopped. Maybe he shouldn't go up there.

No. Pete hadn't even known where she lived, and he had been uncomfortable about intruding on her. That wasn't the dynamic of two people having an affair.

And Pete was married. Nate knew that didn't matter to some people, but it would to Pete...and it certainly would to Cheri.

Both dogs were upstairs watching Pete and Lacey make up the beds. Lacey's ponytail was low at the back of her neck; it had swept over her shoulder when she bent to tuck in the sheet. As soon as her husky noticed Nate, he came over to the door, his ears up, his tail wagging. Clearly he was a very friendly animal.

"How can I help?" he asked.

"Go to the bathroom down the hall. There should be some extra toothbrushes in one of the drawers. Then you can see what kind of men's clothes Mrs. Byrd's grandsons left in the other room. They stayed with her when I went to my brother's wedding."

The toothbrushes were sealed into little plastic cases imprinted with the name of the dentist Nate had gone to when he was a kid. These giveaways were what his family had always used. He had his own toothbrush, but he got one out for Pete. In a drawer he found some mismatched men's sweats, the kind a guy would leave at his grandmother's house, knowing that one of his cousins might need them too.

Thanks to the time change, Nate's day had been three hours longer than usual. He could use a shower. He had clean underwear rolled up in the corner of his backpack, but not a whole change of clothes. He assumed that the grandsons wouldn't mind if he declared himself a cousin for the sake of clean laundry.

Back downstairs, Lacey was alone in the living room, sitting in one of the big nubby-covered chairs, working on her crossword puzzle. Her dog was sleeping at her feet, curled up in a ball, his tail covering his nose. She had taken off her shoes and was rubbing her sock-covered toes into his dense coat. Nate watched her feet for a moment. They rose and fell with Tank's breath.

"Is there wood?" he asked. "Can I build a fire?" He shared a chalet on the grounds of Endless Snow with his two friends Seth and Ben, and its fireplaces, like all the ones at the resort, were fake. Gas jets spurted flames over inflammable, artificial logs. The flames were real, and they looked pretty enough, but a real wood fire crackled and smelled like Christmas.

She nodded. "Mrs. Byrd had some trees taken down last year. The wood is stacked by the garage, but it will be covered in snow."

"I'll manage."

It was still snowing. The back-door light glittered against the snow on the ground, and the snowflakes that fell inside the light were puffy and white against the dark night.

The snow brushed right off the wood; the wet hadn't soaked in. He stacked a couple of loads in the mudroom and raided the recycling bin for paper.

In the living room, Lacey was now on her phone. Nate picked up some old publications from the American Veterinarian Medical Association and twisted them into sticks to use in place of kindling. He laid the fire and then crumpled up a few sheets of the local newspaper and struck a match.

"That was Mrs. Byrd," Lacey said when the call was over. "She's says that it's fine that the two of you are staying here and that your sister should have gotten married in town."

"My sister? Jill? But we had already moved to Oregon by then. That's where she met Rick. His whole family was from around there."

"Apparently that is an inadequate excuse."

"Inadequate excuse for what?" Pete asked as he and Hex came into the living room.

"My sister's wedding."

"Well, yeah. She was a homecoming princess. Those girls are supposed to get married in town. But no one should expect it of your sister, not after the way the paper treated her."

"I think she's over that," Nate said mildly. He didn't really know much of this story. He hadn't been around during his or his sister's high school years, but Jill was certainly a high-functioning individual now.

"Good. I was just talking to our class's little homecoming queen"—he was referring to Cheri—"and she is about to murder me for not letting her know that you were coming. She's always trying to find an excuse to come out."

"Does she want to move back?"

"She thinks she does, but housing is a bitch. Her mom's friends are already renting out their spare rooms. The company gives me a trailer on the site, but sometimes other guys have to crash there. It's no place for her."

"Could her mom manage the garage on her own?"

"If we needed her to, but she worked so hard out here, a single mom with her own business, that I like the idea of giving her a break."

The fire was doing well. Nate was pleased with himself. The smaller logs were catching. Soon a pleasing fruity smell was spiraling out from the flames. Pete said that the wood must be from an apple tree.

Nate liked interesting smells. He always had, but he couldn't identify the source of firewood by the scent of its smoke.

"This is nice." Lacey sighed. "Mrs. Byrd and I never made fires because she was sure that all the heat went right up the chimney."

The flames were airy ribbons of orange and red, twisting and crowding each other trying to reach up into the dark chimney, led on by the pale smoke. The dampness on the logs' rough bark sizzled and popped.

This wasn't about thermal efficiency.

"If you get up," Nate said to her, "I'll move your chair closer to the fire."

"I don't want you to go to any trouble."

"It's more trouble if you don't get up," he pointed out. He circled around to the back of her chair and leaned over her to grasp the chair's rolled arms.

"No, no," she squealed. "I'll get up."

She was looking over her shoulder, laughing. Her laugh was light and bell-like. Some wisps had escaped from her ponytail, and her hair smelled like oranges and something deeper—amber, perhaps.

Then he saw Pete. His friend, his longtime friend, was staring at the fire, his lips narrow. Pete couldn't flirt with Lacey. He couldn't tease her, bend over her to pick up her chair. He was married.

And there was no way Nate was going to make it any worse for him. No flirting with Dr. Lacey Berryville.

"What do we hear about the weather?" Nate gestured toward the TV. It was old and bulky with the bulging back that TVs used to have.

"We only get five channels," Lacey said. Not surprisingly Mrs. Byrd didn't have cable or an Internet connection. "But the cell reception isn't bad."

Pete was checking the weather on his phone. This would be the last blizzard of the season, but the stalled wind pattern was turning it into a bad one. Visibility was poor; the highway patrol was blocking the bridge over the river and the entrances to the bypass; people were being urged to shelter in place and be prepared for prolonged power outages because ice could be coming in the early hours of the following morning and maybe again in the late afternoon.

"Do the Byrds have a generator?" Pete asked.

"A small one, but it's primarily to keep the pipes and pump from freezing."

Nate put another log on the fire. The flames instantly started to circle up around it. He had built a good fire. He stood up and reached into his pocket for his phone. It was an automatic gesture. He wasn't sure what he was going to do, check his messages, play a game, check the new releases on Netflix, whatever he would usually do sitting around the VIP frequent-flyer lounge of a snowed-in airport.

But he wasn't at an airport. This room, with its crocheted afghans, the ribbon-tied baskets of dried flowers, and the hulking TV, was a time machine back to a friendlier way of life.

As long as he was here, he wanted to really be here, to have West Virginia be someplace different.

"How about if we play a game?" he said to the others. That's what they had done at his grandparents' place.

"No way." Pete said. "You're too competitive. You'll do anything to win."

That was true. "What about Scrabble?" That was the one game his sister and brother would play with him. "I am really bad at it. I can't win."

Lacey was pretty sure that Mrs. Byrd had a Scrabble game. She went to get it. Nate lifted the coffee table up over her chair and set in front of the fire. Pete shoved an ottoman over for himself. Nate figured he would sit on the floor. He could tend the fire more easily from down there, and since he was no longer wearing a body brace and a cast from ankle to thigh, he could get up and down without a forklift.

Lacey came back with a faded maroon box held together by duct tape. She unfolded the board, and they drew out their seven tiles.

It was immediately clear to Nate that the other two were indeed much better than he was.

As the game progressed, it was also clear that they were playing not to lose rather than playing to win. That gave him a chance. He looked at his letters, a bunch of crappy one-pointers. He needed a five-letter word to go off of Pete's *B*. He laid down *LINT. Blint.* That looked like a word, didn't it?

"'Blint'?" Lacey asked. "Is that a word?"

Nate had absolutely no idea. "Are you challenging it?"

"What's the penalty if I am wrong?"

"I think you lose your turn," Pete said.

"Oh." Lacey looked at the score sheet. "Then I won't. It doesn't give you that many points."

"But it does me," Pete said. Adding an *S* to Nate's word, he spelled out *SPACKLE*, the *A* covering the Triple Word square. "And that's a Scrabble. Fifty extra points to Petey-boy."

This was exactly what Nate had been hoping for. "I'm challenging it," Nate said.

"What, 'spackle'? You know what spackle is."

"But I don't know what 'blints' are. That's what I'm challenging."

"Oh my God." Lacey leaned back in her chair, laughing, raising her arms to release her hair from the ponytail. "You are the most complete and total jerk. You knew that 'blint' wasn't a word."

"I did not," Nate protested. "At least not one way or the other. Why would I know a thing like that?"

Pete found the official Scrabble dictionary on his phone. "'Blints' is not a word, so Petey-boy loses his turn." He started picking up his tiles. "'Blint' isn't either, but I suppose the statute of limitations has passed on that one."

"I'm fine with letting it go," Lacey said, "because look at me. I'm going to rock this one." She laid down a *Z*, making *blintz,* then followed the *Z* with an *A* and an *X*, the *X* hitting the Triple Word square. "That's seventeen points for 'blintz'…and nineteen times three…seventy-four points in all. Beat that, fellas."

Nate had not considered the possibility of a *Z*. "'Zax'?" He puzzled out how to say that nonword. "And you say *I* make things up?"

"Are you challenging it?" she asked, teasing him, daring him.

Her eyes were sparkling, the corners crinkling. This pretty lady liked him.

But before he could do something stupid, Pete spoke. "Don't. It is a word. It's a tool for working with roofing slates."

"Why did you tell him?" Lacey complained. "Why didn't you let him lose a turn?"

"Because he doesn't have a prayer of winning."

"Don't count on that," Nate said brashly, even though he agreed with Pete completely. Lacey had left them in the be-spackled dust. "I am not a quitter."

Twenty minutes later, the two men made her pick up the game as the penalty for winning.

"That was really fun," Nate said.

"You didn't mind losing?" Lacey asked as she scooped up the tiles. "I would have thought you liked to win."

"I like to *compete.* As long as I've got something to fight for, I'm going to have fun."

"You don't care about the outcome?"

"Sure. Winning is even more fun. But if you've done your best and someone is better, what are you going to do about it?"

He stood up quickly. He didn't want her to ask the question the pretty ladies always asked. They would lean forward, their voices would lower, their faces would get all soft and pitying. *But aren't you going to miss snowboarding?*

Was he going to miss the one thing he had built his entire life around? Did he want to pass out participation certifications, matter only because of what he had done, not because of what he was doing? Well, duh...

And why would anyone ever ask a question like that? What earthly business was it of theirs?

But apparently it had never occurred to Dr. Lacey Berryville to ask the question. She was instead talking to Pete, asking him if he had heard rumors about dogfights out at the RV park, and Pete was all of a sudden going on and on about how Lacey should never go out there by herself. She should send Dr. Byrd.

"I don't 'send' Dr. Byrd anywhere," she pointed out. "He's my boss."

"Then call me," Pete insisted. "If I can't go, I'll get one of my guys to go with you. There are some tough customers out there now."

"I appreciate your concern," she said evenly, "but I can take care of myself."

It was a brush-off, and Pete didn't like it, but what could he do? He was married.

Chapter 3

Tank was a three-year-old, gorgeous, purebred Siberian husky, but in personality he would forever be a human two-year-old: curious, mischievous, absurdly friendly, and randomly stubborn. Lacey treated him firmly and consistently, and one of the rules was that Tank slept in his crate in the kitchen. But when Lacey stood up after the Scrabble game, he trotted confidently up the stairs, not pausing to look back to see if she was planning on enforcing those silly little rules of hers.

Had he been a German shepherd like Pete's Hex, he would have been trying to protect her. There were strangers in the house; a German shepherd or a Rhodesian ridgeback would think he should sleep outside her door. But Tank was a husky. He wanted to see what he could get away with.

She had let him win, although she did make him sleep on the floor. She wasn't going to have him snoring in her ear all night. But the next morning she regretted letting him in the room at all. At 4:38 a.m. his nose on her hand woke her up. He must have heard something in the house.

"Relax," she told him. She wasn't going to get up. "It's Pete and Hex. It's nothing to worry about."

But what if Pete and Hex were having a party? Tank wouldn't want to miss that. They might have snacks. Tank loved snacks. He pattered over to the door and gave a sharp little howl. So much for not getting up.

Lacey let him out. She reached for her bathrobe, then stopped. Pete would be dressed. She needed to be dressed too. She couldn't go to the kitchen even in her thick, fleece-lined, incredibly unalluring bathrobe.

Pete was attracted to her. When he had first brought Hex into the clinic, he had treated her with the reserved respect that blue-collar guys often show toward women. Such women, because of their education and authority, were from such a different world that they barely seemed human.

Although she wouldn't admit it to herself, Lacey was lonely. She quickly discovered that Pete was intelligent and open to new ideas. She admired his work ethic and the way he fought for the guys who he supervised. She liked his military posture and sense of command. As they worked together to open the kennel, she treated him like an equal, which, of course, he was. In the beginning she had asked him about the green construction techniques at Almost Heaven, and then they moved on to other environmental issues. He was better informed on those matters than she was.

They grew comfortable with one another, and he became aware of her as a woman. He watched her. He longed to help her in the way that a man helps a woman, carrying even the smallest load that she might be bringing to the kennel. He tried to hide it. Not only was he married, but he was a high school graduate while she was Dr. Berryville. She was invited to dinner by the people whose houses his mother had cleaned.

As much as he tried to hide his feelings, she could tell. She had been flattered to have a man like him admire her, and she did have moments of wanting to be more aware of herself as a woman. In retrospect, she could accuse herself of encouraging him, knowing in her heart that he was safe.

Above all, he had been safe. He was reserved, respectful, and definitely married, going out of his way to mention his wife in all their early conversations. Having a man like that admire her had lit a spark, igniting her awareness of herself as female, even feminine. So, yes, she might have encouraged him because he was safe. He would never presume. The distance between them was, in his mind, too great.

But what had been safe for her had been painful for him.

So, she had forced herself to be careful. When he had offered to check one of the tires on her truck, using the compressor at the site, she had refused, driving into town to the air hose at the gas station. She wouldn't let him help her anymore. She was a colleague, a pal, but never a woman. He was already too aware of that, and it was her fault.

She looked out the window as she pulled on her clothes. The snow had stopped. The pale wintry moonlight reflected up off the snowy fields and washed everything with a silvery gray glow. The T-shaped uprights of Mrs. Byrd's clothesline poked out of the snow. The ropes between them sagged and glittered. The ice must have come in. She would need to put the chains on the tires.

Pete was at the kitchen counter, waiting for the coffee to brew, talking on his cell phone.

"Yup…yup…" he was saying. "Mile marker seven…you'd better give me thirty, thirty-five minutes to get there...seven…see you there."

Even at this hour, he had found a way to get to work. That didn't surprise her. He was responsible for all the construction company's equipment; if those trucks were going to help out on the public roads, Pete would be the one to authorize it.

"I owe you an apology," he said as soon as he got off the phone. "I looked up the Scrabble rules last night. You only lose five points for a bum challenge, not your whole turn."

"I'm so risk-averse that I probably wouldn't have challenged him even then. It sounds like you're heading out. Are you going to make it to the road okay? The snow's pretty deep."

"I'll be fine. I'll have Hex break the path. But then I'll have to send him back because I have no idea where I am going to end up. So, can he stay at work with you and Tank, and can you drop Nate at the Pritchards'?"

"Of course. Just leave the gate open so Hex can come to the door. Don't you need something to eat? I could make you a sandwich, pack you a lunch." She tried to think of what she had in the refrigerator. Eggs, but he wouldn't want to wait while she hard-boiled them.

"No, no. There's no need. I'll find something."

Right. A half box of stale doughnuts, a squashed PowerBar, and a can of tuna fish he would eat out of the can with a plastic fork—that was the sort of nutrition he would have to fuel an eighteen-hour workday. But what could she do? Even if she did have sandwich makings, he wouldn't want her making one for him. It would be too domestic, too much a husband-and-wife sort of thing.

He had brought his coat in and draped it over the kitchen radiator, warming it. He started to put it on. "Feel free to put Nate to work. He can shovel the drive. He's plenty strong."

Lacey had noticed that. Oh yes, she had. And not just his strength, but the pulse in his throat, the shape of his fingernails, the freckles on the backs of his hands, the tiny scar on his left thumb, the fit of his jeans—they had been cut for a less-toned man.

Why hadn't she told Pete the truth? *No, it is not fine. No, you cannot leave this man here.*

This had never happened to her before. Of course, she had been aroused in the past, but never like this. She had never felt such instant, overwhelming physical yearning. The little flush she had felt with Pete was a wispy birthday candle compared to this.

She had been on one knee, greeting Hex, her fingers tunneling into his wet cold fur. Down at the dog's level, she had first seen Nate's boots. They had been covered with snow. The knots in the laces would be too stiff to untie. She'd had time to think that, time to notice that while she was still scratching Hex, still looking at Nate's boots.

Then she had looked up…and immediately, instinctively flexed her hands open, afraid that her touch might burn the dog.

She had seen pictures of Nate; the clinic kept copies of magazines in which he was featured. The pictures had shown his chiseled features, his unruly, curl-twisted, sun-streaked sandy-brown hair, his dark green eyes. But the camera hadn't captured his crackling energy, the quick play of expressions dancing across his face, and the alert intelligence in his eyes. She had felt the blood rushing to her skin as if everything in her was struggling to get closer to him, to become a part of him.

She didn't remember standing, but she must have, because suddenly she was in front of him and he had taken his gloves off and his right hand was reaching for her.

Yes. *Yes.*

She gave him her hand. Why didn't he jerk his away? Didn't he feel the burning?

For all his strength, he was lean and flexible. He was shrugging off his coat with an easy grace. He balanced effortlessly as he pulled off his boots. His shoulders were broad under his sweatshirt, and when he turned to hang up his coat, she saw that the back pockets of his jeans sagged. His gluteal muscles must be taut and sculpted.

Pete was strong. All the construction workers were strong. They were the guys who charged the trenches first, who worked double shifts, who tested a bridge with their own weight. She herself was strong. She could lift an eighty-pound dog onto an examining table.

If Nate Forrest were only a hunky piece of beefcake, she would have laughed at herself and moved on, but he was more than just a physically compelling individual. He seemed completely alive. He was quick, witty, glowing, incandescent. Larger than life.

She and her younger brother had only met a few of the musicians who her mother had worked with, but some of them were like this, radiating a kind of power that only celebrities had. Lacey had been mesmerized by what seemed like a magnetic field surrounding them, but her brother had hated them. "Mom isn't herself when they come."

And her brother was right. People like that turned you into something that you were not. Look at her. She had already told him more about her parents than she'd ever told anyone.

So, no, it was not fine for Pete to leave him here. *Take him with you. Lock him in the car, tie him to the fence. I'd have you arrested if you did that to a dog. But I don't care, just don't leave him here.*

She could not be alone in the house with him.

What was she thinking? Of course, she could be alone with him. She was Dr. Berryville. She could treat a pet canary one day and a farmyard bull the next.

She poured herself a cup of coffee and sat down at the kitchen table with her phone. She would check the weather. She was Dr. Berryville. That was all she needed to do, to keep reminding herself of that. The weather mattered to the dairy cattle and the chickens.

Seven inches of snow had fallen yesterday, the blizzard winds bringing occasional periods of near-zero visibility. Then a layer of air had warmed, and the precipitation had changed to ice. A round of sleet was expected in the next hour or so. She went on to the town's municipal website. The big roads and the river bridge were closed to everyone except the Highway Department staff and its volunteers trying to help stranded motorists. Both the city and county plows had been working all night; the construction company was going to help, but so many people had abandoned their cars that it had been impossible to make much progress.

Tank had gone back to sleep. The room was warm enough that he was sprawled out on his back; in very cold weather a husky would curl himself up, his tail covering his nose. In a few minutes she heard Hex's bark at the back door. He was heated and panting, having run home, but he was relaxed. If something were wrong, if Pete needed help, then Hex, good German shepherd that he was, would be barking and yipping at her, nudging her toward the door. How nice it would be to have a dog you could trust like that, but a husky like Tank could almost never be off-lead. They were bred to run; running along a road or across an open field was more fun than anything. A loose husky wouldn't be running away; he would simply be running for the joy of running.

Nate Forrest must be like that, she guessed, born to move. Professional athletes had to be. And if he was born to move, he was probably born to move on. But she was going to move on too.

She knelt down to dry Hex off, but Tank wanted to get involved. Wasn't this towel-drying a fun kind of game? She pushed his flank with her shoulder. When that didn't work, she gave a firm command. He acted as if she had hurt his feelings no end, but he did obey. She was drying Hex's paws when her phone rang. It was her boss, Bill Byrd. The mayor was asking businesses not to open. People needed to stay inside until the weather calmed down and the road crews could get things under control. "So, unless the Mattson bull gets worse, you need to sit tight for the day. It's too bad that this had to happen on a Monday. We're not boarding anyone, are we?"

"No." Their vet tech lived close enough that she could have walked to the clinic if they had had any animals there. "I'll call Valerie. She will have today's schedule."

Valerie was their office manager. She always made a photocopy of the next day's schedule before she left in the evening.

Dr. Byrd kept up with advances in veterinary medicine, but he was not a good businessman. The clinic ran as it had when his father had opened the practice. The appointment book was a big green spiral-bound ledger, and the staff had to make individual reminder calls about upcoming appointments. With more of the construction workers bringing their dogs to town, Lacey and Dr. Byrd added hours to their schedules, but the office manager hadn't wanted to hire more help for the front desk. She said the new clients were temporary, that things would go back to normal when the construction was finished. So, the staff was overworked. Mistakes were made in the appointment book, and the reminder calls didn't get made.

The clinic desperately needed to upgrade. Clients were frustrated at how long they spent on hold when calling for an appointment. Dr. Byrd had purchased some software that would allow clients to book routine appointments online. It would be linked to the phone line so that patients would be reminded of appointments through robo-calls, emails, and text messages. On a day like today, it would only take one command to take care of the whole schedule.

But he had made the purchase two months ago, and so far, no one had had the time to figure out how to install it. All of today's calls would still have to be made one at a time. Lacey called the office manager to be sure that was going to happen.

"I will certainly call everyone on Dr. Byrd's schedule," Valerie said in her usual thin voice, "but you can call your own clients, can't you?"

Of all Dr. Byrd's poor business practices, his handling of Valerie was the worst. He let her assume too much authority. She was the sort of person who, having no children of her own, felt qualified to judge everyone else on their parenting skills. From the beginning, she never let Lacey forget that while Lacey might have a DVM behind her name, she was still just another employee, one who was much less senior to Valerie.

So, Valerie did not want to make Lacey's calls for her.

"I don't have any of the numbers," Lacey pointed out. Valerie did not have the capacity to scan and transmit anything from her home; she could barely do that at work. "You would have to read them all to me over the phone, and that would take a long time."

"But less time than having to make the calls."

Less time for her, but the aggregate time would be considerably more. Lacey was not going to be manipulated into this. "Dr. Byrd doesn't like him or me making non-medical calls. Clients try to get us to diagnose too much over the phone."

"Well, okay..."

Lacey knew better than to end the call with Valerie feeling put upon. The woman would find some way to punish her. So, Lacey handed her an olive branch, a tiny bit of gossip. "Pete Willston was stranded here last night. You know him. He started the kennel—"

"Of course, I know who he is. They say his dad had a big drinking problem. Was Pete out there by himself?" Valerie's voice was full of eager disapproval.

Pete's dad...a drinking problem? Lacey hadn't known that. She had known that his father had died, and his mother had gone to live with his sister in North Carolina. This was the first she had heard of a drinking problem.

No, it probably wasn't the first time she had heard of it. It was more likely that she had heard and forgotten. This was the sort of thing Valerie would have mentioned the first time Pete's name had come up, but in Lacey's early days in West Virginia, she had determinedly ignored gossip, not having yet realized that gossip could be valuable. The more she knew about a family, the better care she could provide to their animals.

"No, Pete wasn't by himself." That would have been a juicy piece of gossip for Valerie. "His friend Nate Forrest was here."

"Rick and Peggy's boy? The snowboarder one? What's he doing in town? His sister didn't get married here."

"So I have been told."

"What's he doing here?"

"Visiting Pete."

"Where's he staying? That construction company has booked the whole motel, hasn't it?"

"I think he is staying with one of his parents' friends"—and Lacey anticipated the next question—"but I don't know who."

"It would have to be Marge Pritchard or Pris Clemson, wouldn't it?"

"As I said, I don't know."

"Or it could be one of the teachers from the schools, couldn't it?"

It took another few rounds of Lacey not knowing and one more reference to Nate's sister's wedding before Lacey could finally hang up and feed the dogs.

She stepped back and watched them eat. What good-looking dogs they both were, powerful and well-formed. Hex was proudly German shepherd, black and tan. Tank, her beautiful Tank, was copper and white with his eyes glittery blue.

He must have sensed her gaze. He looked up at her questioningly. She made a little gesture. No, everything was okay. He went back to eating.

Hex was bigger than Tank, more loyal and certainly smarter, but Tank… Lacey couldn't believe how much she loved him. For all that she was a veterinarian, he was her first pet. She and her brother had always wanted a pet; they had envied families who had pets, but her parents didn't want to be bothered. After Lacey left home, she knew she couldn't afford one. Now she couldn't imagine her life without him.

As badly as she felt that Mrs. Byrd probably wouldn't be able to live in the farmhouse again, she did feel a deep thrill of relief. Both of them loved Tank, but with Mrs. Byrd unable to come home, when Lacey left Forrest in August, Tank would be coming with her.

Not long after that she heard footsteps overhead, then water running in the bathroom, and finally Nate's tread on the stairs. Expecting to leave, he was carrying his backpack and was dressed in his own clothes again, a gray hooded sweatshirt and the jeans made for a guy with a flabbier butt.

She wasn't going to look at him. No, that would be rude. She could at least look toward him. The logo on his sweatshirt had black writing—*Street Boards.* Between the two words *"& Snow"* was inserted in red letters.

Then the logo moved toward her, the words swelling. He was breathing. Why was he doing that? She let her eyes move up a bit. His pulse beat lightly beneath his skin just as it had last night. The vertical muscles rose from beneath his collarbone, powerful and well defined.

West Virginia was built on muscle. The Indians hauled dirt and stones in baskets on their backs to the tops of their massive earthworks. Oxen had strained to pull wagons over mountains; pioneers had dug boulders out of fields. Men had plunged into the earth to dig the coal. The mines, railroads, and factories had sweated together to win two world wars.

Here all that was again, that muscle, that power.

She needed to stop romanticizing this. He had a strong neck because he was a snowboarder. Snowboarders wore helmets. They turned their heads a lot. Their necks got strong. Period.

"You're up early," she said pleasantly. "Pete's already left. He got one of the company's big trucks to pick him up by the side of the bypass. What would you like for breakfast? I have eggs. I always have eggs. The farmer down the road brought them to Mrs. Byrd, and he kept it up. They are so much better than you can get in the supermarket. The yolks are more yellow, they stand up higher."

She was talking too much. How could he possibly care about the yolks of some eggs?

"I'll just help myself to some coffee if that's all right," he said, gesturing toward the pot.

It was a nothing of a gesture. He'd bent his elbow, flipped his wrist, and pointed his finger…but he had almost touched her.

The Sistine Chapel…God's finger a millimeter from touching Adam's, the touch that would launch all of human history.

Aren't you making a bit much of this?

Not necessarily.

Nate gestured to the pot again. "May I?"

"Oh, of course. Definitely."

He spoke over his shoulder as he poured the coffee. "I'd like to get out and do some shoveling, if that's all right with you."

"I would appreciate it, but there's no rush." She explained about the roads being closed. "I'm afraid you're stranded here for the day."

"All the more reason for me to start shoveling. I was the sort of little kid who could almost behave during school except when they cancelled recess. I could not handle that."

"Did you drive your teachers nuts?" It was fun to think of him as a squirrely little boy.

"Lord, yes. Especially my first-grade teacher. She was my mom."

He must have had a different sort of mother than she had. "Then you go shovel." She was going to spend the day cooking.

She had never been a kitchen person until she had moved to West Virginia. Her parents had eaten out a lot, both of them believing themselves far too creative to cook. But Mrs. Byrd put a proper supper on the table every single night, and Lacey felt obligated to help. When Mrs. Byrd came down with a cold she couldn't shake and then an uncomfortable case of eczema, Lacey had taken over. She had found that she also enjoyed other aspects of homemaking, selecting place mats and napkins that looked nice with the dishes, stopping on her way home from work to pick a few wildflowers.

She had originally been mystified as to why Mrs. Byrd hung out her laundry when she had a perfectly good electric clothes dryer in the far corner of the mudroom. But Lacey quickly discovered the pleasure of pegging laundry on a sunny day, smoothing the sheets over the line, hanging the whites in the brightest sunlight, watching the wind ripple through them. In the winter she did use the dryer, finding pleasure instead in folding the clothes while they were still warm instead of waiting until they were cold and wrinkled as she had always done during vet school.

Cooking was still a science to her; she wasn't experienced enough to be creative with a recipe. But she had always liked her lab science courses, and Mrs. Byrd had plenty of cookbooks.

Mrs. Byrd bought a side of beef every year because that's what she had always done. The neighboring farms kept her well stocked with pork and chicken. Lacey shivered her way through the mudroom and down the cellar steps to forage in the big chest-style freezer. She got the microwave to work on defrosting, and she started chopping. It seemed like the perfect thing to be doing on a snowy morning.

While her onions were browning, she went to look out the front window. Hex was running free, but Tank was secured to the driveway fence with a long chain. Nate was shoveling. The dogs were fine. There was no reason to stand at the window watching.

But she did.

Nate was like a perfectly trained, perfectly balanced animal. He took small, quick bites at the snowbank, bending at his knees, keeping his back straight, letting his legs do the work. The snow arched off his shovel in a neat spray. He reached his arms forward the exact same amount each time; he lifted the shovel to the exact same height each time. Each step he took was the exact length of the one he had taken before. But it didn't look robotic; it was the dance of a Lipizzaner stallion. She couldn't move away from the window.

Fortunately, her phone rang. Otherwise she might have let the onions burn.

The call was from her boss. He wanted to know what antibiotics she had with her. She was very well stocked. Whenever bad weather was forecast, she always gathered up extra supplies. "Are you worried about Mr. Mattson's bull?"

He admitted that he was. "You'll be able to get out, won't you?"

She was miles closer to that farm than he was. "I'll put chains on the truck, and if the roads don't get plowed, I'll get out the dogsled."

"Tank would love that, wouldn't he?" He had a soft spot in his heart for Tank.

They had found Tank tied up to the railing of the clinic's back steps when he had been about six months old, just when a husky's need for exercise started to overwhelm some owners. There had been a note in a child's handwriting: *His name is Tank. We have to leave him behind. You will love him.*

How many times had she and her brother come home from school to find the car packed? *We're moving, kids. Come on, it will be fun, an adventure. No, we won't have space for this... Why would you need that?... We can buy another...*

At least this family had cared enough to pretend to their children. *The people at the animal hospital will take care of him,* they would have told them.

"This really isn't fair to us, is it?" she had asked Dr. Byrd.

"No," he said reluctantly. "But he does look like a purebred, and with these workmen coming to town, it wouldn't hurt you and Mother to have a dog in the house."

"But a husky?"

"Well...it might not be the best breed for protection—but look at him... he's a beauty."

So Tank had come to live at the farmhouse.

Huskies were the sailors of the canine world. They loved the one they were with. If Tank got lost and another family took him in, he would forget about her just as he had forgotten about the family who had tied him to the back steps of the clinic.

But if that happened, it would be years before she would stop thinking about him.

When it was time for lunch, she put her coat on and went out the back door. Not only had Nate finished the driveway, but he'd shoveled the path to the back door as well. It would have taken her the whole day to do that, and she would have been exhausted.

His coat was hanging on a nearby fence post. The snow along the fence had been trampled down by the dogs' paw prints. The sunshine, although thin and watery, made the snow glitter. It was beautiful, but anything that melted today would refreeze tonight, making the ice even worse in the morning.

Nate and the dogs were on the other side of the garage. Tank was now fastened to the windmill. As soon as he saw Lacey, he strained at his leash. Why should he be chained when his pal Hex got to romp around?

Nate was clearing the garage door. Without his coat on, she noticed something different. Again, he was using his legs, protecting his back by reaching deep rather than forward, but there was just a moment when he was throwing the snow off his shovel and there was a slight break in the smooth rotation of his spine. The energy should have flowed from his lower spine in a smooth, even snakelike uncoiling; instead there was a hesitation, a tiny hiccup. It didn't cause him pain; the movement was identical time after time, but it was an imperfection in what had seemed like a perfect body.

She walked down the drive to look at the county road. The plows hadn't been through yet, so the road was a smooth ribbon of snow. Nate had cleared a track a couple of feet beyond the end of the driveway, clearly hoping to make it easy to turn into the plow's eventual path...which would work unless the driver decided to shove all his scraped-up snow into this conveniently empty spot.

Lacey turned back toward the house. Fresh snow lay in soft white pillows on the branches of the cedar trees. The faded red of the empty dairy barn was bright against the snow, and the creamery, which Lacey had thought of as being white, had a gentle pink glow. The snow changed all the colors. She didn't use to be the sort of person who noticed things like that.

She was now. How lucky she was. She had taken the job with Dr. Byrd because of the financial advantages; she had paid attention to little else. West Virginia's wild beauty was the most unexpected, undeserved blessing.

How she wanted to stay—the apple blossoms, the sharp smell of the wild ramps, the blaze of the maple trees, the way kids tugged at their mothers' coats when they saw her on the sidewalk—"oh, look, look, there's the Berry-doctor lady." But there was no point in thinking about it. She couldn't stay. She had to leave in August. Dr. Byrd's next assistant needed to be someone who could eventually buy the practice. As much progress as she had made on her loans, she still had some debt. Her next job needed to be in a bustling suburban practice where clients were willing to spend thousands and thousands of dollars to keep their pets alive for another few months.

This would be her last snow in West Virginia.

Nate and the dogs followed her back inside. "It smells so good," he exclaimed as soon as he got in the kitchen. "I sure hope that some of this is for lunch."

The beef stew needed to simmer some more, and she was going to freeze the meat loaves unbaked, but the chicken curry was ready.

Lacey used to pour orange juice and fill a cereal bowl for her little brother when their parents weren't out of bed yet. David had always thanked her, but he had been a delicate child without much of an appetite. He rarely finished his Cheerios.

There was nothing delicate about Nate Forrest. He took a glorious animal-like pleasure in the food she had prepared. He asked if there were enough curry for him to have more. Lacey wished she had another potato to add to this evening's stew. She had forgotten how much some men could eat.

He helped her do the dishes, then said, "It's really nice out. Are there any other outside chores that need doing?"

The hay barn needed to be painted, and the chicken coop reroofed. It didn't seem like ideal weather for those chores, but Lacey had a feeling that if she had paint or shingles, Nate wouldn't have let the weather stop him. "I do need to put the chains on the tires."

"Great," he said eagerly. "Let's go."

This wasn't Lacey's favorite job. It involved laying out the chains, backing the truck over them, and then crawling around to fasten them, but Nate did all of the crawling while she stood there watching his deft moves.

"Now what?" he asked, dusting off his hands.

She thought. "There's nothing left to do outside. I'm sorry."

Why was she apologizing? Why was she trying so hard to keep him entertained? Because he was a high-spirited, good-looking celebrity?

Yes, of course. She was a woman, wasn't she? How could she not act a little differently around such an attractive man?

But she had no room in her life for larger-than-life men. She thought of some women she had known in vet school. One had fallen in love with a man who insisted on living in San Francisco, a city so expensive that she had no hope of paying off her loans. Another had transferred out of their school, one of the best in the country, to finish at a much less prestigious school—because she had fallen in love with someone who wanted to open a bar on the beach.

Of course, there were plenty of good stories, happy stories, but the potential bad decisions were what stuck with Lacey. She had debts to pay. She had no one else to rely on. She felt fortunate to have done as well as she had. Now was not the time to get sidetracked by a pretty boy.

"I need to go inside and do some computer work," she said. Then because she couldn't help herself—he was a guest, after all; she could make some effort—she went on, "You can take the dogs out. It is not humanly possible to give Tank enough exercise."

Nate liked that idea. He liked it a lot. When it came to effervescent enthusiasm, clearly he and Tank were soul mates. Lacey wouldn't have been surprised if the very dignified Hex became embarrassed to be seen in public with them.

They were gone for well over an hour. When they returned, Hex's flanks were heaving, and Tank attacked his water bowl as if they had been running through the Sahara. And Nate had been wearing snow boots. That was impressive.

She had made no progress on the software, and it didn't take Nate long to figure that out. "Are you having problems? One of the guys I hang out with is stellar at things like that. Let me call him. He'll get a big charge out of feeling useful."

Lacey shook her head. "It's supposed to be easy to do."

She had a code that was supposed to let her download the software. Thank goodness the clinic paid for her cell phone. Who knew how much data this would eat up? She set up her phone to send a signal to her computer, logged on, found the right website, and then nothing. She looked for someplace to enter the code. She read the same introduction over and over, waiting for a box to appear. It didn't. She checked the Terms and Conditions box. That didn't help.

"It can't be this hard. It simply can't be." She hated feeling this helpless. "I'm sure there's one little thing that I'm not doing right, but I cannot figure out what it is."

"Then let Ben figure it out." Nate reached across the table, grabbed her computer, and pulled it toward him.

Whoa. Lacey sat back, startled, not sure what to do. She didn't like this, not at all. Trying to pick up her chair while she was still in it had been a joke. This wasn't. This was her work computer. You didn't just grab that away from someone.

Okay, this was a long way from wanting her to change schools or move to San Francisco, but still...why did some men think that their Y chromosome gave them an all-access pass to everything? Being a celebrity would only make things worse; people probably let Nate Forrest get away with lots more than this.

But what would be served by grabbing the computer back? She had no idea how to get this program to download.

At least he wasn't acting as if he knew everything. He was already talking to his friend. Ben Healy was another guy he had grown up snowboarding with, Nate explained while Ben was logging on to his own computer. "But Ben's done with the sport and is turning himself into a computer nerd. It's kind of whack, but he's good at it."

Ben wanted to open the website on his computer. Nate gave him the URL. "Ben wants to know if you have asked their help desk."

"We tried that last week. They don't call back."

He repeated that to Ben. Ben didn't like it.

Lacey had no interest in sitting here, looking at the back of her computer. If she was going to be treated like the little woman who stayed home and baked cookies, she would do just that, bake cookies.

She got up to look through Mrs. Byrd's recipes. Nate had Ben on speakerphone, and as she was getting the eggs out of the refrigerator, she heard Ben say, "You need to download the test version and then activate the full version from here."

Lacey almost dropped the eggs. So it *was* simple. "Where on earth does it say that?" she demanded.

"Nowhere." Ben had obviously heard her. "They're assuming that you knew."

"None of us did."

While the two friends were each waiting for the test version to download, they started talking about other things. Ben was still on speakerphone, so Lacey could follow the conversation. They were obviously meeting up in North Carolina next weekend for another friend's wedding.

Ben was able to download the program in much less time than Nate. "We are getting the signal through her phone," Nate told him. "The house doesn't have Internet."

"What are you doing at a place like that?"

"I don't know, but something has started to smell good."

Lacey had just opened the cinnamon and the ginger.

Finally, Nate was able to activate the full version. Ben could see enough on his own computer to help Nate customize it for Dr. Byrd's clinic. Except for repeating the clinic's address and phone number several times, Lacey was able to concentrate on her cookies. Eventually Ben had to hang up, but he told Nate that Nate could ride without training wheels. Nate was still working when the first batch of cookies was out of the oven. Lacey used a spatula to put a few on a plate, and as she set it in front of him, she told him that they were hot and that he should wait.

He didn't, and a second later he was blowing on his fingertips, shaking them in the air.

Some people were good about waiting for fresh baked goods to cool; some weren't. Nate Forrest was clearly in the "weren't" category.

As Lacey was drying the mixing bowl, he linked his hands behind his head. He had taken his sweatshirt off. His shirt was long-sleeved, a black T-shirt knit with a henley collar. Its logo was for the Endless Snow Resort, the one his family owned. His eyes still on the screen, he started to stretch, pushing his elbows back and then pulled them forward, but in the forward movement his range of motion was greater on his left side than his right.

He dropped his arms and patted the chair next to him. "Come look."

She sat down and leaned forward to look at the computer. He pulled his left arm back so that his shoulder wouldn't block her view of the screen. His breathing was slow and steady. He must have trained his body to use oxygen efficiently. He must have—

No. She needed to concentrate.

The computer was open to the clinic's website; there was a new tab: "Schedule an Appointment." Nate had created a password for her. T4NKTH3D0G—Tank the Dog with the vowels replaced by numbers. He had her dummy up a schedule for herself. From his own phone he was able to book an appointment for his pet zebra although in the comment section he described an animal with such grievous afflictions that Lacey recommended he cancel the appointment and shoot the poor beast.

They still needed to install this on the clinic's computers and set up guidelines that would help clients select the right kind of appointment; someone would have to enter all the existing appointments into the new system and hook up the robo-calls. But this was great progress.

"I really appreciate this, Nate."

"Ben deserves the credit. If it were up to me, we'd still be looking for a place to enter the code."

"But you stuck with it. For a little boy addicted to recess, you've done a good job of sitting still."

"It's not my natural mode," he acknowledged, "but if I have a task, I stick with it. I am a bit of a dumb beast in that regard."

Professional athletes had very little of the dumb beast about them. They had remarkable kinesthetic intelligence. "Do you have shoulder issues?"

"I used to." He didn't seem surprised by the question. "I kept dislocating the right one. They cut into me and fixed it."

"And what about your spine. Is it impaired?"

"Not anymore. I had two vertebrae fused. They made me stop competing after that."

"That can't have been any fun," she said mildly.

"No, but I was already dropping in the standings. That wasn't any fun either. And going down in smoke and flames is more my style than quietly fading away."

Lacey had been referring to the fact that spinal fusion surgery could be painful. He had assumed she was talking about having to stop competing. She supposed that that wasn't surprising.

"So, what's next for you?" she asked. "I assume you aren't planning on being a computer geek like your friend."

"At least tomorrow I will be as geeky as you can imagine. I'll come in and do the clinic's computer tomorrow. Then my other friend Seth is getting married down in North Carolina. So I am going there. That takes me to Sunday afternoon. Then I'm thinking of surfing, seeing if Ben wants to go surfing. We've never tried that, but you'd think we wouldn't be too bad. Apparently, Portugal or Costa Rica are the places to go at this time of year."

"You might up and go to Portugal or Costa Rica next week?"

"Sure. Why not?"

Lacey could think of many, many reasons, but none of them were at all interesting.

"But I suppose," he said, "you were really asking what I want to be when I grow up."

"It's none of my business." And she wanted to keep it that way. She had grown up with parents who didn't know how to get what they wanted. At least her parents had known what they wanted. Nate didn't seem to even know that.

She reclaimed her computer, wanting to get to know the software better. She saw that now it was set up, it would be easy enough for the staff to learn how to use it. At least it would be for Katie, the receptionist. She was young and eager to learn. Valerie, the office manager, hated change, so she was bound to hate this too.

Suddenly the room went dim...and silent. Her computer was still glowing, but everything else—the overhead light, the green numbers on the stove—had clicked off. The high flutter of the furnace and the chug of the refrigerator motor had stopped. The power had gone out. Heavy, ice-crusted branches must have crashed down on the power lines. They were probably lucky that it hadn't happened earlier.

She shut down her computer. Dr. Byrd had equipped her truck with an inverter hooked directly to the battery so that she could recharge it if she had to, but it took a lot of juice even when the truck was running, so she was careful.

Nate had been in the bathroom. He emerged, his hands still sudsy. The water, powered by a pump at the wellhead, must have stopped before he finished rinsing them. "This serves me right," he announced cheerfully. "I was trying to wash my hands like you do, and now I'm stuck with a handful of bubbles."

Lacey wasn't entirely sure what he was talking about, but she told him he could use the water pitcher to rinse. They would have running water as soon as they got the generator started.

She got out the instructions that Mrs. Byrd kept in the kitchen drawer. Down in the cellar, she switched off most of the electrical circuits, leaving on only the ones marked with green dots, not the red or yellow. She told Nate to turn off the water to the upstairs and then open all the faucets on that level. Then she asked him to come out to the garage to help her start the generator. Filling the gas tank involved holding a five-gallon gas can at an angle that was awkward for her, but easy for him.

Conserving fuel was important, because you never knew how long the power would be out. Since the fireplace in the living room was worthless as a heat source, the easiest room in the house to keep warm was the small library on the other side of the stairs. It was carpeted and had heavy floor-length draperies that were kept closed all winter. One of the green dots was for the outlets and overhead lights in that room. Another set of green dots was for the outlets, lights, and stove in the kitchen. To protect Mrs. Byrd's Armageddon-esque meat supply, the freezer in the basement was kept running, but the kitchen refrigerator was left off. Lacey put the produce near the windows in the mudroom and the dairy products in an ice chest on the back steps. She had Nate carry all the food she had made that morning down to the freezer.

Yellow dots marked the circuits for the furnace and the hot water heater. You were only supposed to turn on those circuits if you knew you could get into town for more gasoline. Even though the house was old and not well insulated, Lacey wasn't going to run the furnace.

Sorting all this out took a while, and often the power would come back on before the work was finished, but not this time. For dinner she left her favorite ivy-patterned dishes in the cupboard and got out the paper plates. She washed the forks and the glasses in water she had heated on the stove, wanting to save the water in the hot water heater so they could take showers. As long as the pump kept running, they would have water pressure.

"Now we plug in the space heater in the library," Lacey said. "And hope for the best."

There was a sofa bed in the library. One sofa bed.

Nate must have a scar on his back from his spinal surgery. Somewhere between his broad shoulders and his tight glutes would be a little red line, a ridge of hardened tissue.

Maybe Dr. Berryville's medical knowledge wasn't such a good thing. But she had nothing to worry about. There would be no scar exploration if Tank was in the room. If anything started to happen in a bed or elsewhere, Tank would come over to see what the fun was.

"We'll want the dogs in the room with us," she said. "They'll be warmer, and so will we."

"Shall I take them out?"

"I'd appreciate that." Lacey carried the space heater into the library and carefully arranged it so that it wouldn't have any contact with the curtains or anything else flammable. She took the cushions off the sofa and, lifting aside the curtains, propped the cushions against windows. The single-pane windows were cold to the touch; the cushions would provide a little more insulation. Nate returned with the dogs as she was spreading the sheet out. He went to the other side of the bed to help. He made a bit of a mess of his corners.

Someone needed to say something, clear the air, spell out the ground rules.

Apparently, it wasn't going to be her. She had no idea what to say. She picked up one of the pillows.

"I'm usually the sort," he said evenly, "who takes advantage of situations."

"That doesn't surprise me."

"So how far should I go in testing the waters?"

She had the pillow tucked under her chin; the pillowcase was in her hand. She forced herself to go on working, shaking open the folds of the case, easing it up over the pillow. "As far as you like. I have a kit out in the truck for testing the water in the farm ponds. Feel free to go get it."

"But will the kitchen door be locked when I come back in?"

"Good chance."

He laughed. "Should I be all gentlemanly and offer to sleep on the floor?"

"Do you snore?"

"Not that I know of."

"I tried sleeping on the floor first time there was a power outage, and it got really cold. I had to give up and crawl in bed with Mrs. Byrd."

"You slept with Mrs. Byrd? Old Mrs. Byrd?"

"I didn't have sex with her, but yes, I did get in bed with her. She made me feel like the biggest prude in the world for even trying to sleep on the floor."

"Sharing a bed with an eighty-year-old lady? That seems really creepy somehow."

"She's eighty-seven. Do you want to use the bathroom first or shall I?"

Lacey put two of Mrs. Byrd's cast-iron skillets on top of the stove. When they got hot, she wrapped them in towels and put them under the covers at the foot of the bed. With the bed warm, they could save fuel by turning off the space heater. She did leave a small lamp on. If it turned off, hopefully one of them would wake up. She didn't want to sleep through the generator stopping and the pump freezing.

The skillets were so hot that, even wrapped in towels, Lacey couldn't put her feet on hers, but the space around it was nicely warm, and she snuggled into her pillow, turning on her side away from the center of the bed, trying to make the situation as impersonal as possible. She was wearing long underwear, heavy sweats, and socks. Put on a bra and shoes, and she could have gone into town to pick up a few groceries.

She felt a little current of air when Nate lifted the blankets on his side. Tank suddenly appeared next to her, needing to see what was going on.

"Oh, does he sleep with you?" Nate said, and before Lacey could protest that no, he never did that, that she didn't allow it, Nate patted the bed, inviting Tank up. Tank leapt up and scrambled over her. The mattress sagged as he found himself a nice spot in the middle of the bed. A moment later Hex was at the edge of the bed, looking lonely. Nate, apparently as overly friendly as a Siberian husky, patted the bed again.

"Are you out of your mind?" Lacey demanded as Hex tried to squirrel himself between the skillets. He weighed fifteen pounds more than Tank. The sofa-bed mattress was larger than a double, but smaller than a queen. Even in a king-sized bed, Lacey would not have wanted to sleep with two full-sized dogs and a man who had the shoulders of a warrior.

The dogs got themselves comfortable, and Lacey yanked on the covers, trying to get enough for herself.

"See, we all fit, don't we?" Nate said.

"Define 'fit.'" She turned her back on men and dogs.

She could feel Tank breathing against her. He let out a shuddering sigh.

"That wasn't me," Nate said.

Chapter 4

A noise. *Trill, trill.* A bird? No, it was her phone. She fumbled for the nightstand. Her hand hit something soft. *Trill, trill.* Where was her phone? She always put it on the nightstand. *Trill, trill.* That was her boss's ringtone.

Oh right. She wasn't in bed. She was in the library; that was the arm of the sleep sofa she had hit. Her phone was plugged in on the other side of the room. Tank had his head on her feet. She shoved him aside. Hex—sensible German shepherd that he was—had left the bed to sleep on the floor. He was already on his feet, looking from her to the phone.

She glanced at the time display before accepting the call. It was a little after midnight. "Is it Big'un?" That was the name of the Mattsons' bull.

"I hate to make you go out on a night like this, but your road has been plowed, and I called the Highway Patrol earlier. They'll keep plowing to the Mattsons'. I'd go if I could, but the bridge—"

"Stop it, Bill. My driveway's shoveled. The chains are on. I can make it."

"Is Pete Willston still out there? I'd sure feel better if he is."

"He managed to get out, but his friend is here."

"Rick and Peggy's boy? Then take him with you."

"I'll be fine." She had gone out in bad weather alone before. "What options you have discussed with Mr. Mattson?"

Earlier in the day Bill had talked to one of the professors at Virginia Tech. Lacey was listening intently to how she should give Big'un a full dose of the medication he'd had before, then half of the new one, wait fifteen minutes, then give the second half. She heard the library door closing. Nate had left. She supposed he was going to the bathroom.

At least that meant she could put on her jeans and hook up her bra without having to pretend about being modest.

She hurried through the chilly house, the dogs coming with her. In the mudroom she pulled on her boots and clipped Tank's leash to his collar, then reached for her keys, usually on a hook by the door. They weren't there. That was strange. She lifted the little curtain over the window in the door and looked out. Her truck was in the driveway. The lights were on, the engine was running. Nate must have done that.

Dr. Byrd had bought a big double-cab Chevy Silverado for her to drive. The bed was fitted with a locked "vet box." In its drawers and pull-out trays, she carried syringes, medications, supplies for wound care, and a portable ultrasound machine to use when she made large animal visits. She put the dogs in the cab and then unlocked the box to get what she would need. It would be easier to do it now than at the side of the road.

She was locking it back up when she heard Nate. He was coming up the drive, carrying a snow shovel. "We're in luck. The road's been plowed."

"It isn't all luck." The Highway Patrol knew where she lived. The streets the medical doctors and the hospital's two senior nurses lived on got plowed first, followed by the town's chief engineer and some of the utility workers. She and Dr. Byrd were next. When it came to emergency access, she was among the ten most important people on this side of the county.

Her parents would have loved that. In their own minds they were special, unique, interesting, important, and they were desperate to have other people believe that.

Lacey and her brother had grown up thinking that they weren't creative and artistic, not like their shimmeringly talented parents. And maybe they weren't. But Lacey was a veterinarian, David a pediatrician. They weren't wasting the space the planet had allotted to them.

"I grew up around here. I know these roads," Nate said. "I can drive."

"No, you won't," she said flatly, opening the driver's side door for herself. "It's not my truck. I don't lend out other people's property."

"Okay," he said and went around to the passenger side. He tried putting the orange snow shovel in the back with the dogs, but he ended up holding it upright between his legs.

She had a support for her phone mounted on the dashboard. She called the Mattsons. Mrs. Mattson answered, relieved to be hearing from Lacey. The fastest way to the barn would be to come up to the back gate. One of her sons would meet her there with the tractor.

"What would you have done if the road hadn't been plowed?" Nate asked when she finished the call. "I saw some old snowshoes in the garage. Wouldn't that have taken forever?"

"Dr. Byrd found me a little aluminum dogsled for exercising Tank in the winter. I could have hitched him up. He would have gotten me there."

"A dogsled?" Nate was suddenly interested. "That sounds like fun. Like the Iditarod and all, us racing to save a dying town."

"It would be more fun if Tank had more training. He always wants to run along the windbreaks. I don't know if he is trying to knock me off or if there is just something about the trees. And it wouldn't have been fun for you at all. It's a one-person sled. I would be out saving the world while you would be home wringing your hankie."

"That would suck," he admitted.

Even with the chains on the tires, it wasn't an easy trip. She had to drive slowly, and the chains made for a spine-jarring ride. "Does this bother your back?" she asked.

"This?" he scoffed. "No, not at all. I'm as good as new."

That probably wasn't true, but a little self-deception was better than professional victimhood.

The Mattsons' back gate did face the plowed road, but there was only one narrow lane clear. If Lacey left the Silverado here, it would block the whole road.

"Just turn toward the shoulder," Nate suggested, "and ram into the snow as far as you can."

She looked across the center console. He had pulled his dark green stocking cap carelessly down over his head; curls escaped over his forehead and the puffy collar of his sleek down jacket. She hadn't thought of his hair being curly, but apparently it was. "That sounds like a really bad idea." They did have to get back home.

"No, it's not. I'll get us dug out and turned around while you're in with the bull." He patted the handle of his shovel. "But you can hop out now, and I'll take care of it."

"I suppose you think that ramming into a snowbank would be fun."

He grinned. "I wouldn't know. I've never done it deliberately before. But I'm certainly not afraid of a little snow."

"Then I will let you be as crazy as you want. I'm sure that the Mattsons' tractor is big enough to get us out of the ditch."

He made a face at her and got out of the truck, letting Hex out, but lifting his arm to keep Tank in.

While she came around the truck with her supplies, Nate and Hex began breaking a path to the big farm gate. Hex went first, forcing his powerful body through the drifts while Nate followed him, stomping the loose snow. The gate was sixteen feet, made of tubes of galvanized steel.

To open it even enough to let a person slip through would have taken a lot of shoveling.

"You're going to have to climb it," Nate said. "You okay with that?"

She could hear the rolling rumble of the tractor coming closer. "Of course."

"Let me go first then."

She couldn't have stopped him. He already had one foot on the second lowest rail and his hands on the upper one. From there he lightly swung himself over and reached though the tubes to take her bag. Then he started stamping out a landing pad for her. When she swung her leg over the top rail, he moved out of her way. With the snow on either side of the gate tamped down, Hex wriggled through the fence.

The lights of the tractor swept across the snow. A boy was driving. He cut around so that the tractor was parallel to the gate. The engine sputtered and then raced when he put it in neutral. He flipped down a small, after-market passenger seat. Lacey pushed her bag in and found some handholds to swing herself up. The boy, who looked to be in high school, engaged the gears and eased back into the track he had made while coming in.

He did a good job. He obviously knew what the ground was like under the snow. "You're the younger one, aren't you?" she asked. "Tyler?"

"Yup. Trent's at Virginia Tech." His gloved hands looked to be gripping the steering wheel hard. "Big'un... He's really sick. And it was fast. Three days ago, he was fine."

"That happens with some infections."

"Will you make him well?"

"We will do everything we can. I can promise you that. We know how special he is."

Big'un had turned out to be an unexpectedly valuable animal. His daughters had a high-milk yield. As a result, straws of his frozen sperm were in demand. Mrs. Mattson turned out to be savvy at Internet marketing. His sperm was shipped all over country, and now international markets were opening up. Not only was his sperm valuable, it was plentiful. When it came to sperm production, he was an industrious gentleman.

Because of him, the Mattson farm provided a far more comfortable living than a herd of a hundred Holsteins usually would. The older Mattson son was studying dairy science over at Virginia Tech. The bull and his ejaculate were paying for his education. People might talk about Nate Forrest being the most important thing to come out of Forrest, but it was actually Big'un. That's why the Highway Patrol made a special pass on the road to the Mattsons'.

Big'un was insured, of course, but even with the current sophisticated genetic testing now done on dairy bulls, there was no guarantee that his replacement would equal his success.

The Mattsons had—again, thanks to Big'un—put up a new steel barn right after Lacey had come to town. Big'un had his own "suite," a roomy stall, heated in the winter, misted for cooling in the summer, with free access to a small paddock. Beyond the paddock gate was his acre of private pasture.

He was a magnificent creature, rippling muscles under a gleaming black and white coat, a godlike embodiment of testosterone. At least that's what he was usually. Today, inside the straw-scented barn, he was a sad boy, his eyes rimmed with red, his chest heaving with his labored breathing. He was chained, but the restraint seemed unnecessary. He looked too weak to lift his head.

"Oh, you poor thing," Lacey cooed. He might be ten times her size and a hundred times stronger, but he was suffering. She put a hand on his flank. "You poor baby."

"I hate to see him like this," Mr. Mattson said.

"We're a long way from any decision like that." Lacey knew what he was worried about.

She put on gloves and prepped the three syringes. All were intramuscular injections that she would put into his neck muscle. She first gave him the med he had had before, followed by half a dose of the new one. She set the timer on her phone.

The three Mattsons were too nervous to chitchat. As warm as it was in the barn, Mrs. Mattson kept pulling her coat closer. Lacey touched her arm.

The timer dinged. Lacey hadn't expected that Big'un would instantly rise up and stagger toward the front of the revival tent, but nothing bad was happening. She put on another pair of gloves and gave him the third syringe. This one did have a stimulant to give the meds a bit of a kick and a steroid to reduce the inflammation.

She set her timer again and stripped off her gloves. "As long as I am here, why don't I take a look at the girls?"

The milk cows had almost no contact with the bull; they were artificially inseminated. But as the origin of Big'un's infection was unknown, it was probably best to monitor the entire herd.

The cows' share of the barn was divided into stalls, but except when they were in the milking parlor, the Mattsons' cows weren't restrained. They could move around the barn freely, walking to the water tanks or the feed troughs, visiting their friends, doing whatever was the dairy-cow equivalent of neighborhood gossiping. Most of them were sleeping now. In the dim light, the barn was a jumble of black-and-white bodies, some lying on their left, others on their right. Some had their legs splayed out; others had them neatly tucked in. Their pink udders were filling; they would be milked in a few more hours.

Lacey felt lucky to have started in a mixed practice, seeing both pets and farm animals. In a practice that served only large animals, a veterinarian got to care for cows, sheep, horses, and goats. It was interesting work, but such a doctor was on the road for hours each day. The money was in a companion-animal practice, and her next job would almost certainly be in one of those. Lacey liked dogs and cats; she had enjoyed getting to know the owners more than she had expected. But she would miss working in the sunlit openness of the green pastures and the warm earthiness of the barns.

Back in the bull's stall, Mrs. Mattson claimed that Big'un's breathing was easier. That might be the steroid kicking in; more likely it was wishful thinking on her part. But the bull certainly wasn't getting worse. There was no reason for Lacey to stay. Dave Mattson had grown up on this place; he'd been running dairy cattle his whole life. He could manage the additional injections and the follow-up care.

It was sleeting when she came out of the barn. The Mattsons didn't have a cab on the tractor. They didn't spend the long hours on their tractors like the farmers who raised crops. She pulled her hood tight. Tyler looked as worried as ever, and Lacey wished she could tell him that everything would be fine, but she wasn't going to make false promises.

Not only was overpromising poor medical care, it was also what her parents had always done. *Oh, it will be even nicer there,* they would assure Lacey and David. It usually wasn't.

Nate had gotten the Silverado turned around. The snow between the gate and the road was churned and marked with tire tracks. He had clearly used the weight of the truck to muscle through the snow, pushing forward, backing up, turning the steering wheel to pivot a few inches, then accelerating hard to push forward a few inches more.

She hoped he had found it fun.

"Are you sure that you don't want me to drive?" he asked. "I got a good feel for how the truck handles."

She shook her head, and for a moment, she thought he was going to argue with her, but he simply opened the driver's door for her. She appreciated that.

Tank was much too happy to see her. Squirming joyfully, he tried to crawl between the front seats to sit on her lap as if he were a little lapdog.

"This dog goes in his crate when we get home," she announced to Nate. "Everyone will sleep better."

"It was getting a little cramped," he admitted.

The sleet was making driving even more difficult than it had been an hour ago. She wished she had let him drive. He might find it fun.

We never have any fun. Two different men had said that to her. It was true, but it wasn't only her fault. They hadn't been any more fun than she had been.

But how could she be fun when she was always the one who had to think about consequences? She had once grabbed her brother by the arm and refused to get in the packed car unless her parents stopped by the school and picked up their records. She had had too much experience with her mother having to charm administrators into enrolling them without records from their previous schools.

She stopped the truck in the drive. "Would you put the truck away? And dry off Hex and put Tank in his crate? I want to take a shower."

"Leave me a little hot water if you can," he said.

She scurried upstairs to get clean sweats and fresh underwear. The old single-paned windows left the second floor icy, but the downstairs bathroom, thanks to not having windows, was slightly warmer.

Veterinary clinics were full of smells—harsh cleaning products, the animals' wet coats on rainy days, their breath if their teeth weren't taken care of, their feces and vomit when they were ill. During vet school she had found it challenging enough to keep herself clean, much less fuss with her hair or curate her earring collection.

But after her first few months here, she reminded herself that she wasn't a student anymore. She started trying harder. Instead of the scrubs she had worn in school, she ironed white shirts, which she wore with dark-wash jeans under her lab coat.

She also wanted to smell as good as she could. Her brother's now-husband designed websites. One of his clients was a fragrance company, and Tim deluged Lacey with complimentary products. The company thought women ought to change their scent seasonally, something that had been news to her. But she was willing to buy in to the concept, especially as she didn't have to "buy" anything. This winter she was using soap and perfume that had a deep undernote of sensuous amber resin.

Wanting to be careful with the hot water, she turned it off as soon as her hair was wet. Before she rinsed the shampoo out, she propped each foot against the fiberglass wall of the shower stall and shaved her legs.

She wasn't shaving her legs for him, she told herself. She always shaved her legs…although maybe not at 2 a.m.

Okay, she was doing it for him. But why not? What had she been so worried about? He might be a larger-than-life, computer-grabbing celebrity, but in a couple of days, he would be going on with his life, attending that wedding in North Carolina and surfing in Portugal. How much harm could he do in a few days?

Swaddled in a towel, she smoothed the richly scented lotion on her arms and legs. The heavy sweat suit felt like a blanket, cuddling the smells close to her skin.

Both dogs were in the kitchen, Tank sleeping in his crate, Hex on the floor next to him. Hex woke up when she came out of the bathroom, but she signaled to him to stay there.

Nate was back in the library, sitting in the chair, the white cord to his phone draped over the arm into the outlet. She could see that he immediately noticed her scent even though her hair was wrapped up in the towel.

"This crap is going to stop soon," he said, "and temperatures are going to slowly warm up."

"That's good. Then I'm going to try to get to work early, like five thirty or six." They had gone to bed so early that with a few more hours' sleep she would be able to function normally. "Unfortunately, unless you come with me, you'll be stranded at the farmhouse."

"I'll come into town with you." He picked up his backpack. "Is there any hot water left?"

She nodded. "Use as much as you want." If the power was still off, she could bring more gas with her after work and switch on the water heater.

Knowing that she didn't have to be so careful about the gas supply, she plugged in her hair dryer. The warm air heated her scalp and the wood handle of her brush. As she worked, she noticed two lumps under the blankets on the sofa bed. While she had been in the shower, Nate had reheated the cast-iron skillets.

How thoughtful he was, warming up the truck and backing it around, now this. She wouldn't have expected that from someone with his status, but she supposed that with a mother who was a first-grade teacher, pretty high standards got set.

The door to the library opened. He, too, must have gone upstairs to find clean clothes. The grandson's sweatshirt was tighter across the chest than his own clothes had been. "I think there's still plenty of hot water," he said, putting down his backpack.

"Do you have condoms with you?"

"*What?*" He was startled. She could hear it in his voice, but the lamplight was shadowy, so she couldn't read his expression. When he spoke again, his voice was careful. "Yes."

"That's good." She wasn't sure what else to say. Of course, asking about condoms had been insanely matter-of-fact, but that was who she was.

He sat down on the bed next to her. "Is that a general question, or are you changing your mind about testing the water in the farm pond?"

The mattress must have sagged when he sat down, forcing her closer to him. "I think it would be fun."

"I hope so. But you know that I am leaving on Thursday?"

And then going to Costa Rica or Portugal. "I know. It makes everything simple, doesn't it?"

"As long as it's clear. I don't want to mislead people, particularly women."

"This works for me."

Couldn't she have figured out some way to make this a little more romantic? Apparently not.

Nate had his arm around her, and he kissed her, his warm lips touching hers, his tongue touching to part them. He tasted of cinnamon. He must have used his own toothpaste. Hers was mint. She luxuriated, letting the kiss happen, the gentle touch of his tongue tracing the outline of her lips.

She slipped her hand under his shirt and found the scar first from his spinal fusion. The scar tissue was slightly raised, but not ropy or knotty. He had had skilled surgeons and good follow-up care.

She had to hunt for the shoulder scar. She didn't know where they went in to repair shoulders.

"I fractured ribs twice," he said. "I don't think you can feel where the breaks were, but you're welcome to try."

"Am I being too clinical here?"

"Maybe a little. I could lie and tell you I had to have a groin muscle repaired, but that seems to be one thing I didn't tear. I do have pins in one foot, but let's not waste time with my feet."

He had paid for his life, for being able to dash off to Portugal or Costa Rica. "Are you in pain?"

"Nope. But the doctors say that I have a pretty high tolerance for that kind of crap."

"I imagine that they don't say 'pretty high'."

"Okay. 'Off the charts' is what I hear. But why are we talking about this?" He started to lift her shirt, then stopped. "You're going to get cold." He stood up to turn back the covers.

The lamp was still on, but under the blankets she had to rely on her sense of touch, and for once it wasn't enough. She could feel the strength of his back and chest muscles, the power of his legs, the size of his penis, but she wanted to see him. Yet still what was happening was wonderful enough, a glowing light building inside her. Within moments the light suddenly shattered, leaving her limp and golden. She had never before responded so quickly.

Now she turned to pleasing him, pushing his shoulders back against the bed, kissing his chest, using her hands to cup and caress him. The mattress shifted as he got out of bed. She turned toward the light, eager to see him.

He might have battle scars, but he still had a young man's body, a young warrior's body, the muscles promising force and strength that women could rarely possess.

And his erection, springing from the twists of hair, darker than that on his head. For a moment Lacey understood the phallic cults, how right it would have felt to kneel before this, worship it in whatever way it wanted to be worshiped, being willing to offer it anything. The room was suddenly enchanted. The pool of lamplight was a soft gold; the mattress was a flying carpet carrying her to a place she'd never visited before.

He moved over on top of her, supporting his weight himself. When his hand went down to guide his penis into her, he left it there, his fingers searching. The first pressure made her gasp—it had been more than three years—then she softened and eased.

Wasn't this supposed to be sex at its most casual, a physical act meaning almost nothing? Yet here they were, their heads so close, his breath, still scented with cinnamon, on her cheek. Each touch of his was so…so personal, so designed to please her. He was being tender, protective, tucking the blankets around her to be sure that she stayed warm.

But afterward she realized that those blankets had trapped her, had kept her from being able to move.

Chapter 5

It was strange in the morning after feeling that her world had become a place out of a fairy tale, with everything heightened and intensified, spun with glowing light, that Nate would be talking so matter-of-factly about taking turns in the bathroom.

Do you have condoms with you? Wasn't she the Queen of Matter-of-Fact? He must have thought this was how she wanted things. And she did, didn't she?

She had no idea.

He said that it was too early for him to go to the Pritchards'. He would come to the clinic and get started on the software. "Let's see how much I can do before I have to wake up Ben."

The clinic was in a freestanding building on one of the side streets, a block off Main. The clients parked in front, and although it wasn't even five thirty, two cars had already pulled into spaces, their engines running, the interior lights on. They must be longtime clients who knew that the clinic would open as soon as the roads did. Lacey stopped the truck at the entrance to the lot, asking Nate if he would get out. "Tell those people that I will be at the front door in a minute."

She pulled around to the back of the building. The man who had plowed the front parking lot had also plowed back here. The picnic table that sat next to the back lot was still blanketed with a marshmallow-like mound of snow, and the fenced-in dog run was equally untouched. "If you need to poop, you'll have to do it on the concrete," she told the dogs as she brought them in through the back entrance. She went through the clinic, turning on lights as she went.

Nate and two women, both of them familiar, were waiting by the glass front door. One woman had two cat carriers, and Nate has holding a midsized mixed-breed dog. The dog looked dehydrated. "Can you get their files?" she asked Nate as she held the big glass door open. "Alphabetical order by owner's last name."

So, the day started, and it didn't let up. On top of two days' worth of appointments—and Dr. Byrd not coming in until he had checked on Big'un—there were several ADRs—Ain't Doing Rights. Being stuck at home with their pets for two days, owners had noticed—or started fretting about—things they might have otherwise ignored.

Her stethoscope around her neck, her knee-length lab coat with "Dr. Berryville" embroidered over the breast pocket, she went to room after room, seeing client after client, apologizing for having to rush. This was how she had worked when she had started here two and a half years ago. She had prided herself on her efficiency, being able to provide excellent medical care in the shortest amount of time.

Then Dr. Byrd had told her that wasn't what he wanted. She needed to use the full appointment time even if the diagnosis and treatment plan only took three minutes. She should talk to the owners, listen to them, learn what role their animals played in their lives. Yes, it was important that the clinic make money, but other things mattered too.

She had felt awkward at first, but now it seemed natural to ask about clients' families. She had become the sort of person who engaged with other people's lives. It would be hard if her next job required her to go back to assembly-line medicine.

As far as she could tell, Nate had turned himself into a receptionist, working the front desk alone for the first hour or so, signing people in, pulling charts, flipping the flags on doors telling her where to go next. He had probably logged enough hours as a patient with medical doctors that with a little help from the clients, he could figure out the procedure. Katie, the young receptionist, came at seven. By seven thirty, Stephanie had opened up the lab, and KimAnne, the vet tech, was helping Lacey in the examining rooms.

Finally, at ten Lacey had to stop to use the bathroom. Nate was in the break room. He and Katie were working at the desktop computer, his own laptop open next to it.

How could she have ever not noticed how much curl there was in his hair? She remembered lacing her fingers through it. It had been full and soft, not at all coarse.

She needed to stop thinking about this. Katie looked up and handed her a pink message slip. It was from Dr. Byrd. Big'un was stable, maybe a little better.

Lacey stepped into the office manager's small office to ask Valerie a question. "Do you know when Dr. Byrd is coming in?"

"What those two are doing out there, it doesn't make sense to me."

Lacey was not going to get into a thing with Valerie. She repeated the question and, when she finally got an answer, went on to the next examining room. KimAnne had just finished prepping the room across the hall. She stopped Lacey. "Isn't it amazing to have Nate Forrest in there helping out? I mean, *Nate Forrest.* You hear so much about him."

"He does seem conscientious."

Conscientious? What kind of word was that for a man whose muscled silhouette in the lamplight had made him look like a pagan god?

"And do you know what he told us about Valerie? That she gave out raisins at Halloween."

Lacey pulled the chart of her next patient out of the Plexiglas holder attached to the door. "I guess that's pretty bad."

"It certainly is. What kind of kid wants raisins at Halloween?"

She didn't know. She and her brother had hardly ever gone trick-or-treating.

She suddenly wanted to ask Nate what his Halloweens had been like. What had he dressed up as? Had he gone out with his sister and brother or with Pete? She wanted to imagine him walking through Forrest swinging an orange plastic pumpkin.

But there was no time. She had to see the next client.

Dr. Byrd got in around eleven, feeling more confident about Big'un. At noon Katie thrust a sandwich into her hand. Lacey ate it, standing up, flipping through charts. She kept up the pace the rest of the day, and because Katie had the sense to reschedule a time-consuming, but routine teeth cleaning, Lacey got back on schedule. Valerie locked the front door at five thirty, when KimAnne and Katie had to go get their kids from day care. At six thirty, the only animal left in the waiting room was on Bill's schedule.

Lacey was finished…and filthy.

Over the course of the day, she had been vomited on, urinated on, and had a near-miss with a diarrhea explosion. Normally she was more careful, but today she had been rushing, and so it had been a three-lab-coat day.

The staff bathroom had a shower where everyone stored extra clothes for the moments when the diarrhea explosions couldn't be avoided. Lacey kept the bathroom stocked with products that her brother-in-law had sent. She got out of the shower, smelling like a tropical orchid.

It was nice to be clean, but the clothes she had left here were…well, the sort of clothes that you left at work for emergencies. The jeans had never fit right, and the flannel shirt was baggy and frayed. The bra was a thick-strapped sports bra that hooked in front and gave her a mono-boob. And the underpants…she was no sexpot when it came to lingerie purchases, but seriously, why had she ever bought granny panties?

She got Hex and Tank out of their crates. Tank was used to this routine, and he usually went straight to the back door, but tonight he headed to the front of the clinic, his nails clicking against the tile floor.

Indeed, there was a light on in the break room, and she heard Nate's voice. "Hey, Tank. Where's your doggy-mom?"

"I'm right here." *Doggy-mom underwear and all.*

Nate was at the computer again. He had changed clothes. His jeans had a different wash, but he was sitting so she didn't know whether or not the back pockets sagged on this pair too.

"Katie picks up things quickly. She's not from around here, is she?"

Lacey shook her head. She was surprised Valerie hadn't told Nate all about Katie being a single teen mom who had come to live with her aunt and uncle. "We're lucky to have her. It looks like you got over to the Pritchards' okay."

Of course he had. That house was only four or five blocks from the clinic.

"Yes, and they put me to work right away. Mrs. Pritchard gave me a list of people to check on and sent me off on her neighbor's snowmobile."

"That was noble of you." She imagined that he had had a grand time.

"Indeed it was. I took it out to the farmhouse. The power was on. So I turned on the furnace."

"Oh good. No, wait. How did you get in the house? I'm sure I locked up."

He shrugged. "Your keys were in your purse."

"You went in my purse?" She couldn't believe it. He had gone into her purse. How could he do that?

Her mother used to do that: open Lacey's purse and "borrow" money, leaving Lacey trying to explain to a bus driver why she and her brother couldn't pay their fare.

"Is there something wrong with that? I put them back."

Something wrong? Her purse had a leather flap and a zipper. He would have had to have lifted the flap and undone the zipper. She always put her keys in one of the interior pockets, but the other pocket had her emergency supply of tampons.

"I took the truck keys off the hook last night." He still sounded a little bewildered. "That didn't seem to bother you."

She hadn't even noticed that. And what was she so upset about? She'd had sex with him, hadn't she? Surely that was a more intimate, more trust-requiring act than this?

She tried to sound pleasant. "I don't suppose that as long as you had my keys, you took the chains off the truck."

He drew back. "Was that a mistake?"

"I was joking. You didn't really do that, did you?"

"Of course I did. The ice is gone. The chains would chew up the roadbed. And the parking lot out back is turning to slush. Did you really want to go out and do that now?"

No, of course not, especially since she was now clean.

"If you're ready to go," he went on, "are you too tired to go out to dinner? We may have to go over to the county seat. Mrs. Pritchard said that every place would be packed because people are so happy to be able to get out."

Driving twenty miles made no sense. In fact, doing anything this evening made no sense. In the middle of the night she had gotten up to treat Big'un and then had worked a twelve-hour day. But she suddenly felt fine, and she certainly wanted to be with him.

"Why don't you come back to the farmhouse for dinner?"

He liked that idea. He said that he would walk over to the Pritchards' to pick up his rental car.

It was as dark out as it had been when Lacey had arrived at the clinic in the morning. Lacey was really glad that he had taken the chains off.

She knew that Mrs. Pritchard was a talker, so even with having to load the dogs in the car, she got home first. The farmhouse was indeed deliciously warm. The refrigerator was running, and Nate had put the produce and the dairy products back in. Lacey turned on the oven and went down to the freezer in the cellar to get one of the casseroles she had made on Monday.

Piled on top of the washer were the sheets from the sofa bed and the ones from the beds he and Pete had slept in Sunday night.

She had the stew in the oven and was feeding the dogs when he arrived. He had brought a bottle of wine. "I hope there's a corkscrew," he said. "I should have thought of that."

"There's one somewhere." Lacey started rummaging through the kitchen drawers. "Thank you for stripping the beds."

"Three of us trained together as kids. For a long time Seth's mom traveled with us because my mom taught school and Ben's mom had a bunch of little kids at home. If we stayed in a motel, Mrs. Street made us strip the beds to help the maids. Somehow that was supposed to keep us from being spoiled brats, but I don't know if it worked."

"It seems to have." Lacey handed him the rickety corkscrew and rinsed the dust off the wineglasses.

After giving her a glass, he reached forward and clinked his against hers. It was a nice gesture.

"I don't know much about wine," she said a minute later, "but I like this."

"I didn't have a lot of options, but I thought you'd enjoy this one. It's more earthy. You seem to like that sort of thing."

Mrs. Byrd's cooking had tended toward the high-sodium farmhouse-bland. When Lacey started cooking regularly, she wanted to get away from using so much canned cream of mushroom soup. Scientifically minded as she was, she researched flavors and spices and discovered that she liked the "bass spices"—cumin, paprika, cinnamon, and cloves, especially when combined with umami, the meaty flavors.

So, it wasn't only his sense of smell that was keen. He had noticed the cinnamon in her chili, the extra cumin in her curry.

He was leaning back against the kitchen cabinets, his left arm stretched along the countertop, his right hand holding his wineglass.

And his sense of touch…that had been pretty well developed too.

"Do you still have condoms?"

"That's really romantic, girl." But he put down his wineglass and started toward her.

Tank woke up, and Hex was on his feet, his ears pricked, his tail lifted.

"I am not going to hurt her, boys." Nate grabbed Tank's collar and started pulling him toward his crate.

"I should warn you," Lacey said. "I have on the ugliest underwear you will ever see."

He looked up from latching the crate. "Do you honestly think I care what your underwear looks like?"

Ten minutes later he was sitting on her bed, having pulled her to stand between his legs. Her shirt was so old that the placket started to rip when he tried to unbutton it. She grabbed the tails and gave a hard jerk. The shirt ripped open, exposing her sturdy, boob-crushing bra.

"Okay, this is pretty bad," he said. "It could be a mood killer."

"So is it?"

"No. I am a stalwart fellow, and it unfastens in front." He had already slipped his fingers under the band to unhook the bra. "A gentleman can forgive a lot in a bra with hooks in the front."

It was very different this time. She had never before been with a man with Nate's sexual self-confidence, and the warmth of the room allowed them to move boldly. No need for the missionary position this time. They didn't have to worry about staying warm.

Lacey pushed him down on his back and straddled him. Thinking she was inviting penetration, he reached for her hips. She instead laced her fingers in his and, relying on her knowledge of body mechanics, pressed his hands down, trapping his elbows at his side. He could only use his lats and his triceps while she could use her body weight as well as her arms, her back, and her core muscles. In this position she was more powerful than he was.

It made him laugh.

He commented on it afterward. "You're strong."

"Of course I am. I lift dogs all day long."

Lacey knew that she was attractive in an outdoorsy kind of way, but since she had grown up being told that she would never be as beautiful as her mother, she never took any real delight in how she looked. But her strength she was proud of. She had earned that. She hadn't been this strong when she had started vet school, but she didn't want to be like the women who had to stop in the middle of an appointment to call someone in to lift a heavy animal.

She was pleased that he noticed, but compliments made her uncomfortable. It was her mother who was supposed to get the compliments, not her. She changed the subject. "Are you hungry? The casserole should be ready soon."

"Do I have time for a shower first?"

"No rush." She got out of bed and started to untangle their clothes. She had just picked up his shirt when Mrs. Byrd's landline rang. She thrust her arms into the shirtsleeves and hurried out to the niche in the hall where the one upstairs extension was.

It was Pete. Oh Lord, *Pete.* She had not given him and all of the complexities a minute's thought.

"I tried your cell," he was saying.

Her cell had been downstairs while she had been up here romping with his oldest friend.

He apologized for leaving Hex with her so long, but he finally had time to come get him. He could be at the farmhouse in fifteen minutes.

"Fifteen minutes? Ah...sure. Can you stay for dinner? Nate's here."

"Nate? What's he doing there?"

"It's a little complicated. We lost power last night, and he was helping me turn the generator off and all that." She had turned off the generator before leaving for work.

She knew Pete wanted to ask about the power, but he was in his truck, getting closer to the farmhouse with each breath. And he was a super-prompt person. If he said fifteen minutes, it would be ten or less.

"We can talk about it when you get here," she said and hung up.

A little frantic, she banged on the bathroom door, but Nate couldn't hear her over the sound of the shower. She opened the door, and he stuck his head out from behind the shower curtain.

"Pete's coming to pick up Hex. He'll be here any minute. Can you hurry?"

"Yes, but I'm going to need my shirt back."

"Oh, of course." Lacey jerked it off and, feeling self-conscious about being buck naked in Mrs. Byrd's house, scurried into the bedroom to scramble into some clothes. On her way downstairs, she knocked on the bathroom door again. Nate was standing on the bath mat, drying himself.

"Nate, about this…you and me—"

"I get it," he interrupted. "I won't say a thing."

I get it. What did he get about her and Pete? How much had he realized? Too much, apparently.

A few minutes later a car door slammed in the driveway. Where was Nate? The last thing she wanted was to be offering Pete a glass of wine and have Nate saunter into the kitchen, his hair wet. It was going to be hard enough to explain why he was here; it would be impossible to account for him having had to take a shower.

Pete was obviously tired; there were grayish shadows underneath his eyes. He thanked Lacey and then dropped down to one knee to greet Hex. The usually restrained German shepherd burrowed his muzzle into Pete's chest, then circled around him, rubbing his flank against Pete's back, squirreling himself under Pete's other arm, trying to get even closer.

"There's no need to be so crazy," Pete told him. "You knew I was coming back, and it sounds like you had a great time with Nate and Hex."

Lacey looked down at the two of them; they were both so happy to be together again. She remembered what Valerie had said about Pete's father's drinking problem. Clearly she and Pete had more in common than concerns about the environment. They were both the infinitely reliable offspring of flawed parents. They were familiar with the constant undercurrent of anxiety and uncertainty, the coming home from school not knowing what you would find.

Nate Forrest, with his Norman-Rockwell, Hallmark-card family, could never know any of this. Things had come easily to him. And now she had become one more thing that had been easy for Nate and unattainable for Pete.

Can you betray a married man with whom you are not having an affair? Apparently so.

Pete looked up at Lacey. "That's Nate's rental car out there, isn't it?"

"Yes. He is—" What? Getting firewood? No, Pete would have seen him if he'd been outside. And he'd be coming down the stairs. What could he be doing upstairs? Lacey's feelings about being a traitor now spilled into anxiety about getting caught. She got out a wineglass for Pete to give herself time to think. "He's putting the Christmas decorations back in the attic. It's hard for me to do it alone, the boxes and the ladder and all." Mrs. Byrd's grandsons had done it in early January. "But Nate said that he is good at that sort of thing, climbing ladders and all." A snowboarder couldn't be afraid of heights, could he?

"I suppose he is."

A minute later Nate came into the kitchen. Suddenly Lacey launched into thanking him for putting away the Christmas decorations. "Until she broke her hip, Mrs. Byrd and I would do it together. I would get on the ladder, and she would hand me the boxes. I would shove them up and then go into the attic and organize the boxes."

"It was no problem," he said. "Honestly, it wasn't."

She didn't dare look at him. She would have laughed.

Over dinner Pete apologized to Nate about having disappeared all day. "But when I mentioned to one of the management guys that you were in town, he got all excited. I'm supposed to see if you will take a meeting with them."

Nate picked up the wine bottle and topped off the glasses. "Probably not."

"Why?" Lacey asked. "You don't even know what they want."

"I'm pretty sure that I do. They want my name. I don't want to be A Name."

"They want more than that," Pete said. "They would like you to be involved in their instructional and coaching program."

"They shouldn't," Nate said. "I'm a terrible teacher. I don't know how I do things. I just do them. My only advice to anyone is to go faster and higher, be stronger and more flexible. That doesn't seem to be very helpful. No, they just want to put my name up on their signs."

Lacey's parents would have loved that, people paying them to be celebrities. It would have validated their worldview.

"But you've done ads before, haven't you?" she asked.

"Sure. I was still competing. But now I'd feel like a fraud out there pretending to be the person I used to be. What comes after that? Reality TV?"

"I'm not arguing with you," Pete said mildly. "But isn't this what your brother said that you didn't want?"

"The only thing my brother wants is for me to be out of the business. He wants to be the Number One Son."

Lacey was surprised. Maybe Nate's family wasn't so picture-perfect after all. This was another side of him, a layer that he had been hiding beneath his carefree good cheer. He had depth and dimension that she hadn't seen. He was more than the fantasy celebrity who had swept into her life for a few days.

But how much more? Could she let herself be curious about him? Or was that too much of a risk?

Chapter 6

The evening ended early. Pete was exhausted, and Lacey had suddenly been overwhelmed by a bone-deep fatigue. She sent the men home, and with a silent apology to Mrs. Byrd, went to bed without doing the dishes.

She was doing them in the morning when her phone chirped. It was a text from Nate.

How did he have her number? He hadn't asked her for it. He must have gotten it when he had installed the clinic's new app on her phone.

The message was to both Pete and her. *Picnic after work today?*

A picnic? she texted back. *In the snow?*

An instant later her phone rang. His name and picture flashed onto the screen of her phone. He must have inputted his own number when he was working on her phone.

Didn't he have any boundaries?

"You're up early," she said as a greeting.

"West Coast time. So what do you say to a picnic?"

"Do you know what the ground is like? Or the fact that West Coast time would make you sleep later?"

"Don't nitpick everything," he said cheerfully. The bitterness she had sensed yesterday when he had been talking about his brother was hidden. "And of course I know what the ground will be like, snowy or muddy or both. This will be an indoor picnic. I want to walk through my grandfather's store, and since I now owe you yet another meal, I thought we could have a picnic there. You could bring Tank."

Bringing Tank seemed like a very bad idea. Tank wasn't going to understand picnics. He was trained to leave people alone when they were eating at a table, but if they were doing something that he didn't associate with normal human behavior, like sitting on a blanket with food in front of them, Tank, all fifty pounds of him, would probably want to crawl onto her lap and eat off her plate.

But she loved going places with her dog. "We will both be there."

She needed to take to work some clothes to replace the horrible ones that she had worn home Tuesday night. She picked out a decent shirt and a pair of jeans that were only marred by a bleach splatter. She closed her closet door, then opened it back up. She took a white lace-edged peasant blouse off the hanger. Her brother-in-law Tim's mother had given it to her. Caroline McGuinness didn't have any daughters, and she relished buying little gifts for Lacey. This blouse was to slip on "if you go out for a drink after work." Lacey had never worn it because she didn't go out for drinks after work.

But here she was, going out not just for drinks, but dinner. Of course, it was a picnic with the dogs, and a lace blouse might not have been a perfect choice, but she didn't care. She was glad that she had something pretty to wear even if it wasn't quite weather-appropriate.

The commercial part of Forrest was crowded into the flatland at the edge of the foothills, stopping at the river. Main Street had four bars, a Subway sandwich shop, and a Laundromat as well as offices for the lawyers and insurance agents. The grocery store, the hair salon, the liquor store, and Dr. Byrd's clinic were on side streets. At the south end of town were the police station, the fire station, the hospital, and the Best Western motel. The old high school had been near the river at the northwest edge of town.

The churches were on the west side, the spires rising over the trees. The houses on that side were well-kept. The lawns were mowed, and the screen doors closed neatly. On the east side into the hills and down in the hollers, people lived closer to squalor. Cars were left rusting in the yards, and the gutters sagged.

At least a third, maybe a half, of the stores on Main Street were closed. Lacey had seen a candle shop, a fortune-teller, and a tattoo parlor come and go in the time she had been here. The dental clinic and Forrest Hardware had closed before she had come.

Forrest Hardware closing must have been a blow. It had been a big operation. In addition to the original stone building, the family had eventually taken over the buildings on either side. Now all three had red *For Rent* signs in the windows.

But those signs stayed red; the listing agent replaced them every so often. All the other rental signs had faded into a weathered pink. The other stores had dusty windows, and many of them had sad debris left over from the former business owners: shelving, cardboard boxes, paint cans, odd chairs. But once a month, two women came in to vacuum the floors and wash the windows at Forrest Hardware. Clearly the building's owners still took pride in the property.

Lacey had often peered in the window of the original building, the one in the center. It was stone and had *Forrest Dry Goods* etched over the door. The fixtures appeared to be original. The glass-fronted display cases sat on oak bases. Along the walls were mesmerizing banks of little oak drawers with brass fittings. An oak rack with wide spindles must have held lengths of canvas or oilcloth. The ceiling was pressed tin, stamped with a fleur-de-lis pattern, and the big nickel-plated cash register appeared to have some kind of scrolling design, but Lacey couldn't see any of the detail from the window.

She and Tank had walked over from the clinic. Both Nate's and Pete's cars were parked in front, and she could see them moving inside. She let Tank go in ahead of her.

The building was warm. Nate must have come earlier to turn up the heat. She unhooked Tank's leash and handed Nate her coat. "These fixtures must be very valuable."

"My dad and his sister got offers, but it all seemed so much a part of the town's history that they couldn't bring themselves to have everything stripped and taken away. They really hoped to find someone to run the business."

"Is there any hope for that?" The grocery store had half an aisle devoted to cup hooks, prepackaged sets of screws, and a few flimsy tools, but Lacey had never found anything that she needed for little repairs at the farmhouse.

"Not now," Pete said. "People have gotten used to driving over to Lowe's in the county seat, and an independent can't ever compete with those prices."

"But what about when people move into the new houses?" It seemed such a shame that such a beautiful store sat empty.

"They're even closer to Lowe's, and they'll be able to hop on the bypass and get there in no time."

That was true.

Lacey had expected Nate to pick up food at Subway and, if they were lucky, he would have brought a blanket for the floor. She had underestimated him. In addition to turning on the heat, he had set up a card table and three chairs in an open space at the back of the store, and on the counters were some foil-covered pans. He reported that when he had asked Mrs. Pritchard if he could borrow the card table, she had sneered at the idea of carryout. She had made a ham loaf and scalloped potatoes. While Nate opened a bottle of wine, Pete started showing Lacey around the store, pointing out the board that had mounted samples of the store's knobs, draw pulls, and hinges, as well as four black marks on the floor and the now-patched round hole in the tin ceiling. "In the early days there was a big potbelly stove here. The old-timers used to say it was the warmest place in town."

"You worked here before you went into the service?"

"Since I was eleven," Pete said. "I loved the place."

"Eleven? That wasn't legal, was it?"

"Not a bit. Nate and I were put to work here for a couple of weeks one summer as a punishment, but I kept coming back. Since Mr. Forrest couldn't pay me, when Mrs. Forrest—Nate's grandmother—would go to the grocery store, she would always pick up a few things for my mom, and her definition of a 'few things' included a ham and a crate of oranges. Mom would have made us live on government cheese and canned peaches rather than take charity, but as long as she felt like I had earned it, it was okay."

Lacey had to wonder what it had been like for Pete, having his best friend be live on the west side of town while he had been from the east. He had probably just accepted that that was how things were supposed to be for him.

She and her brother had accepted it. She had stopped longing to be like the girls who stayed in one place long enough to have birthday parties and to become presidents of clubs. She and her brother knew they were different, and that was all there was to it.

"Why did your family leave?" Lacey asked Nate.

"My dad didn't get his contract renewed."

"It was the newspaper," Pete said. "That idiot editor."

Lacey asked him to explain. As the superintendent of schools, Nate's father—Pete called him Dr. Forrest—was faced with dropping revenues and increasingly needy children. He had been creative, getting federal dollars to set up consortiums with the other rural schools to provide distance learning for the smart kids. He was also willing to make hard choices, putting his limited funds into the third-grade classrooms and the vo-tech programs at the high school.

Fred Kayot, the editor of the *Forrest Gazette*, had hated the changes and the compromises. Loathing anything that had to do with the federal government or federal funding, he had spotlighted the distance-learning program. "Every student deserves a live, caring teacher in the classroom, not more *Sesame Street*," an editorial read.

"That wasn't the choice," Pete said. "The choice wasn't between a living, caring calculus teacher and distance learning, but between distance learning and no calculus at all. Dr. Forrest probably could have lived with the criticism, but not when the paper went after Jill."

Nate's sister had been Miss Everything-Smart during her last two years of high school, but whatever she did, her Girl Scout Gold Award, her youth mission with their church, her success at Girls' State, her National Merit Scholarship, was ignored. That she was valedictorian and had given the commencement address at graduation had to be mentioned, but it had gotten two paragraphs inside the paper and her name had been spelled wrong.

"How could the *Forrest Gazette* misspell 'Forrest'?" Lacey asked.

"I'm sure they would have gotten it right if my brother or I had gotten into trouble," Nate said.

Kayot had enough allies on the school board that Dr. Forrest's superintendent contract was not renewed.

"But Dr. and Mrs. Forrest were so upset about what had happened to Jill that they wanted out. They told Nate's younger brother that if he wanted to finish high school here, he could stay and live with his grandparents, but he was ready to go too."

"I didn't know that," Nate said. "Why didn't he want to stay?"

"Cooper was tired of everyone expecting him to be as smart as Jill," Pete said, "and as successful as you."

If Nate's younger brother did want to be the Number One Son, as Nate had said last night, Lacey could understand.

"This seems strange," she said, "that Pete knows all this and you don't. Are you a hometown boy or not?"

"Of course he is," Pete said instantly.

"Not like you," Nate said. "I was only around during the summers. I never went to a school dance. I never saw you play football."

"You seem to have survived that," Pete said.

"Yes, but it's strange to come back and feel as if I was never really a part of things like everyone else." Nate seemed surprisingly reflective. "This is my hometown. I should have all these memories and formative experiences from here, but except for a couple of our escapades, I don't. My sister and brother do, you do, even my dad and grandpa did, but I don't."

"Not every formative experience is all that great," Pete pointed out.

"Yes, but mine were made on the slopes, not here."

Lacey thought about herself. Very few of her memories were anchored in one place. She could remember in sixth grade staring down the fourth-grade boys who were bullying David, but she had no idea where they were living at the time.

What would it have been like to have walked over here and felt that she belonged? That she was more than a visitor on a three-year pass?

She had no idea, but she did know that it was time to go home.

"Do you have to?" Nate groaned. "Listen, can you cut out tomorrow afternoon? Pete swears that he is taking the afternoon off. We're borrowing a pair of snowmobiles. I'm sure we could snare another one. Why don't you come?"

Take the afternoon off? She couldn't do that. What was he thinking?

She had to fight the flash of irritation she felt. He might not have anything to do, but she certainly did.

Pete must have read her expression. "What about dinner?" he suggested quickly. "We're driving down to Ma's BBQ, and then Nate is leaving for North Carolina from there."

Ma's BBQ was an hour south of town. Lacey had heard of it, but she had never been. Dr. Byrd took calls on Thursday nights. She could go.

* * * *

She managed to get out of the clinic on time Thursday afternoon, but as she was standing in front of her closet wishing that she had something fun to wear, her cell rang. It was Valerie, the clinic's office manager. The owner of a dude ranch an hour north of town had called. One of his mares was having a difficult birth.

"Dr. Byrd's on call tonight."

"No, he said you should go. They are your clients."

That was true. Lacey had brought in this lucrative piece of business. During Lacey's first year, the owner of the dude ranch had called the clinic asking for a second opinion because his usual vet's treatment hadn't been working. Lacey had no idea what was wrong either, but at least she was willing to admit it. She had gone to UC Davis, one of the best vet schools in the country, and she had called her equine professor. He told her what cultures to take, and with her describing what she saw, he was able to diagnose the very unusual parasite. The treatment worked, and now, because of Lacey, the ranch used Dr. Byrd's clinic exclusively.

Dr. Byrd took only a small overhead out of the ranch's invoice and very generously gave Lacey the rest. So of course she had to go. She unzipped her good slacks, letting them fall to the floor, kicking them aside rather than hanging them up—something she never did.

This was so disappointing. It was bad enough that she hadn't had a chance to be alone with Nate since Tuesday night, but not to even get to say good-bye to him?

The dude ranch owner was surprised to see her. He was expecting Dr. Byrd. "I thought he was on his way. I guess I should call him and tell him you're already here."

A few minutes later Dr. Byrd called her. He was puzzled about her being there. "I know Valerie suggested sending you, but I told her no. She must have gotten confused."

Oh no, Valerie had not gotten confused. Lacey was very sure of that. This was another one of the woman's pointless little stunts.

"I am sorry," Dr. Byrd continued, "but as long as you're there..."

Her barn boots already had manure and straw trapped in the ridges; her coveralls would have to be put in a special laundry bag so that they could be washed in ultra-hot water and disinfecting detergent. She was now two hours away from Ma's BBQ where Pete and Nate were.

She tried to talk herself out of being angry, but she failed. Valerie was constantly doing things like this—not ordering enough knee-length embroidered lab coats for Lacey so that at least twice a month Lacey had to wear one of the short ones that the vet techs wore. It didn't make a hoot of a difference. The clients knew that Lacey was the doctor, but Valerie clearly felt triumphant every time it happened.

Well, now you've actually hurt me, Valerie. Are you happy?

Chapter 7

When Nate first started going to competitions, he began hearing about two other kids, Seth Street and Ben Healy, who were supposedly as good as he was. He hadn't liked the sound of that. He didn't want any other kid his age to be as good as he was. But as all three of them began competing above their age levels and were surrounded by the heady, masculine, aggressive older riders, they were relieved to have each other's company. Their parents were deeply concerned about their young sons being around such high-spirited men that they coordinated schedules, and the boys did everything together, chaperoned by Seth's mother.

The three of them had been tight ever since, and it was now Seth's wedding that Nate was attending. Seth's hometown was near Boone, North Carolina, about 175 miles from the restaurant where he and Pete had had dinner. But it was an easy trip. And a familiar one. Nate's parents had often driven him down and Ben's family had brought him up from Georgia so that Seth's mom and the three boys could head off toward the snow.

Good memories. Good times.

Dinner with Pete hadn't been so great. They were both disappointed that Lacey hadn't made it, and Nate felt as if Pete was needling him about something, saying how great it must be to take time off without worrying about money, stuff like that. Nate hadn't liked it.

There had been an even more awkward moment during planning the night before. Nate had turned to her and said, "Shall I pick you up at work or at the farmhouse?"

He had said it unthinkingly. It was what you did. Even if you'd only been with a woman for a night or so, you offered to pick her up. Of course you did.

"At the farmhouse," she had answered, and there had been a quick lilt to her smile. They were both thinking the same thing—maybe there would be a little time for...

She was the first to realize how this could sound to Pete. She spoke quickly, "That means you'll have to drive me home, Pete. I hope that is okay."

Then she hadn't been able to come at all.

It didn't matter now. It was over. A fun couple of days and then done. He was driving south. Pete would leave when Almost Heaven opened. The resort was bound to bring in some rich, educated guy who would be a perfect match for a beautiful veterinarian. Lacey deserved that. She really did. She was so great.

But it was hard to imagine her with some other guy.

There was no point in stewing about it. He was driving south, out of the picture.

What he needed to be stewing about was his parents. Of course, they would be at Seth's wedding. The three sets of parents had remained close. In fact, the three moms knew that Seth was going to marry Caitlin well before Seth himself had realized it. That was great. The issue that Nate didn't like thinking about was the family meeting that had left him growling at his brother. His parents must have hated that. At least he hadn't made that crack about Cooper wanting to be the Number One Son. That would have really hurt them.

It would be nice if he could tell them that he was joining the Peace Corps or applying to medical school, but since he didn't have a college degree, neither of those was much of an option. It would have been even better if he had come up with a plan for doing something at Endless Snow.

He kept waiting for this idea to appear. His mind didn't work by slowly calculating the pieces of a rational argument. He would have no idea that he was even contemplating something until a decision would appear. That was how he had always been.

But what was appearing now was a flat, hard truth. Endless Snow did not need him. Whenever his parents expanded a department, they hired really great people, people who loved revamping the retail sales or coordinating weddings. Endless Snow had a great social media presence, managed to get along with all the rival camps in the winter-sports community, and supported obscure little charities that turned out to be in the right place at the right time. That was all Cooper's doing. Jill's programming often struck Nate as completely looney-tunes. A classical music week at a ski resort? How crazy was that? But it had been so popular that they were having two such weeks next year.

The resort didn't need him. That was all there was to it. He was done competing. Lacey Berryville was going to find that rich, educated dude. More businesses in Forrest were going to close. There was nothing to do but accept it all and move on.

* * * *

He arrived at the hotel around midnight, but the front desk was expecting him. Caitlin's family had put together a nice welcome bag; it had maps, protein bars, an apple, an orange, and trail mix along with little bottles of water and wine. The bag had a copper metallic sheen and was tied with a twist of aqua and teal ribbons. Those must be the wedding colors. He probably had an aqua-colored carnation boutonniere in his future.

He liked weddings. He was a good guest and an even better groomsman. He never got hammered, and he never brought a date. He flirted with the married bridesmaids, tried to seduce the single ones, and asked the grandmothers to dance, something that the single bridesmaids found more alluring than more conventional seduction techniques. It should be a good weekend.

Things went downhill from there.

He met Ben at the hotel's complimentary breakfast buffet.

"So today we pick up our tuxes and then become Seth's mother's slaves"—the rehearsal dinner was a cookout at the Street family's lake house—"tomorrow we keep Seth from wigging out. Sunday is the brunch, and any cleanup they need us to do. Did I leave anything out?"

Ben shook his head. "That's it, but Seth isn't going to wig out. It should be Caitlin having second thoughts, not Seth."

That was true. Caitlin and Seth had met while—of all the strange things—serving on a jury together. After the trial had finished, she had had the guts to fly to Oregon to knock some sense into Seth. Everyone there had instantly adored her. Ben had once had a girlfriend, Colleen, who had fit in like that. She had been lively, warm, and funny, but none of them ever thought any woman could be so perfect for one of them until Caitlin had shown up.

What about Lacey? What would the guys think of her?

That was a pointless question. They would never meet her.

"So on Monday," Nate said to Ben, not wanting to think about Lacey, "what do you say we try surfing? We'd probably be pretty good at it. I'm thinking Portugal, Costa Rica, maybe Australia."

Ben shook his head again. "No. I've got a lot of ground to make up before I start boot camp."

"Boot camp" was a nine-month program that would make Ben even geekier than he already was. "Why don't you ask Motorneck or Steve Carter?" Ben suggested. "They're always up for something."

"Those guys?" Keith Matternach and Steve Carter were a pair of trust-fund babies who hung around with the pros, never good enough to compete themselves. They showed up at all the parties with expensive liquor, gorgeous girls, and even more expensive drugs. Nate had zero respect for them. What made Ben think that Nate would want to go anyplace with them? They were major wannabes.

Whereas he was a has-been. Surely on the hierarchy of lame-o's, has-beens were above wannabes. But still lame.

How come Ben had been able to figure out how to move on? He had never ridden with the creative flair that Seth had or the muscle that Nate had. He had more silver and bronze medals than almost anyone on the circuit, but he only made it to the top of the medal stand when someone else messed up.

Ben had two things going for him. First were his looks. He had the black-Irish thing, wild black hair and deep-set green eyes. Lots of people said that he was the best-looking of the three of them. And he was smart, super-smart. He was definitely the sharpest tool in the shed. His elevator didn't just go to the top floor; it went up to the penthouse that hadn't gotten built yet. He could watch a trick and spot the three tiny things the rider was doing wrong, things that no one else would notice. And then he could explain himself, something Nate could never do.

He would have made a great coach, but last summer he had flamed out, publicly criticizing the whole winter-sports establishment, saying that the training programs weren't safe, that parents were being misled about their kids' potential, and so on. A lot of doors slammed shut, hence this computer geek thing.

"So what's the deal with the lady veterinarian?" Ben asked. "Did you completely screw up her software? Is she young? Is she pretty?"

"No, yes, and yes."

"Go on."

Nate knew that Ben wasn't asking about the software. "She's actually awesome. Outdoorsy, strong. She's got a purebred husky that can pull a dogsled, and she climbs fences in the middle of the night to go treat a bull."

"And you aren't going back?" Ben asked.

"No, it was a short-term thing. She's no Colleen."

Ben made a face. "Are you ever going to stop that?"

"Probably not."

One of the dumbest things this very smart man had ever done, maybe even dumber than torpedoing his coaching career, had been to let Colleen Ridge get away. They all thought that, even the moms. Now women were judged as to whether or not they were a Colleen. *She's a lot of fun, but she's not the new Colleen.* Their friend Ryan, who thought he was in love with every woman he had a drink with, was constantly declaring that he had met his Colleen.

All day the two of them took orders from Mrs. Street, obeying her even better than they had when they were twelve. In the middle of the afternoon, Nate had to go back to the hotel to meet his parents, because, idiot that he was, he had charged out of Oregon last week without bringing the right clothes. Caitlin was from a pretty classy Southern family, and he couldn't spend the weekend in a snowboarder's baggy jeans and tattered hoodie.

"Thanks, Mom." He kissed her cheek. "I acted like an ass last week. I wish I had an excuse, but I can't think of one."

"Oh, honey." She patted his arm. "We understand."

They went to sit in a corner of the lobby. The hotel's bar wasn't open yet, but there was a coffee station. Nate offered to get his mother a cup of tea. She refused, but gushed about how thoughtful that was of him.

He looked at her suspiciously. "Lay off it, Mom."

As a West Virginian first grade teacher, his mother had worn denim jumpers over turtlenecks. The turtlenecks were often dotted with a pattern of little flowers. She still dressed informally, but with a crisper, more put-together air: trousers with creases, shirts with buttons. She often added a bracelet or a scarf. Resort guests found her approachable and welcoming, but also like someone you could trust to enforce standards of hygiene.

"So how are things at home?" his father asked.

Twelve years, and Dad was still calling Forrest home. "It's totally whack. There are all these construction workers, but they just fly by on the bypass. The closest they ever get to Main Street is the liquor store. Even the ones renting rooms in town just pick up food at the Subway and then disappear. It is like the town wants it that way. They don't want newcomers. But that's not what you want to talk about," he added abruptly.

"No," his father admitted. "No, it's not."

His mother reached over the table and took his hand. "I don't want you to think that the rest of us don't appreciate what you've done."

"It doesn't seem like Jill and Cooper do."

"I know, but at the same time they don't feel that you appreciate what they've done. Of course, all the marketing is about you, but the guests' actual experience...that's what makes people come back themselves and then tell their friends to come too."

"And I don't have a thing to do with that," he admitted. The food, the friendliness of the staff, the efficiency of the ski lifts, the cleanliness of the rooms—he had never paid any attention to any of that. "I know the two of you would love it if I could come and do the sort of thing that Jill and Cooper do, but let's face it. The resort doesn't need me."

"That was Cooper's point. You would be miserable if we made up a job for you, if you were doing something that wasn't real."

That was true, but Nate didn't believe that Cooper was too deeply concerned about his emotional well-being. "I don't want to be somewhere that I'm not needed."

"We know that," his mother said. "We know that you need to be needed."

Before Nate could protest that he was no Boy Scout, his father spoke. "Actually, Nate, the more I think about it, the more you remind me of Aeneas."

Aeneas? Who the hell was that?

His parents knew, in theory, that he didn't have the big-time liberal arts education that everyone else in the family did, but they never seemed to realize how much had been left out of his GED curriculum.

"Was he one of those ancient Greeks?" Nate guessed. Hadn't there been a movie about that?

"Actually, he was Trojan, and the *Aeneid* was written in Latin."

Close enough. In fact, pretty damn good. "So why do I remind you of him? Did he keep breaking his bones?"

"Actually he would have. He wanted to. "

His father outlined the story. Aeneas's mother, who was the goddess Venus, had given him a mission; he was to sail off to Italy and found the city of Rome. To do that, he had to stay alive. So when Troy was burning—that was the whole wooden-horse thing from the movie—instead of standing with his fellow soldiers and dying nobly, he had to slink away. Throughout the rest of his adventures, he had to go against all his warrior instincts to be sure that he stayed alive.

"What does that have to do with me?"

"You knew how much the resort depended on you during those first couple years. We needed you to go on winning, and you did. Then we needed you and your friends to hang around the lobby being cool, and you did. We needed you to stay out of trouble, and you did. But now everything

THE LAST SNOWFALL   85

is on solid ground. We don't need you to go on competing, and even if you got in trouble, the resort would be fine."

"That's good, isn't it?"

"For the rest of us, but maybe not for you. You'd always go right up to the edge, but never cross over it because you knew that we were depending on you. Nobody's depending on you now. I'm afraid that without that, you'd be restless and dissatisfied, and you'd get in trouble."

"You are so loyal," his mother said. "Seth didn't keep up with any of his hometown friends, and Ben only sees his brothers. You've never let your friendship with Pete go."

"I suppose." Nate had to agree, but as in everything, he probably went too far in the loyalty department, like putting up bail money for an ex-girlfriend's new boyfriend. That might have been too far, but fortunately his parents didn't know about that.

"Seth is intensively competitive," his dad was saying, "which explains why he made the Olympic team. Ben loves figuring out new things. You'll probably scoff at this idea, but you need to feel like you are doing something good. All that crazy, wild energy of yours is wonderful when you've harnessed it. You like risk, you thrive when you are taking risks, but if you hadn't had a mission for all these years, you'd probably be dead."

"With five illegitimate children," his mother added.

"Mom!"

"Peggy!"

Nate and his dad had spoken at the same time.

"Okay, maybe only two," his mother corrected. "But it would have been okay. We adore Jill's girls."

"So is that the mission you're giving me? To have a bunch of little bastards? I can probably do that."

"No, Nate." His father was still being serious. "The mission part is something you will have to figure out for yourself."

"But didn't you say that Aeneas's mother stepped up to the plate for him on that one, gave him a mission? Maybe I'd be better off if my mother were a goddess."

"Oh, son." His father reached back and put an arm around Nate's mother. "Your mother is a great deal more like Venus than you could ever know."

Nate pushed back from the table. "I don't think I want to hear this. No, I know that I don't."

That conversation had done exactly zero good. If the standard was now founding a major European capital, what hope was there for him?

* * * *

The Streets' lake house property was a perfect setting. The evening cooled off quickly once the sun faded, but the Streets had studded the property with rented propane heaters. Earlier in the day, Nate and Ben had enlarged a fire circle and people gathered around a bonfire. And there was nothing wrong with an event where the pretty ladies needed to huddle up under a blanket…although as it turned out, the pretty ladies that Nate was keeping warm were Seth's little nieces. But he didn't mind. They were sweet kids, all excited about their flower girl dresses.

Nate and Ben had flipped a coin to see which one would be the best man, and Ben had won—or lost, depending on how you looked at it. So Ben had to keep track of the rings, which Nate could have done by harnessing his warrior energies and all. But the best man also had to give a speech, a job that Nate was happy not to have.

It was one thing to deliver a speech on behalf of a sponsor or take questions from the media after winning a gold medal. But Seth and Caitlin were so great, he was so happy for them, and their coming together meant so much to him…he couldn't imagine trying to talk about that.

"This is for the best," he had said when Ben was starting glumly at George Washington's receding hairline on the face of the quarter. "You'll do the whole Irish 'kiss the Blarney Stone' thing, whereas I would have just stood up and said, 'Here's to the new Colleen' and then sat down."

Ben made a face. "Don't think I wouldn't slug you. I know you claim to be stronger than me, but I know the location of all the screws and plates and duct tape that hold you together. I'd be able to do some damage."

* * * *

Nate supposed that all brides looked good, but Caitlin was something else. She had clouds of dark hair and beautiful dark eyes. She was wearing her hair down because Seth had said that fancy updos scared him. Her white dress was floaty and glittery, shimmering in the soft lights of the country-club ballroom where the reception was.

The two bridesmaids, Caitlin's sister and a cousin, were wearing dresses that started aqua on top and then shaded into a dark teal at the bottom. Nate supposed there was a word for that, but he didn't know it. They looked pretty, but both were married. The flower girls had been swept off to bed, and Caitlin's friends who had come in from San Francisco seemed to all be gays and lesbians.

"If we were really as progressive and edgy as snowboarders are supposed to be," he said to Ben at one point in the evening, when they were standing on the little mezzanine where the bar was, looking out at the crowd of dancers, "wouldn't we ask one of the gay guys to dance?"

"I can do that. No problem. They're going to play some Irish music later on, and guys in Ireland jig together all the time."

Then Ben was going to beat him on that one. "Your speech was good. I was impressed."

"It wasn't bad, you're right. My sister did a good job."

"Your sister wrote it?"

"I certainly didn't."

Cooper probably could have won a Nobel Prize in best-man speechwriting, but it would have never occurred to Nate to ask him for help. Maybe that was what super-smart people had going for them; they knew when to ask for help.

The dance floor was a swirl of moving bodies. Caitlin was the only woman on the floor wearing white, and in this crowd, Nate's eye always went to her even if it was to the drift of her shimmering skirt. He supposed that was the point of weddings, everything being about the bride.

He wondered if Lacey would invite him when she married the rich, educated dude. A number of his ex-girlfriends had invited him to their weddings.

But did she even qualify as an ex-girlfriend? They had only had a few days together.

"It's interesting," he said to Ben, "Caitlin's and Colleen's name being so similar. They kind of look alike too, don't they?"

"Not at all," Ben said crisply. "Caitlin has all that hair and those amazing eyes. Colleen's are nothing special."

Colleen was plenty pretty. "They're both short."

"My sister said that we should call short women 'petite.' It sounds better."

"Okay."

Nate himself wasn't one for petite women. He had once gone out with a very tiny, delicately boned woman. She was barely five feet tall and probably didn't even weigh a hundred pounds. Halfway through the evening, he had realized there was no way he could have sex with her. All he could think of to do with her was to put her on a shelf and dust her every so often.

Lacey wasn't petite. She was five seven, maybe even five eight, and she was strong. Caitlin was clearly fit; she looked great in her strapless wedding gown, but Nate had seen Lacey scoop up her dog effortlessly, and Tank probably weighed fifty pounds.

And then there was that time in bed when she had trapped him with his arms folded so he had absolutely no leverage. He wasn't into bondage or anything like that, but her being so strong…he had liked that.

And the feel of her hands on him, he had liked that too. Her touch had seemed so trained and knowing. She had kept her hands arched; only the pads of her fingertips explored him, searching out each scar, her sensitive index finger tracing the little ridge of hardened tissue. She didn't flatten her hand against him until near the end, until she was fully aroused, and then she had spread her fingers wide. It was as if she couldn't get enough of him. That had been great, really great.

Why hadn't he asked her to come to the wedding? His invitation had had a "plus one." It would have been fun to have her here. He wanted the guys to meet her. They would like her.

She was down-to-earth; she was a problem-solver; she liked to figure things out. And the things she figured out were important—diagnosing valuable farm animals or people's much-loved pets. She confronted suffering every day in her job.

She wasn't as spontaneous as the rest of them. And the way she had, completely out of the blue, asked him if he had condoms—she hadn't known how else to do it. But when she had first looked up at him, everything about her seemed to glow with warmth. Her hair was the color of nuts in the autumn; her skin was golden with flecks of russet freckles, she was a creature of the outdoors, the earth. And the way she cooked, those deep warm spices…even her chili was sexy. That caution of hers, he couldn't believe that it was really bone-deep. He had to believe that he hadn't seen the whole person yet.

He had been thinking about her all weekend. That had to mean something. When something wasn't important—a fan whining that his people had swept him away when it was almost her turn to get an autograph—he forgot about it. When there was nothing he could do to change things—getting a bronze medal when he was sure he had earned the gold—he forgot about it.

But he wasn't forgetting about Lacey Berryville. That must mean that she was important. And perhaps that there was something he could do about it.

And of course there was. He could go back.

Chapter 8

"Peggy Forrest's son, he was such a pretty little boy."

Once Mrs. Byrd had moved to the rehab center attached to the hospital, Lacey visited her every Sunday afternoon. One of the changes Lacey had suggested at Dr. Byrd's clinic was Sunday walk-in hours. The construction workers were happy not to have to make appointments, and Lacey and KimAnne, the vet tech, were happy to have the extra work.

This made it easier to visit Mrs. Byrd than if Lacey had had to get dressed and drive into town. Lacey never regretted the visit. She did like the old lady.

"I wouldn't call him 'pretty,'" she answered, "but he is an attractive man if you like the rumpled snowboarder type."

"And do you?"

The question startled Lacey. She and Mrs. Byrd had lived together for more than two years, and they had never completely dropped their company manners to discuss anything intimate. This had probably been Lacey's fault. She had been cautious at first, knowing that she was intruding on Mrs. Byrd in her home. By the time she relaxed, the pattern had been set.

"I like the look." Lacey decided to tell the truth as far as she could. "But I'm used to people who have goals. He doesn't have a clue what he's going to do with himself."

At work on Friday morning, Valerie had pretended to apologize for having sent Lacey to the Mattsons'. "It's this new business with people making appointments on the computer. Nate Forrest did warn us that there would be an adjustment period."

This had nothing to do with the new system. The dude ranch owner had called the after-hours emergency line. But Lacey wasn't going to bicker with

Valerie. She ignored her and checked the pockets of her lab coat to be sure
that she had her prescription pad and favorite pen.

"And how was I to know that you had dinner plans with those two boys?"

So Valerie had known. She had somehow learned that Lacey had evening
plans and had wanted to ruin them.

Why? What on earth was the point of doing something so petty and
malicious? *If you truly hate me, have the guts to do some real damage.*
Valerie could have switched the label on an injection Lacey was about to
give. She could have changed the pharmacy records and made it look as if
Lacey were selling pain meds on the sly.

Lacey took a breath. She only had to live with this until August. That
was the one good thing about her departure. She wouldn't have to put up
with Valerie anymore.

In the middle of the morning on Friday, Nate's name flashed across the
screen of Lacey's phone. He had sent her a text. *Great spending so much time
with you. Hope your magic worked on Big'un. Take care of yourself. Nate.*

She read the message again. Was this what happened after casual hookups?
A breezy text and a "take care of yourself"? When hadn't she taken care of
herself? It wasn't as if anyone else ever had.

Mrs. Byrd wanted to know how the farmhouse had done during the
snow. "I never thought I would ever say this, but it was a bit of a relief to
be all cozy here."

Lacey told her about the power going out, but that Pete and Nate had been
there. She didn't go into any detail about precisely who had been there when.

"I'm glad you had some help. This is the end of winter. As soon as the
snow is gone, spring will come fast."

Spring would bring the thickening tips of the redbud trees, the brook trout
in the cold mountain streams, the deep sweet scent of the honeysuckle, and
the pinks and purples of the rhododendrons blazing on the hillsides.

This would be Lacey's last spring in West Virginia.

The fastest route from the hospital to the farmhouse would be the bypass
road, but the bypass had been graded for speed while the county roads rose
and fell with each change in the earth. The back roads passed by a burnt-
out barn, the collapsing roof of an abandoned farmhouse, the piles of rocks
built up by long-ago farmers who had tilled the fields with plows drawn by
horses, mules, or oxen, and a cemetery.

The small graveyards next to the churches had been full for generations.
The Protestants had joined together to build this one on a few acres of donated
pasture land. It was surrounded by a low board fence, a stone arch marking

the entrance. The Boy Scouts had painted the fence white last summer. It blended into the melting snow.

Mrs. Byrd's husband was buried here, and Lacey had come with her to visit his grave. The first time Lacey had come, she had marveled at the number of headstones commemorating people named Forrest. She hadn't realized that the town had been named after an actual family. She had seen *FORREST DRY GOODS* carved in the stone above the closed hardware store, but she had assumed that the store had been named after the town, not the other way around.

Lacey pulled off onto the shoulder of the road. Tank stuck his head over her shoulder, curious as to why they had stopped. She would like to get out, go see if she could find Nate's grandparents' graves, but the afternoon sun was warming the section where she remembered the Forrest family graves being. The ground would be slushy. If she got out with Tank, his paws and underbelly would be a mess.

So she stayed in the truck, looking through the stone arch. There was one small column-like obelisk; the rest were upright headstones with oval or square tops. When the snow melted, there would be some faded plastic bouquets and a few foil-covered pots with the twiggy remains of a flowering plant. Would there be, near Nate's grandparents' graves, space for Nate's parents even though they had moved away? What about Nate and his sister and brother and their families?

She envied them. If her father died, how would she find out? She wasn't even sure where he lived. She crossed her arms across the steering wheel and listened to Tank's steady, even breath, the sound filling the cab of the truck.

Mrs. Byrd had had a home. She had grown children who fussed over her and grandchildren who could tease her. She had neighbors who brought her eggs and tomatoes and a minister who asked for her advice. She had graves to visit.

How did a person make that kind of life for herself? Lacey had no idea.

* * * *

She saw the car first, the white rental, parked in the farmhouse driveway. It was Nate's car. Nate had been driving that car.

She felt giddy, flooded with golden, sparkling champagne. This was what she hadn't dared let herself think about, Nate coming back, the laughter, the magic. This was too good to be true.

But…but…in her experience things that were too good to be true were always, always, *always* untrue. When had it been any different? She suddenly felt sour. Something was wrong. It had to be. It always was.

He had left room for her to pull the truck into the garage, but as she came up the drive, she saw him coming down the front walk, moving with his broad-shouldered, snowboarder-cool assurance. She stopped the truck behind his car. He had the gate open by the time she and Tank were out of the truck.

"Nate, what are you doing here?"

"I came back to see you. And, of course, my buddy, Tank." Nate was already down on one knee, greeting Tank. The front walk was almost dry. He must have shoveled it while he was waiting. "I left without saying good-bye to my Iditarod pal."

"No, Nate, be serious. What are you doing here?"

"I came to apologize." He stood up easily, gesturing for her to go through the gate so he could close it. "I should have asked you to come to Seth's wedding with me. It would have been fun to have had you there."

"What? You can't just invite someone to go to a wedding two days beforehand."

"Why not? Caitlin's mom is chill."

"You said that this was a dinner dance at a country club with place cards and all. Nobody's mother is that chill."

"Okay, I probably wasn't serious about that."

Tank was pulling at his leash. Lacey checked the gate and let him free. He immediately started to race through the melting snow, running the perimeter of the yard.

"Then why are you here?"

"I came to see you. What's wrong with that? We had fun."

Fun? Was that what it was? *Fun?* "I thought you were going surfing."

"That didn't pan out," he said casually. "Ben couldn't go."

She was right, so right, about this being too good to be true. He was bored. He didn't have anything to do. So he'd come back here. She was supposed to entertain him. "So I am Plan B?"

He drew back, startled at her tone. "No, Lacey, it's not like that, not at all."

"And why not? Ben couldn't drop everything and be your playmate. What makes you think that Pete or I can either?"

"That's not what I had in mind."

"Then tell me, what did you have in mind?"

Lacey got angry when someone mistreated an animal. Increasingly she was angry with Valerie, and now, suddenly she was angry again. She was angry at Nate for coming back like this, for sauntering in after a weekend of dancing and champagne, for being so confident about everything, for being so good-looking.

It felt good to be mad at him. Breezy texts…that's what you did when you didn't care. Anger, this much anger—oh, you cared.

"I thought you would be glad to see me." Clearly this wasn't what he had expected.

"When have I ever done anything to give you the impression that I like being surprised?" Did he really know her that little?

"Okay, so I didn't think this through, but I am here now."

"And is that enough?" she snapped. "That you decided to come back? Don't I have a say in it?"

"What are you talking about? Didn't you have a good time when we were together? Are you prepared to forget about that?"

Of course, she'd had a good time. That was something else to be mad about, that he had swooped in and made her have a good time. She didn't have time to have a good time.

Or something like that. She was too mad to think straight.

Tank was near one of the fence posts, looking back to see if Lacey was watching him. He wanted to dig. Huskies loved to dig. Lacey had spent a year teaching him that that was not acceptable. She stepped toward him and clapped her hands sternly. He pouted for a moment and then started to run again.

"It was a great couple of days, Nate, but that's all it was, that's all it could ever be." Those were the rules. He had said he was leaving and wasn't coming back. He was breaking the rules. She didn't let her dog break the rules. Why should she let him?

"What's wrong with spending some more time together? Don't you think you could use some more fun in your life?"

How dare he say that? "Don't tell me what I do or don't need." This was what she had worried about, big, bold, overconfident men telling her what she needed. "You don't know me that well, and it's none of your business."

He started to speak, but she held up her hand, stopping him. She wasn't done. "I grew up with people who spent their lives trying to get what they lost, what they thought they deserved. Never again."

"Oh, don't you start on the whole 'what are you going to do with the rest of your life' thing?" Now he was getting mad.

"Why not? Aren't you here because you don't know what else to do? That you're expecting me to take the place of snowboarding? I can't do that. Pete and I have jobs. We have to have jobs. We can't drop everything to be your playmate."

"Are you turning this into some kind of class struggle? You know, I'm getting a little sick of this whole Golden Boy thing. The whole 'Oh, Nate had it so easy.' Pete's suddenly got into that big-time."

"That doesn't have anything to do with me."

"Sure it does. Why else would he suddenly have this big chip on his shoulder? Because he knows I can help you. I can shovel your drive, take your chains off, put away your Christmas decorations—"

"You did not put away the Christmas decorations. Mrs. Byrd's grandsons did."

"Whatever. When it comes to you, he wants to be in my shoes…although I guess I wasn't wearing shoes for the best part."

That was it. That was so totally over the line. "That statement may not be beneath you, but it is beneath me to have to listen to it. You say that you don't feel a part of this town. That's right. You don't deserve this place."

She didn't mean that. She really didn't. Why had she said it?

It was too late.

"I thought there was a side of you that wasn't afraid to take risks, but was I ever wrong about that. Here." He whistled for Tank and then grabbed his collar. "Hold on to your dog because I'm leaving."

Automatically Lacey curved her fingers around Tank's collar. She could feel the raised stitching, the cool metal buckle, the pebbly grain of the leather.

The gate clicked shut, the car door slammed, the engine turned and caught. He had to pull forward and then angle back to get around her truck. Once he was on the road, he shot off, the roaring of the car echoing off the melting snow.

What had happened? What had she done?

Of course, he was right. She didn't take risks. How could she? And how little did he know her to think that she could?

There were moments when Lacey would glance in the mirror and feel that the image was all wrong. She should have pale skin and black hair. She should have a narrow face and a sharp nose. The mirror should show hard-edged, even cold contrasts. Wasn't that who she was—distant, unapproachable, a person who saw only black and white, right and wrong, nothing in between? Instead her coloring was earthy and forgiving. Her hair swirled with shades of brown, wheat, chestnut, loam. Her eyes were hazel. Her natural skin tone always had a hint of summer sunshine. She looked like a person who was warm and loving.

And she was warm. She was loving.

Except that she wasn't. She was cold and frightened.

Chapter 9

What was wrong with her? Nate jammed his foot against the accelerator, fighting the rental car's sluggishness. Why couldn't Lacey see this—him and her—as an exciting adventure, something to take a chance on? Why was she making such a big deal out of him not knowing what he was going to be doing at 9:01 a.m. on Monday morning?

He started up the access lane to the bypass road, then saw traffic ahead. Oh yeah, the Sunday afternoon thing. He jerked the steering wheel, swerving back onto the county road. He charged northward, blowing through the intersections, the telephone poles whipping by. Suddenly he was on the knotted mountain roads, his rear tires squealing as he took the curves.

It felt good to be driving this fast. So what if he got stopped? So what if the world found out that he drove too fast? A snowboarder indulging in risky behavior? When had that ever happened before?

And wouldn't it be a bit of a relief, to be a bad boy, to stop keeping his nose clean all the time? Then no one would want to pay him to be a professional has-been. Maybe Ben's big flameout made some sense. He had taken the has-been option away from himself, forced himself to figure something else out.

Nate felt the calf muscles in his right leg contract; his ankle flexed down, and the ball of his foot pressed harder on the accelerator. He didn't look at the speedometer. He didn't care how fast he was going. Even in this crappy car, he could be one with the road, just as he had been one with the snow. The car was like his board, an extension of himself.

Suddenly every muscle was tensed, the knuckles of his hands were white as he gripped the steering wheel. He had slammed his foot on the brake before his conscious mind even knew why.

A battered red Ford was angled off the road, the front headlight crushed against an ash tree. A woman and a boy were at the front of the car, staring at it helplessly.

By the time he could stop, Nate was well past them. He pulled onto the road's narrow weedy shoulder and backed up slowly. In the rearview mirror, he could see that the tree was dying. It must be an ash. They were all infected by some kind of beetle. Another thing people couldn't do anything about.

Both the woman and the boy had phones in their hands. "No signal here?" he asked pleasantly as he got out of the rental car.

"No. We're between the mountains," the woman answered. It was a deer, she explained. The animal had leapt into the road, and she had swerved to avoid it.

Nate went over and looked at the car. The front fender and the tire were goners, but the situation wasn't hopeless. There'd been a lot less snow in these parts. The car wasn't too deep in the mud. "You have a spare?" he asked. He might not be Pete, but he did know how to change a tire.

She nodded. She had one.

Her son was a spindly looking kid, maybe twelve or thirteen. There was a good chance that his mother was stronger than he was, but he probably wouldn't be in love with the idea of people thinking that. So Nate suggested that the mom steer while he and the kid pushed.

The lug nuts looked like they were rusted on pretty tight, so Nate loosened them, but the rest of the job he shared with the boy. The kid didn't say much of anything until he had finished putting the hubcap back on.

"You're Nate Forrest, aren't you?"

Nate nodded.

"It was good of you to stop, real good."

"Anyone would have," Nate said.

But clearly, in the boy's eyes, Nate was not just anyone.

The nearest town was four miles away, the woman said. She'd get cell service in another two miles. She would call her mother.

Nate said he would follow them in case more was wrong with the car than they had thought.

The Ford was indeed wobbly. The woman had to drive slowly so Nate had time to think, something he hadn't done in a while.

The first of these thoughts was that he was grateful to have a professional athlete's reaction time. What had he been thinking, driving like that on mountain roads? Even if he did want to self-destruct, he didn't want to be taking this mother and son with him.

Second, he didn't actually want to self-destruct. The respect he had seen in that boy's eyes—did he want to lose that? Hell, no.

He wasn't Ben, who managed to shoot himself in the foot whenever things got good. Anyone who pushed away a woman like Colleen Ridge wasn't much of a role model to the rest of the world.

There had to be something between being a D-list celebrity on reality TV and facing criminal charges. He supposed this was the whole finding-a-mission thing that his dad had talked about. It had felt good, helping this family, but he couldn't roam the mountains for the rest of his life, looking for people who had swerved to avoid a deer.

Since it was Sunday evening, the service bays at the filling station were closed. The woman left her keys with the pump attendant. Nate waited until her mom pulled in; the mom was driving a car as old as the red Ford. Nate picked up the service station's business card. In the morning he would call and have the repairs put on his credit card. The tired look around the woman's eyes suggested that having the bill taken care of would make her Monday a lot brighter.

He set off on foot. The town was smaller than Forrest. The only places open on Sunday evenings were the bars. He headed toward the one most brightly lit in hopes of getting something to eat. He came to a little gift shop. He cupped his hands to look in the window. It had handcrafts, soap dispensers made out of mason jars and plant stands carved from local wood. A couple of stores were vacant, of course, but even they had placards in the window advertising an upcoming Spring Festival. The vestibule in the bar still had some faded notices about last summer's fishing competition and vintage car show.

This town had not given up. It was still trying to attract a little bit of outside money. Unlike Forrest. Forrest had given up. The high school was gone; half the stores were closed; the young people were moving out. It was like people were just waiting to see what would die first, them or the town.

Almost Heaven would be hiring, but a fancy resort would want its employees to be young and toned, with perfect skin and perfect teeth. That didn't describe the labor force in an aging coal-mining town. The jobs the residents could get hired for were in the kitchen and the laundry where they would need to be on their feet all day. The people who could do that had long since left Forrest.

He might not feel that he was really a part of Forrest, but he still felt bad about how things were there.

On his way to Seth's wedding, he had driven through Boone, North Carolina. It was a vibrant place, the economic hub of the Blue Ridge

Mountains. Of course, it had more going for it than Forrest; it had a university and a bunch of spots on the National Register of Historic Places. But there were so many thriving little shops, selling things to the people coming to the mountains.

By next Christmas, all these rich tourists would be coming to Forrest. They would be staying five miles outside town, and no one was trying to get them to come to Main Street. Why not? Why not get Forrest Hardware on that historic registry? The original dry goods building was every bit as historic as half the places in Boone.

Okay, Nate Forrest wasn't likely to give the world another Rome, but couldn't he do something for the town with which he shared a name?

You don't deserve this place. That's what Dr. Lacey Berryville had said. He would show her. His something-great-grandfather had pitched a tent and started the town. Gramps had brought cast-iron skillets and dried beans. Nate was going to bring the tourists. He might not have an Olympic medal, but he knew how to draw a crowd.

He asked for his burger wrapped to go and paid for his beer without touching it. At a much more sedate pace, he headed west, finding a motel on the outskirts of Charleston. First thing Monday morning he drove to the State Capitol building, climbed the broad limestone steps, and asked the security guard how he could find someone who knew about the tourist industry.

Yes, the idea had come to him, full-blown and clear, as ideas always came to him. But he knew that the idea wasn't enough. He needed a plan. He should have had a plan when he showed up on Lacey's doorstep, and he knew a lot less about entrepreneurship than he did about courting women. He needed to be smart and ask for help.

Receptionists kept asking if he had an appointment, and of course he didn't, but his smile, his name, and—oh yes—his mission got people to talk to him. And they were helpful people, state employees who truly cared about West Virginia, who understood which rules protected the citizens and the environment and which rules were going to get in the way.

He told his parents where he was, but not why. Finally, after four days of listening, talking, planning, and strategizing, he called his dad.

"How much rent do you and Aunt Amy want for the store?"

* * * *

Mrs. Byrd was right. As the snow melted, spring came quickly. The weeping willow down by the farm pond was leafing out, a delicate blur of yellow-green softening the stark outline of the branches and twigs. The new growth on the other trees was thickening and starting to show buds. The pastures were developing a thin green glaze over the stubbly brown earth.

What if her next job were in Florida or someplace where April didn't arrive with all of this glowing promise?

She was used to having to leave places. How many times had she sat in the back seat of her mother's car, her hand on her brother's arm? Leaving was what she knew. She had never come to school and found a friend's desk empty. She didn't know what it was like to be the one left behind... not until she had sunk down on Mrs. Byrd's front steps and watched that mud-splattered white car surge off.

For the first time someone had left before she had.

But you sent him away. You were afraid.

Despite all of spring's promise, the world did seem small and dim.

The clinic's new software was working well. The system gave Lacey a regular lunch break instead of the randomly spaced brief intervals Valerie used to leave for her. New clients could download forms and fill them out at home. Katie still had to print them out—Dr. Byrd was a long way from having a paperless office—but the typed forms were much more complete and far easier to read than what the clients scrawled while sitting in the reception room with a sick animal on their laps.

Valerie was now realizing that she had made a mistake. Not a "mistake" like sending Lacey to the dude ranch, but a real mistake. She hadn't known what a system administrator was, and rather than admit that to Nate, she had airily agreed to let Katie have those privileges. She learned how to add an appointment to the computer, but when she went to put one of her own friends into an already-taken slot, the computer wouldn't accept it. Only the system administrator could double-book. And Katie refused.

So Valerie told—not asked, but told—Lacey that there would be a Post-it note on the computer screen adding Mrs. Dorf to Lacey's Thursday morning schedule and that Valerie would handwrite in the name when the schedule was printed.

Lacey checked the Thursday schedule on her phone. How great it was to be able to do that. "There's an opening in the afternoon."

"But I told her she could come at ten." Valerie had a slight underbite, so when she was angry and tightened her thin lips, her cheeks bulged, toad-like.

"I'm not going to see her at ten. We need to give the system a chance."

But later that afternoon Lacey saw that there was a Post-it note on the computer monitor. Mrs. Dorf had a ten o'clock appointment the next day, but her appointment was with Dr. Byrd. Bill Byrd hadn't been able to say no to Valerie.

There was nothing Lacey or the rest of the staff could do.

"What do you want to bet," Katie grumbled to Lacey at the end of the week, "that two months after you leave, we are back to the old way of doing things?"

Lacey shrugged. That seemed sad, but what could she do? She would be gone.

Like Nate. He had left twice now.

She wasn't going to feel sorry for herself. Her next client was the most adorable little mongrel of a puppy. He was big-eyed, healthy, and trusting, with a soft coat and a delicate jaw. This really was the best job in the world. She was so lucky. If one thing had gone wrong in the last ten years, if a professor had failed her for refusing an advance, if her car had needed a major repair, if she had been kicked by a horse and needed time off, if any one of those things had happened, she might not have been able to recover. To have gotten where she was without a safety net, how could she complain about anything?

And how could she risk all of this for a man?

Those fine thoughts didn't keep her from thinking about him. "I hope you've told Ben Healy," she said to Katie, "how much we appreciate his help." She knew that Katie had had to call him several times with questions.

"I do every time I talk to him, and I also told Nate this morning."

"Nate? Nate Forrest?" Why had she said that? What other Nate would Katie have talked to? "You talked to Nate this morning?"

"He asked if I could run over and look at the Fischers' garage after work, see what I thought about it."

"The Fischers' garage? Why does Nate care about the Fischers' garage?"

"Oh, they've turned it into an apartment. Nate's looking for a place to live. He's thinking about coming back. Didn't you know that?"

No, Lacey had not known that. After everything she had said to him, how could he be thinking about coming back?

He's not coming back for you. You lost your chance.

Several times during the week, she had noticed the feel of her jeans against the flesh of her inner thigh. Her breasts had strained against her bra, and she had thought of him, of how he had looked nude, standing next to the sofa bed. The first time they had made love—no, no, it was having sex, not making love—her hands had felt his orgasm throughout his, the tensing of his muscles, and she heard it through her ears, the gasping of his breath. But the next day she had taken her hands away so that she wouldn't be distracted by her sense of touch. She had held her breath, and she had been able to feel the throbbing release of his penis inside her.

At her next break between clients, she called Pete. "What's going on with Nate?"

"He hasn't called you?"

"No." People were assuming a lot. "There's no reason he would. He's your friend, not mine. Is he really moving back?"

"It looks like it, but I can't tell you much. Things are crazy out here, so I've just been trading texts. He asked me to go take some measurements at his grandfather's store."

Measurements at the store? "He's not planning on opening a hardware store, is he?" That seemed impossible. Not only had Pete said that the big box store in the county was taking all the hardware business, but Nate? A store?

"He says not, but I don't know what he is planning."

On Monday, Lacey overheard in the grocery store line that Nate had left a message with the now-retired history teacher from the old high school, but since the speaker was only a neighbor of a friend of the history teacher's wife, there was no more information than that. On Tuesday, a client, who, along with her husband, owned the town's used car dealership, gushed about how great it was that Nate was buying a car from them. "Surely he could have afforded a new one"—all those dealers were in the county seat—"but Teddy's out at the repo auctions, seeing what he can find for him."

So, Nate was coming back. He had talked to Pete, to Katie, to the Fischers about an apartment, to the used car dealer about a repo, and to the history teacher about God only knew what, but he hadn't said a word to her.

In a town this size, there would be no way to avoid him. She would see him on the street, at the grocery store, and at the gas station. She didn't know how to do this, how to avoid someone. She had never been in one place long enough to need to. It seemed like avoiding him would be like inching around a fiery chasm, trying not to fall into its depths glowing red with awkwardness and pain.

No wonder her parents left town every time anything got difficult. If only she could do that. But she had signed a contract; she had debts to pay. So, there was nothing to do but put on a clean lab coat, load the pockets, check the schedule, and be Dr. Berryville.

One Sunday she dutifully went to visit Mrs. Byrd. Mrs. Byrd talked about the progress she was making in physical therapy, about how good the cherry pie had been at dinner on Friday, about one of the residents needing more surgery, and about a call she had gotten from her former hairdresser.

Lacey wasn't bringing her best listening skills to this conversation.

The hairdresser had a daughter who had moved away and would like to come home for a bit because her husband was working on the construction site. The daughter had heard that Lacey was living in Mrs. Byrd's house and so had asked her mother to ask Mrs. Byrd—

Lacey started paying attention.

—since Lacey was out in the country all by herself, if the daughter could stay—

*Hairdresser mother...husband on the construction site...*Mrs. Byrd was talking about Pete's wife.

That couldn't be possible. "Are you talking about Cheri Willston?" Lacey wasn't sure what to say. "Doesn't she want to stay with Pete?"

"He lives in a company trailer on the site. That's no place for a girl."

That was right. Pete had said that when Nate asked. "How can she get away? Doesn't she need to run their business?"

"Her mother is out there. When Paula owned the salon, Dr. Byrd always said it was one of the best-run businesses in town." Mrs. Byrd always called her late husband "Dr. Byrd" when talking about him.

When Lacey didn't say anything, Mrs. Byrd raised her eyebrows and looked at her carefully. "Would you rather she not come?"

"Oh, no. Not at all." Lacey had absolutely no idea if that was true; she didn't know how she felt about this. "I was just surprised, that's all."

And how she felt didn't matter. The farmhouse was Mrs. Byrd's. Lacey wasn't even paying utilities, much less rent. If Mrs. Byrd wanted to invite the Mormon Tabernacle Choir to stay, it would have to be fine with Lacey.

But Nate and Cheri both coming to town...this couldn't be a coincidence.

Chapter 10

The rehab facility and a small nursing care unit were connected to the town's two-story hospital by an enclosed hallway. Lacey always parked in the back corner of the hospital's lot, leaving the better spaces for people who didn't like to walk. In bad weather she cut through the hospital, going in and out its rear door. On spring days like this, she took the sidewalk that skirted the buildings.

She was used to seeing her Silverado parked by itself, but today a green pickup was next to it—Pete's green pickup, the one with company plates. Pete himself was leaning against the tailgate, and Hex was sniffing around the nearby grassy strip. Pete must have come straight from the job site. His olive twill work pants were splattered with mud, although there was a clean spot at his thigh where his tool belt had been.

Lacey supposed that he had known what Mrs. Byrd was going to ask her.

She spoke brightly. "Your wife is coming out. You must be happy about that."

"I hope she won't be a burden to you."

His tone was flat. He was looking past her shoulder. Well, crap. He didn't want his wife to come.

Surely he wasn't worried that she would say anything that would jeopardize his marriage. He had to know her better than that. And what was there to say? Even when he took a heavy box out of her arms, he was careful not to touch her.

No, Pete, no. You have to be happy that she is coming. This is a good thing for you. You need to stop thinking about me.

Even if he hadn't been married, he would not have been the right man
for her. He had a darkness, a heaviness about him that she didn't need in
her life. She needed sunlight.

I need Nate.

No, that was absurd. She did not need Nate Forrest. He understood
nothing about her, nothing about how careful she felt she needed to be,
nothing about what a burden it was to have student loans, nothing about
what it was like to grow up with parents she couldn't count on. Why would
she ever need a man like that?

* * * *

Nate was coming on Friday evening, flying to Charleston from Oregon,
where he had apparently been most recently. He was taking a shuttle to
the county seat, and Pete was going to pick him up there. They would
have dinner at the new Mexican restaurant. Pete asked Lacey if she would
like to come. He was, Lacey knew, using Nate as an excuse to spend time
alone with her.

She wanted to say no. She didn't want to be alone in a car with Pete,
and she certainly wasn't eager to sit down and have dinner with Nate.

But wouldn't it be for the best? In front of Pete, she and Nate would
need to pretend that nothing had happened on the sofa bed during the
snowstorm or that Nate hadn't come back for a few hours on a Sunday
afternoon. They would need to pretend that they hadn't had sex, that they
hadn't had a horrible fight. Maybe if they pretended about that enough, it
would start to feel true.

So she agreed to go, but Friday at noon Pete called her, full of apologies.
Something had happened at the site, an injury; he couldn't get away. Did
she mind picking up Nate?

"No, of course not."

So now, instead of being alone in a car with Pete, which wouldn't be
great, she would be alone in a car with Nate, which could be awful.

She didn't have to do it. The used car dealer was so happy about selling
a late-model Escalade that he and his wife would have been quite willing
to drive the twenty miles to get Nate. They would have even driven all the
way to Charleston. All she needed to do was call.

But then she would have to explain that to Pete, make up something about
an emergency, and it was very hard to get away with lies in a town this
size. She should just go and get it over with. She was going to do exactly

what she had planned, wear her work clothes and leave Tank at the clinic so she would have an excuse to end the evening early.

But…but…after her last appointment on Friday, she saw the tiniest fleck of something on her jeans. She didn't think it was from one of the animals, but she couldn't be sure, and Nate had such a sensitive sense of smell. So, she really should shower and change, shouldn't she? Especially since she now kept nicer clothes at work.

The Mexican restaurant was freshly painted with bold shades of terra-cotta red and yellow. Scrapes hung on the wall, and the vinyl tablecloths were turquoise and patterned with red chili peppers. It seemed like a happy place. That was nice. So much of Forrest seemed tired.

Nate was already at a table. His hair was more crisply trimmed than before, and he was dressed in khakis and a polo shirt. She didn't think she had ever seen him wear a shirt with a collar before.

He was doing something on his phone, absorbed enough that he didn't look up as she crossed the room. Then suddenly he reacted. If he had been an animal, his ears would have perked forward, his tail would have lifted. Instead he pushed back from the table and stood up.

"Lacey…the soap from the clinic. I knew it was you."

Strong smells of spices and meats were swirling in from the kitchen. The limes from the margaritas at the bar had a high, piercing scent. And yet he had still noticed the orchid perfume of the shower gel and lotion that she kept at the clinic.

"Another messy day at work," she said easily. "I hope I haven't kept you waiting long."

"It was nothing." He took hold of the back of one of the wood-slatted chairs, pulling it out a little, inviting her to sit down. "It was good of you to come, especially after the way I flung myself at you the last time I was here. It was thoughtless of me. I was wrong, and I am very sorry."

Lacey dropped into the chair. When he had pulled it out for her, he had reached for the one nearest to himself, not the one on the other side of the table. She was ninety degrees from him, closer than she would have been otherwise.

"What?" he asked. "Are you surprised that I apologized?"

"I assumed that we would pretend it never happened."

"And that works for you?" He shook his head. "When you screw up as much as I do, you learn the value of apologizing. I also know that apologies aren't enough. Now, I've already ordered nachos to start with," he said.

She blinked at the change in subject. "That's fine. In fact, I won't need to order anything else. Nachos are usually enough for me." Then she heard herself start to ramble about the fat content of a nacho platter, the avocado, the sour cream, the cheese. It was all so delicious, but very filling. She sounded like an idiot. But him apologizing—she hadn't expected that.

"I told them you like cilantro," he said when she stopped for air. "I hope that's still true."

So he remembered.

Which didn't mean anything. Enough people hated cilantro that it was a good idea to remember who did and who didn't.

His polo shirt was black, and the embroidered Endless Snow logo was also black, very subtle. She might not have noticed it, but while she yammered on about dietary balance, she was watching him breathe; the black knit that spanned his chest rose and fell with his deep, easy breaths. The pulse in his neck throbbed with a slow rhythm as it had done that first night of the snowstorm when she had sat across the kitchen table, fascinated by him.

How constrained her breasts felt by her bra. The quarter moons of flesh that rose above the lacy cups seemed to be swelling, reaching toward him.

She always wore a bra in public. Always. But what if this once she hadn't? What if she had buttoned her shirt over her nakedness? Would Nate have noticed? The dense pattern of the shirt's print would have hidden her nipples, but there would have been movement, vibration. Would he want to cup her breasts with his hands? Or would he have stayed seated and pulled her to stand between his legs so that his breath would be hot against her body?

She had never understood women so urgent for penetration that they would go with a man into alleys or dark corners, even into public bathrooms, but at this moment she felt that if Nate took her hand and led her to—

No, of course, she wouldn't go. She was Dr. Berryville. And he was a man who was completely wrong for her.

"I'm hearing such mysterious things about your doings," she said brightly. "The hardware store…a history teacher. You have people curious."

She had rehearsed that. She didn't want to demand to know why he was here. She had tried that once before, and it hadn't gone well.

"I'm happy to tell everybody," he said easily. "In fact, people may get sick of hearing from me. But first I need to say something. I'm not here to stalk you."

Lacey started to murmur that she knew he wasn't, that she hadn't been worried about that, but he held up his hand. "No, let me finish. I said some things that I shouldn't have, and I regret it. Please believe me. I'm not here to torture you."

Not torture her? A minute ago, his breathing was torturing her, and as for saying things she shouldn't have, she had done her share of that too.

She couldn't bear to rehash every moment of that awful conversation. She nodded and said, "Okay." That would have to do.

"Now, the second thing I want to say may seem to completely contradict the first, but you look really good in that shirt."

"Thank you. My brother—or his mother-in-law—picked it out. They both say I shouldn't wear black and white, that I should wear brown and ivory. But I want to wash my work blouses in hot water and Clorox so—" She stopped herself. She was yammering again. "So now, are you going to tell me what you're up to?"

"I'm going to try to get something happening in the business community of Forrest, to take advantage of the opportunities that the resort is giving us."

He explained. He had a two-pronged approach. The first would be to lure the tourists into town for a few hours during their visits. The second would be to try to keep the residents, both the current ones and the new ones, from driving over to the county seat every time they needed to buy something. "I can't take credit for all this," he acknowledged freely. "We've got some people working in the state government who are really good. Who would have thought that the government was here to help us?"

"I imagine everyone who works in the government believes that."

"Snowboarders generally don't."

To get the tourists to come to town, he was going to turn the stone dry goods building of Forrest Hardware into a living history museum. "People in old-timey costumes will talk about what it was like to live in coal-mining country back in the day. Apparently rich people taking expensive vacations want to believe they are giving their kids something educational."

"So, this is where the retired history teacher comes in?"

"You don't think I know about this, do you? Anyway, he's already having a great time and is researching grants and getting on a National Register of Historic Places."

Once the tourist families had been appropriately educated, they would be encouraged to go next door into the largest of the three buildings, the one in which Nate's grandfather had displayed the power tools and gardening supplies. Nate had already hired an architect to draw up plans to add bathrooms and carve the space into stalls where people could sell local handicrafts, jams, and such. "We've going to have ice cream at the back. And the older Mattson kid, he's graduating from Tech this spring. He's all hot to see if it would be feasible to make local grass-fed ice cream."

"You talked to him?"

"Sure. What do I know about ice cream?"

"Nate, I'm sorry, but what do you know about any of this?"

"More than I did three weeks ago." He continued explaining his plan. To keep people in town, he was going to open a variety sundries store in the building that had housed the paint display and the Weber grills. The store wouldn't carry any big-ticket items. People would to still drive the twenty miles to Lowe's to buy their power tools and paint. It would have the little things—light bulbs, plastic anchors, vacuum cleaner belts, notebook paper, thumbtacks—things that people needed at the last minute.

"But the grocery store carries some of those things, doesn't it?"

"I've talked to Mr. Stonefield and managed to make him see that if his produce were as good as his meat, the new people might stay in town more."

"And he was willing to take that risk?"

"Yes, because I am helping him refinance his loan. There're some sweet government programs he didn't know about. Financing, getting cheap money, is the key to all of this." Nate was glowing with energy. "My parents made me promise that I wouldn't use my own money for any of this. When they took over the resort, they decided that they couldn't invest anything that was in their retirement accounts. Mom had to teach for the first two years because they couldn't pay themselves, but if the resort had failed, they wouldn't have gone down with the ship. So I am not paying myself, but I'm also not investing my own money. And I'm not encouraging anyone to quit their day jobs. Nobody's going to get rich off of this, and there may only be a couple of full-time jobs, but it is getting things moving."

Chapter 11

Nate had come on Friday. Cheri was arriving Sunday afternoon, and Lacey had invited Pete to come to the farmhouse for supper that evening. On Saturday she called him, asking if he would like her to invite Nate. It turned out that Cheri had already invited Nate.

"Oh."

Even over the phone, Pete sensed her surprise. "I'm sorry," he said. "Cheri can be a little impulsive. It's okay, isn't it?"

"I called you to suggest it. So obviously it's fine."

On Sunday, before going into town to staff the walk-in hours at the clinic, Lacey had set the table and finished as much of the cooking as she could. When she got back from seeing Mrs. Byrd, she decided to tidy up the front yard, picking up the sticks and twigs that had broken off during the snowstorm. She should have done it weeks ago, but she hadn't had time. As she worked, she spotted one of Tank's tennis balls under the bushes. Once green, it was now faded and looked sodden. When she nudged it with her foot, it squished unpleasantly. She decided to leave it there until she was wearing different gloves.

She heard a car. A shiny black Escalade turned up the drive. It must be Nate. She pulled off the cotton work gloves, called to Tank, and grabbed hold of his collar, keeping him close while Nate opened and closed the front gate.

He was carrying a bag from the liquor store and one from the grocery store. Tank bounded over to sniff the bag.

"You're going to think these are boring," Nate told Tank, "but hopefully your doggy-mama won't. Stonefield's had limes," he told Lacey. "I brought rum and tequila. Do you want daiquiris or margaritas?"

When the grocery store did have fresh limes, they were expensive—too expensive to be used for juice. But Nate had money. He had bought a bagful of limes. He was driving a used car only to be a good citizen. He could have bought a fully loaded Escalade brand-new. Lacey couldn't imagine what that would be like.

Anything made with freshly squeezed juice would be a great treat, she said. She didn't care which cocktail he made. She asked about his apartment. It was small, but surprisingly nice, he said.

By now Tank had retrieved his soggy tennis ball and was nudging Nate's thigh hopefully.

"Don't take it," Lacey advised. "It's been outside all winter. It's disgusting. And I'm a veterinarian. I know gross."

Nate laughed and started to try to persuade Tank to take no for an answer. Tank wasn't having any part of that, but fortunately another car turning into the drive distracted him.

A sleek little red coupe was stopping next to the windmill. Nate set down his bags and hurried through the gate. Lacey held on to Tank's collar in case Pete's wife was afraid of dogs.

The car door opened, and a tiny, light-haired sprite of a person came running toward Nate, her arms out. He didn't just hug her, he lifted her off the ground.

No one ever picked Lacey up. It wasn't something that people did.

"So I made it," Cheri said to Nate. Her voice was high and feminine. "And I didn't speed once."

"So, you finally figured out your cruise control." Nate was laughing at her. "Now, come meet your new roommate."

Cheri was birdlike, delicately boned, with shining blond hair and a lovely smile. As soon as the gate closed, Lacey let go of Tank and stepped forward. Cheri took both of Lacey's hands in hers. Her hands were tiny. Lacey felt like an elephant. "Oh my God, you are gorgeous. Nate"—Cheri twisted her head over her shoulder to talk to him—"you didn't tell me how beautiful she was."

"Ah…thank you." Lacey wasn't sure what to say.

"No, really, you're striking. You must know that."

"I don't think she wants to talk about it," Nate said.

"Oh, I don't believe that for one second. Not everyone around here tries, and she is." Now she addressed Lacey. "You have makeup on. Your jeans aren't baggy. Your belt is first-rate, and you've got this little bit of lace on your cami, right above the top of your cleavage, a perfect touch to the sexy ranch-hand look. You look really good. She does, doesn't she, Nate?"

"Yes, but she's a little overqualified for a ranch-hand position."

"But not for sexy." Cheri whacked him across the chest with the back of her hand. "No woman is ever overqualified for that."

Lacey was starting to regret having put the camisole on under her shirt. She wasn't a lace-trimmed sort of person. One of her roommates during vet school had bought it and didn't like the fit; she wanted it to be tighter. Since Lacey had a more generous build and less need to display herself, the roommate had given it to her. "Why don't you come in? Do you need help with your stuff?"

"Oh, I'll let Pete do it. He likes being useful."

Cheri was wearing a peach-colored cardigan. As soon as they were inside the house, she pulled off the sweater, turned sideways, and pleated up the back of her shirt in her hand, pulling it close to her body. "Look, what do you think?" She was obviously talking to Nate.

Now it was his turn not to know what to say. "You're as pretty as ever?"

"No, dummy, look. Look at my boobs."

"Okay...I don't usually need to be told to do that." He was still at a loss.

"Did you get implants?" Lacey asked.

"Of course." She clapped her hands over her breasts. "That's one of first things I did when money started coming in. I didn't look this good even when I was fifteen...and you should remember." Again she was talking to Nate.

He made a feeble little gesture. Clearly he still didn't know what to say.

Lacey decided to rescue him again. "I don't know what you looked like before, but the result is tasteful, in proportion to your build. Some of our clients are the women who come to dance at the strip clubs. Even when they are just dressed to bring their pets in to the clinic, they don't look right in normal clothes."

"A strip club? Here? In our little hometown?"

"No, things haven't changed that much." Nate had rediscovered his vocal abilities. "The strip clubs are down by the state line."

"So why do people come up here? Isn't there a vet down there?"

"There is, but everyone likes Lacey, and the strippers, I imagine, are probably particularly sick of men. They like that she is a woman."

Cheri rolled her eyes as if she couldn't imagine ever being sick of masculine attention.

"Some packages came for you," Lacey said. "I put them upstairs." Lacey had decided to put Cheri in Mrs. Byrd's room. It had a queen-sized bed. "Do you want me to take you up?"

Nate said that he was going to start squeezing limes.

"Those boxes," Cheri said to Lacey on their way up the stairs, "I hope you didn't say anything about them to Pete. They're a surprise."

Lacey shook her head as she directed Cheri to the front bedroom. "I haven't seen him all week."

She had cleared out the rest of the drawers in Mrs. Byrd's room and packed away the clutter that had been on the surfaces, neatly labeling the boxes even though three-quarters of the stuff was junk that needed to be thrown away. She had washed the curtains and the quilted bedspread and had left the windows open for most of the week, so the room no longer had a musty old-lady smell.

"I wished I could have gotten flowers," Lacey apologized. "But there's no place in town to buy fresh flowers, and the wildflowers haven't blossomed yet."

Cheri waved a hand. "I don't care. It's so good of you to let me stay here." She sat down on the bed and bounced a little, testing the mattress. "The strippers who come to see you, did you talk to them about their jobs? What it's like to have people watch you? Do you ever think about that?"

"Think about being a stripper? No, never. But I imagine that I would be terrible at it. I would stand up there and take my clothes off as if I were at the doctor's office, and I don't think that would be very alluring."

"But you've slept with different men, haven't you?"

What a very odd question to ask someone you had known for fifteen minutes. "I'm almost thirty, so of course."

"I got married at eighteen, and believe it or not, I have been faithful to my husband. But what's it like? I mean, how do you decide when to have sex with someone?"

"Sometimes you make mistakes."

"Oh…that sounds interesting."

"Actually it isn't." Lacey felt she needed to put a stop to this conversation.

"But it's not like Pete's the only guy I've had sex with. Nate and me… we were each other's first."

Lacey had been moving toward the door. She stopped. "Nate? You and Nate? I thought—"

"It was in high school. Pete and I had broken up for a bit one summer. Since then I have been a faithful wife."

"I'm sure that's important to Pete."

Cheri laughed. "If he ever thinks about it. It might never have occurred to him that either one of us might be unfaithful. Now, tell me what you think of Nate. He's cute, isn't he?"

Cute? "He is planning on doing a lot of good work around here."

"Don't be silly. You know that's not what I was talking about."

Fortunately Nate called up from the bottom of the stairs. The drinks were ready.

"Oh good." Cheri jumped up.

The drinks were wonderful, not as sweet as the mixes and certainly without the chemical aftertaste. They were a little strong…but Lacey wasn't driving anyway, so why not?

Cheri was talking to Nate, her voice light and teasing. "Lacey's been trying to tell me that she wouldn't make a very good exotic dancer, but I am not sure that I believe her."

"Oh?" Nate raised his eyebrows. "I thought there was a lot of potential in the sexy ranch hand."

"I have a Burdizzo out in the truck," Lacey said. "I could swing that around." Clearly the other two didn't get her joke. "A Burdizzo is a pincher tool for castrating livestock," she explained. "Every sexy ranch hand should have one."

"Oh." Nate apparently didn't like the idea of the pincher tool. "Maybe you should keep your clothes on."

Lacey hadn't had much lunch. The alcohol was already making her feel quite splendid. "Or I could do a snake act," she continued. "I'm not afraid of snakes. But I guess you would have to research the exotic pet regs in every county you went to. And then there's the issue of maintaining temperature control when you're traveling. You can't let boa constrictors get cold. This actually might be harder than one might suppose."

"Is she joking?" Cheri asked Nate.

"I think so," he answered. "But I can't be sure. Reptilian temperature is something she might take very seriously."

"You smell like limes," Lacey told him.

Tank suddenly let out a little howl. "Is he laughing at your joke?" Cheri asked.

"No, he doesn't find me funny either. He probably heard Pete's truck."

"Oh, great!" Cheri jumped up. Lacey and Nate followed her to the door. By the time they got outside, Pete was letting Hex out. Cheri called to the dog, and as soon as Pete opened the gate, Hex came dashing toward her, his tail wagging. He jumped up on her with such enthusiasm that Nate had to catch her by the shoulders to keep her from falling.

Hex jumping up on someone? That was unexpected. Lacey sobered up a bit. Hex was as well trained as Tank, and as much of a social butterfly as Tank was, he would never jump up on someone.

"Down, Hex, down, boy," Pete called out. "Lift your knee, Cheri. Give him a shove."

"Oh, you know I don't mind." Cheri was turning her face from side to side, trying to keep Hex's exuberant tongue from licking her mouth or eyes. "Now I'm covered with dog spit," she said when Pete reached her. "You aren't going to want to kiss me."

"That's for sure." He gave her a quick hug while she pretended to wipe her face off on his shirt.

She went inside to wash up. The others stood around, waiting, apparently unable to say much without Cheri.

"I have big news," she announced when she got back. "I got a job. You said I couldn't come"—she was clearly talking to Pete—"unless I had a place to stay, which I do now, and a job. I called Mother's salon—not that it's hers anymore—and I was on hold so long that it was pretty easy to convince them that they needed more help."

"Are you a stylist?" Lacey asked.

"I don't have my license. My mother was pretty upset that I didn't finish beauty school. But I was married, and so I figured it was up to Pete and me, not her. It's an assistant manager–type job. It sounds like the new owners haven't changed how things were done, and I started helping out in there when I was seven. Nate said that I could ask you"—now she was talking to Lacey—"about working at the vet's, but I'm really not an animal person. Now, Pete, you have to come inside. Nate has made the most marvelous drinks."

At dinner the other three were reminiscing. Both men had pushed their chairs back from the table. Nate had his hands linked behind his head. Pete had one hand on the back of Cheri's chair. Cheri was perched forward, her elbows on the table, her chin resting on her clasped hands. Pete looked young for a change, closer to his actual age. Cheri had turned off most of the kitchen lights, so the soft glow of the stove and the counter lights blurred the roughened skin of his face. The giddiness Lacey had felt after the first daiquiri had melted into a lovely golden warmth.

The other three were talking about football games Pete had played in. Nate hadn't been to any of the games, but he had heard about the particularly spectacular plays. Then they went on to something about Cheri and another girl's lipstick. And the time one summer when Cheri and nine other junior girls had dared themselves to play strip poker. At the mention of that, Nate moaned and covered his face while Cheri started to laugh so hard she had to lean against Pete's arm.

"But it was just girls?" Lacey asked. She was fascinated by the conversation, by all the history that these three shared.

"Yes, it makes no sense, particularly since we showered together in gym class three times a week. I can't possibly explain why we did it...except to let the guys know we were doing it."

"It had the intended effect," Nate said. "It was all we could think about. We were in the back of—was it Jeff Sterling's pickup?—drinking Pabst Blue Ribbon. I still can't even look at the label without wanting to puke."

Pete ran his hand down Cheri's back. "Too bad none of us had video-phones back then—Matt holding on to J.T.'s belt so J.T. wouldn't fall out of the truck while he hurled."

"And I was between J.T. and the side of the truck," Nate said. "It was too horrible for words."

"How did you do in the game?" Lacey asked Cheri.

"I was amazing. These two made me sit down and memorize this table of odds and learn when to double down. I did more math that afternoon than I had done all semester, maybe all year. So I only had to take off my cardigan and my shoes. Anyway, we were clearly poster children for why they're right to ban underage drinking."

Lacey turned to Nate. "I thought you said you didn't have many memories of Forrest."

He smiled. "Maybe I should have changed that to 'memories I'm proud of'."

His smile caught at her, and for a pulsing moment she ached to be alone with him. Then she remembered that Cheri and Pete were entitled to be alone. She stood up. "Nate, I love being outside at night, and it's finally warm enough. Let's take the dogs out."

"Oh..." He didn't quite get it. "Well, sure. Why not?"

But Pete got it. "You don't have to do this," he said softly.

She pretended not to hear him and announced their plans to take the dogs down to the farm pond, then to come home by the road. It would take at least an hour.

By the time they had gotten flashlights and their jackets—it wasn't really as warm as Lacey was pretending it to be—Nate had figured things out. "I know your heart is in the right place," he said once they were outside, "but you're wasting your time. Pete's a bit of a prude. What do you want to bet that we'll go back and find the dishes are done?"

"At least we need to give them a chance." Tank was straining at his leash, unhappy that Hex was being allowed to roam free.

"I'm sorry if we were boring at dinner," Nate said. "I guess most of my memories of here are about summer and Pete and Cheri, so it's easy to get stuck on those stories."

"So, the three of you spent a lot of time together even though they were boyfriend and girlfriend?"

"Only in the summers. It might have been different if I had been here year-round. One of Pete's older sisters got pregnant in high school, which mortified and terrified him so much that he was less inclined to spend a lot of time in the back seat of his car than most guys were with steady girlfriends."

"Then why—" She stopped.

"Why what?"

"Something that is absolutely none of my business." She shouldn't have brought it up, but sitting at the dinner table, so aware of Nate and his broad shoulders and the little hitch in the movement of his spine, she couldn't help thinking about him and Cheri.

"Something about Cheri and Pete?"

"Not entirely."

"Oh, for God's sake…are you kidding me? You and Cheri were upstairs for ten minutes. What did she tell you?"

Lacey shrugged. "Things I would be happier not knowing."

"That is my worst memory of here, but listen"—he was unusually serious—"I have no idea whether or not Pete knows. And I never think about it anymore, but then she made that crack this afternoon that I should remember what her breasts used to look like. It's obviously still a big deal to her."

"How did it happen?"

"It was summer. Summer was a bitch for most kids back then. There wasn't enough work for the adults, much less the teens. Most families couldn't afford to take vacations, so they were here, year in, year out. My life probably seemed pretty amazing. One year I stayed in Oregon until my family could come out, and we went all around the Pacific Northwest for a couple of weeks. We were camping, so it wasn't like we were spending tons of bucks, but it wasn't what anyone else around here did. When I got home, Cheri told me that the two of them had broken up. I saw Pete the next morning, and when I tried to say something about them breaking up, it was clear he had no idea what I was talking about. You can't imagine how guilty I felt, so I backed away and they went right on being a couple. I couldn't wait to leave at the end of the summer. I felt like such a tool."

"One thing people around town say is how loyal you've been to Pete."

"He's an easy guy to be loyal to, and after that, I decided I was never going to mess with a friend's girlfriend—no matter what she says—not ever."

* * * *

Lacey had never been able to be fussy about roommates, so she had braced herself for Cheri being a slob, but she wasn't. She and Pete had done the dishes meticulously, and Cheri had been very clever about figuring out where the pots and pans went. When Lacey went upstairs to get ready for bed, she noticed two generously sized, pink cosmetic bags on the wicker shelves across from the sink.

She was checking the clinic schedule for Monday when Cheri knocked on her door.

"Is it okay for me to leave my stuff on that shelf? I can take it back to my room if you want."

"No, it's fine, but I did clear out a drawer for you."

"Oh my, that was so nice of you," Cheri gushed. "You didn't have to do that, but it was really nice."

"It was nothing."

Cheri was hovering like a little hummingbird. She clearly had something else to say. "I hope you had a good evening," Lacey said politely.

"Yes, yes. Dinner was great. Thank you. You went to a lot of trouble."

"I like cooking."

"Oh, I wish I did. But I hope you will let me do the cleaning. I love making everything sparkle. And Pete said you probably like things super clean, working in a clinic and all, everything being so sterile."

Was this going to go on all night? "Mrs. Byrd's eyesight wasn't what it used to be, and of course, I couldn't say anything, but I am used to how clean we keep the clinic."

"You have nothing to worry about. Cleaning is one thing I know that I am good at."

Getting to her point clearly was not. They talked about Mrs. Byrd and the clinic for a while, then more about cleaning. Finally, *finally,* Cheri said what she really wanted to say.

"You and Nate...there's something going on between you two, isn't there?"

"Ah...no. No. We're friends. That's all."

"Oh, come on. I can tell. I have a sense for these things."

Why had Lacey ever thought that she hadn't wanted to talk about using vinegar as an all-purpose kitchen cleaner? Vinegar was a good topic. "He was here for three days in March. That's it. We hardly know each other."

"Since when has that ever stopped anyone? You don't have to lie to me. I am never wrong about these things."

"I regret to inform you that in this case you are wrong."

How stiff she sounded. Would she have been more animated if Cheri actually *had* been wrong?

"I don't believe you," Cheri said lightly, "but I guess there's no reason why you would tell me your secrets."

"There's nothing to tell. There are no secrets."

Chapter 12

Media campaigns featuring snowboarders played up their image as risk-taking, fun-loving, slightly insane rebels. The risk-taking part was true. Nate had the scars and fractures to attest to that. And fun-loving also fit. The rest of the image…not so much. The snowboarding establishment no longer had any patience for insanity or rebelliousness, and a successful professional athlete could be laid-back about very little. Diet, practice sessions, competition schedules, even airplane departure times—all had to be faced with unrelenting self-discipline. Some athletes required the cattle prod of competition to remain so disciplined; they fell apart when their competitive days were over.

It had been three weeks since Nate had walked through the white columns of the State Capitol building, and it had been three weeks full of spreadsheets, business plans, and dense regulations—very dense regulations. The tasks had been very schoolwork-y, and Nate had never been a huge fan of schoolwork, but he had had no trouble staying focused this week. Maybe his dad was right. If Nate had a mission, he could anything.

After spending two weeks in the state capital, he had gone back to Oregon to pack up his stuff. It was time to move out of the chalet. Seth was still actively snowboarding. He and Caitlin would want a home when Seth was training at Endless Snow. They would have never dreamed of telling Ben and him to move out, but of course they had to be eager to have a place to themselves.

He had been telling his parents about his plans over the phone, but now he had a chance to sit down with them. His mother had sighed at the notion of him going back to Forrest. "For so long I couldn't let myself think about everything we left behind. We were so angry." She hadn't wanted to return even to see her friends. It hurt too much. "We had to go to your grandfather's funeral, and I wasn't angry anymore, but not being there didn't feel right."

His father had agreed. "It has seemed odd not to have a Forrest living in Forrest. When we left, I never thought about what it would be like when my father died. Our family was always so much a part of the town."

They weren't only being sentimental. Nate's dad and Aunt Amy weren't going to charge Nate any rent on the three buildings. Erasing that line on his spreadsheets made them look a whole lot better.

His sister had at first thought he was joking, but then came around to the idea. "It seems out of character, but you have always tackled whatever you've taken on. It might be harder than you realize."

His brother had concurred with her last thought. "You're going to have an uphill battle with the newspaper."

Nate had expected Cooper to be a little more gleeful. Nate was taking himself out of Oregon. Cooper could go on being the Number One Son.

But when he mentioned this conversation to Pete early Monday morning, Pete suggested that maybe Nate should take Cooper's remark as advice.

"Advice? Why would he give me advice?"

"Because he doesn't want you to fail."

"Oh, come on. Why would he care about that?"

They were in the original dry goods building. Pete had been on his way to the new housing construction on the other side of town.

"I know I wasn't there when you two had it out." Pete was speaking carefully, like the guy who the electricians and laborers all wanted to be working for. "But I may know your brother better than you do. That isn't like him."

* * * *

Nate spent the morning at the buildings, trying to get a handle on the things he wanted to discuss with the architect. Aunt Amy had given him seed money to pay for the architect and the building permits. People in the capital had provided all sorts of material about well-designed retail spaces, and he wanted to get some sense of what would work in the two side buildings.

Occasionally people on the sidewalk would peer in the windows. He felt like he had to stop and go outside to chat. The interruptions made it hard to concentrate, but he supposed that he needed to get to know people.

The trouble was that while they all knew who he was, he had no idea who most of them were. That was fine when you were signing autographs at the rope line. You'd ask someone's name, scrawl it down, sign yours, and then forget about them. That wasn't who he was anymore.

At noon the person on the sidewalk rapped on the window. He looked up. It was Lacey. She had Tank with her.

"I'm sorry," she said as soon as he opened the door. "I shouldn't have disturbed you. I'm sure you've been interrupted all morning."

"I'm happy to see you. Are you taking Tank on a walk?" The clinic software was programmed to give her a lunch break at noon. "Do you want company? I've been inside all morning."

Tank was already inching toward his pockets, hoping he had treats. She said that she was heading down to the river, and that, of course, he could come.

It was starting to seem that she had forgiven him for blasting in on her after Seth's wedding, but he was going to take it slow. He had promised her that he wasn't going to stalk her.

On their way down Main Street, they didn't see too many people, but she greeted about half of them. After the person had moved on, he would quietly ask her their name. It made him feel like they were playing on the same team.

A dirt path ran along the top of the levee. There must not have been any precipitation since the snow; the ground was dry enough to walk on. The river was reasonably high, but its green-brown waters were well below the levee.

"You have a younger brother, don't you?" he asked suddenly.

"Yes."

"Did he ever wish he were the older one?"

She had to think. "He did get tired of me constantly rescuing him. He has said that sometimes he felt he would have rather been bullied than have me swoop in all the time." She shifted Tank's leash to her other hand. "What's this about, Nate?"

He told her what had happened last week.

"Don't you think that the timing of your first blowup with your family was revealing?" she said. "Here you were, on your first day of trying to be a person who wasn't a big-time snowboarder. Is it any surprise that you needed to get mad at someone?"

"Are you saying that it was all displaced?" Anger was a big enough issue among professional athletes that they sometimes had to go to workshops about it.

"Some of it, perhaps. But if you got mad at him, then of course he attacked back. Now you're both stuck feeling competitive and adversarial."

Why were she and Pete both trying to make this out to be his fault? "You were supposed to be all soft and sympathetic," he grumbled. "I bet you are nicer to that bull than you are to me."

"If your sperm were as valuable as his, I would be."

Nate wanted to say that a woman so condom-focused wasn't letting people prove the value of their sperm, but decided that was over the line. When she talked about sperm, she sounded like a veterinarian. If he did, he would sound like a stalker.

* * * *

Whether or not Cooper cared about Nate succeeding, what he had said made sense. Nate needed to get the newspaper on his side. He called the office of the *Forrest Gazette* and made an appointment to see the editor the next morning.

He had gotten the phone number off of the paper's website. It was the most miserable excuse for a website he had ever seen, especially for a newspaper. It didn't even have the current weather, simply a link to an online edition of the paper. It turned out that digital subscribers were being charged so much for access that Nate couldn't imagine that there were any digital subscribers.

The newspaper's office was in a freestanding building on a side street parallel to the one Dr. Byrd's clinic was on. The paper had had to cut back to publishing twice a week, and indeed, the outer office didn't give signs of a flourishing enterprise. The beige-toned linoleum floor was nicked and scuffed; the furniture was worn.

The receptionist told him to have a seat, that Mr. Kayot would be with him shortly. Nate expected that. Guys behind desks wanted you to believe that they were much too busy and important to be worrying about your appointment time.

Instead of sitting, he went over to look at the bank of black-framed pictures that nearly covered two of the walls. They were photos of more than seventy years of Forrest High's homecoming queens. Each picture was virtually the same: girls in long dresses, the queen standing in the center, wearing a crown and holding a bouquet of flowers, while her court—the princesses, the losers—stood on either side of her. The hairstyles changed, and over time the dresses got more daring. Every fifteen years or so the crown changed…although the one in the last picture was at least twenty-five years old. The bouquets had grown skimpier as the town had fallen on hard times. The last picture, dated a few years ago, was in the middle of a row. There was room for more. But there would be no more. Fred Kayot wasn't hanging the pictures from the new county-wide school's homecoming court.

That was a shame. Piled up on an end table were photo albums, and Nate knew what was in them: photos from weddings, reunions, and baby showers, featuring women lined up in the order they had stood in the fall of their senior year in high school. Whenever such a picture came in, the newspaper would publish it. Nate remembered seeing pictures of silver-haired ladies with walkers and wheelchairs. These pictures used to mean something to the town.

What would have been his class was at the start of that last row. Cheri had been the homecoming queen that year. Then he started looking for his aunt, but his eye stopped at the end of the row above Cheri's picture. Out of seventy-plus pictures, this was the only one that showed only the queen, not the other girls.

Because Jill, his sister, had been one of the attendants. And Fred Kayot was not going to print a picture of Superintendent Forrest's daughter.

This was small-town America at its worst.

No, no, actually it wasn't. Not at all. The newspaper had, in fact, saved the town from what was worse, Nate had learned from his parents. Several years ago, a pain clinic had opened up in a storefront on Main Street. It was run by a licensed physician, but it offered no physical therapy, no acupuncture, no biofeedback training, no topical NSAIDs, all of which had helped Nate manage pain. The sole purpose of this clinic was to write prescriptions for addictive opioids and, whenever possible, to overcharge Medicare or Medicaid for the visit. *That* was small-town America at its worst.

The newspaper had gone after the clinic, guns blazing, just as it had gone after his father. But this time it had more than opinion. News articles detailed how often the doctor had had his license suspended or revoked in other states. Editorials called for the state to audit the Medicaid charges and for the local medical community to speak up. The reporting had been solid, and the opinions well-reasoned. After only two months of operation, the clinic suddenly closed, and the doctor disappeared.

Nate sat down and picked up a copy of last Friday's paper. It was thin and tedious. Fred Kayot must be like Nate; he did better when he had something to fight for. The current editorial was about the challenges the last snowstorm had presented to the town budget. The middle school's performance of three one-act plays got a decent feature, but except for the box score from the baseball team's most recent game, there was nothing about the high school.

The paper used to be full of reporting about the high school. Not only were the athletics covered in play-by-play detail, but there had been articles about the band and the stage productions, the community service projects and the engineering club's attempt to build a robot. Forrest High hadn't had as many activities as a bigger school, but everything that happened had been featured in the newspaper. People had liked that. Whenever a kid was mentioned, all the neighbors had saved their copies for that kid's family.

So what if the high school was now twenty miles away? Parents still must like seeing their kids' pictures in the paper.

Nate heard a door opening and he turned around. Mr. Kayot was tall and balding, wearing a short-sleeved dress shirt and outdated pleated khakis.

"Young Nate," he said. "It's been a while."

Nate followed the editor back into his office. It was carpeted, but just as in need of a makeover as the reception area.

"It's a shame that your family up and left so fast," Mr. Kayot said, lowering himself into his swivel chair.

Snowboarders were not renowned for their ability to make nice, but Nate was on a mission. He ignored the remark. "As you've probably heard, I am moving back, and I have some plans that I'd like to share with you."

As he described his plan, Mr. Kayot occasionally nodded, but asked no questions. Nate had no idea what he was thinking.

"Well, this is all very interesting here," Kayot finally said. "But you haven't said anything about your advertising budget and how much of it is going to be for print."

Oh. Was this "pay for play"? "Honestly, sir, I haven't gotten that far. But I know that in the next few months I could use some advice on that," Nate said even though he had a pretty good idea what Kayot's advice would be.

"Good. You do know what happened when your grandfather stopped his daily ad."

Nate felt suddenly cautious. "No, sir, I don't know anything about that."

"Things happened. That's all I'm saying. Things happened."

Like what kind of things? Nate's dad being forced out of his job?

Was this possible? That the hardware store ceasing a daily ad had started all that?

Maybe the pain clinic hadn't advertised. Maybe that's why Kayot had gone after the place. If that scumbag of a doctor had had the sense to advertise in the *Gazette*, would Forrest have become the opioid capital of southeastern West Virginia?

Nate was disgusted. And angry. Really angry. Fred Kayot needed to pay for what he had done to Nate's family.

Nate was going to put that miserable, flea-bitten thing of a newspaper out of business if it was the last thing he did.

* * * *

Half an hour on the Internet told Nate that if he tried to start a newspaper, it would indeed be the last thing that he did. The economics of print production were unworkable. He hated having to climb down from his mountain of outrage, but he couldn't let his anger distract him from what he was really trying to accomplish.

Being a grown-up wasn't always oodles of fun, was it?

Chapter 13

Lacey could feel herself melting.

Several times a week, Nate would "happen" to notice Tank and her walking past his buildings at 12:05 p.m. and would join them on the walk down to the river. Sometimes she would glance through the big windows and see him talking to someone, a pair of work gloves in his back pocket. He would look up and nod, but he couldn't get away. That was disappointing.

It had also become a settled thing that Nate and Pete would come to the farmhouse on Sunday evenings. The evenings were lovely and relaxed. The men arrived when they could. Supper was served when it was ready. Lacey didn't feel stressed about the timing. Occasionally they all played a game although—Cheri was even worse at Scrabble than Nate was. More often they sat companionably in the living room, Lacey doing a crossword, Cheri flipping through a magazine, Nate checking his email, and Pete falling asleep.

Cheri and Nate did most of the talking, of course. Cheri was breathing new life into the beauty salon. Her first weekend she pulled all the chairs into the center of the room and had the stylists come in to repaint the walls. The sinks, the countertops, and the floors now gleamed. The owner had previously wiped them down every night; Cheri scrubbed and disinfected them. She replaced the aging coffeemaker with a sleek, single-serve machine. She threw out the dusty hard candy and opened a fresh box of cookies every day.

Each week Nate had much to report about the architectural drawings, the permit process, and the financing. He talked about it with such boyish enthusiasm that it almost seemed interesting.

The town was buzzing with talk about his projects. According to Cheri and Mrs. Byrd, much of the chatter at the salon or among the nursing home staff was about selling things to the tourists. The women in town who did needlework and the men who had workbenches in their garages were asking questions about stall space in the biggest of the buildings. Mr. Mattson, Big'un's owner, said that his son who was about to graduate from Virginia Tech might be interested in starting an ice cream operation, possibly even transitioning a part of the herd to grass-fed as city people would swoon over locally made, grass-fed ice cream.

The *Gazette* was less enthusiastic about Nate's efforts. The editorials called him "young Mr. Forrest" and argued that while it was nice for the local ladies to have a showplace for their little handicrafts, did the town really want throngs of out-of-town tourists crowding the sidewalks and littering the streets?

"We should be so lucky to have throngs of anyone," Nate grumbled.

He also groaned loudly about having to replace the heating and air-conditioning systems in his buildings. He was going through his aunt's money more quickly than he would have liked. It was going to be hard to find workers to remodel the two side buildings. Anyone with construction skills was working at the resort. Pete promised he'd help Nate find at least part-time workers once the days were longer. In the meantime, Nate was starting on the demolition himself. The dropped ceilings in both side buildings had to be taken down, and the pegboard shelving systems removed from the walls.

When he came out to walk with her, Lacey could tell when he had been doing demo work. There was a lightness in his step and greater ease in his carriage. He had a crowbar, a man's strength, and a seven-year-old boy's joy in destruction. No wonder he felt good.

Lacey still had moments of awkwardness. Of course, people in town noticed them walking together. Working in the salon, Cheri heard everything, and she now had town gossip to add to her "evidence" about a secret relationship.

Finally Lacey had to say something. "Cheri, I know what you think, and I can't stop you from thinking it, but you are making me very uncomfortable."

Cheri looked stricken. She liked a touch of drama, but she hated hurting people. "I am so sorry. I won't say another word. Not one more word."

"And remember, I'm leaving in a couple of months." She had told Cheri all about her contract with Dr. Byrd.

"That wouldn't stop me." Then Cheri paused and thought. "But you...I guess I understand why it would stop you."

* * * *

Lacey had always planned to start looking for her next job in May.

She couldn't bear to think about it. She felt at home in West Virginia; she had changed so much while she had been here. She loved the way Dr. Byrd treated his clients. She liked living with Cheri, and their Sunday night suppers with Pete and Nate—she had never had anything like them before.

Of course, she didn't have a future with Nate. She knew that. It wasn't only an issue of the timing. He was still too impatient—he was going nuts over the continuing delays in getting the parts for the new heating and cooling system. He was still too compelling, too capable of leveling everything in his path. He was still too—Lacey had to force herself to be blunt about this—still too sexy. She hated how vulnerable she felt around him. She hated how distracted she felt when she was with him.

At least she thought she should hate it.

Hunting for a job would be tedious. She would have to find practices that were looking to hire, research them as much as she could, and then go for interviews if they were interested in her. Traveling wasn't going to be cheap or easy. She would have to drive to Charleston, and unless she was going to DC, Charlotte, Atlanta, or Chicago, she would have to change planes.

"That sounds like a bore," her brother said when she was explaining this to him. "I have an idea. You've made decent money out there, haven't you?"

"More than I ever thought I would."

"Then you've got some breathing room. Why not work out your contract and then come stay with us? It would be cheaper and easier to fly out of Chicago."

It was an interesting idea. If she were visiting every new place while still working for Dr. Byrd, she would probably focus only on how much more she was suited to his practice. Maybe if she had already said good-bye to Forrest, she could look at another clinic more clearly.

It was actually a very good idea. She wasn't used to her brother being the solution to her problems. It had always been the other way around. "But I have Tank."

"Our building allows dogs, and if he needs more room, you can always stay with Tim's parents. They love you, and their house backs right up on parkland."

"It's a good idea and generous of you. I'll think about it," she promised.

But really, what was there to think about? Between the cost of travel and missing the extra hours from the Sunday clinic and the dude ranch, she wouldn't be out that much money by doing it David's way.

And she could enjoy the soft colors of the spring wildflowers giving way to summer's vivid colors without wondering whether she was moving to Memphis or Fort Wayne.

The air in West Virginia was different than in any place she had ever lived. During the winter, every breath had been pure and silvery. Now the spring air was fresh and full of the promise of the summer's caressing breeze, which was softened by the lightest whisper of humidity. When she had first arrived, her scientific mind had needed to understand that the richness of the air was the result of the woodland's concentrated photosynthesis. Nearly three years in this beautiful state had taught her that she didn't need to understand the "why" of something in order to treasure the moment.

So she was going to enjoy the remaining months in West Virginia. She wouldn't let herself fret that each sunset brought her another day closer to leaving. She never talked about leaving when she was with Nate, Cheri, and Pete, when they were all doing nothing together at the farmhouse, having a picnic at the river, going into the county seat for a movie. When Pete talked about what was going on at the site, she never let herself sigh that she would not be here to see the resort open. She didn't want to think about leaving, and so she wasn't going to talk about it.

* * * *

It was now May. One Sunday Cheri asked Lacey if she were going to attend the hospital's annual gala.

Although Forrest Memorial Hospital was now owned by a company that ran hospitals all over the state, the community took pride in the small facility. It was certainly the largest employer within the city limits, and its auxiliary committee was the most active fund-raising organization. Their primary event, the annual June gala, was a dinner-dance with a casino theme.

"I haven't given it any thought," Lacey admitted. "But I suppose I'll go. It's the last weekend in June, isn't it?"

In previous years, Dr. Byrd's clinic, as a part of the medical community, had bought tickets for both Lacey and Mrs. Byrd. Lacey had brought Mrs. Byrd, something she was happy to do as it then required her to leave early.

"Is your boss going to buy tickets for her staff?" Lacey asked Cheri.

Cheri shook her head, her light hair brushing against her shoulders. "She said that the salon is super busy that day, and all the stylists are too tired to go. But Nate should buy tickets, shouldn't he?"

"Probably. We should mention it to him."

An hour later when the men arrived, Cheri started talking about the gala again, exclaiming how fun it would be if the four of them went together.

"I don't know about fun," Nate said. "Don't the old people—"

"But you probably thought that people who were thirty-five were old," Cheri interrupted. "And if you are going to be a pillar of the community, you need to buy tickets."

"You can count me out," Pete said.

"But Nate will buy our tickets," Cheri told him.

Lacey didn't recall Nate agreeing to that.

"I don't have a suit here," Pete countered. "The gala isn't our kind of deal. My parents didn't go. Even your mom didn't go."

Apparently, Pete was having a class-struggle moment.

"Mother went sometimes," Cheri protested. "She always bought a ticket and advertised in the program. She just didn't like being the only single woman there. Some of her clients' husbands would grope her. But it can't be like that now. Lacey's been going for a couple of years, and no one gropes her, do they?"

"No, no one gropes me," Lacey acknowledged, "but I pretty much have to go. The clinic buys tickets. I don't know if I would have gone otherwise."

"Lacey!" Cheri turned on her. "You're supposed to be on my side."

"I didn't mean to take sides. I was just explaining why I go."

"If you and Nate are going for business reasons," Cheri said, "then it's important that I go too. The salon is a part of the community. You know what a good job I'm doing." She was now talking to Pete. "I really should go."

"I've never suggested that you couldn't go," Pete said. "I just said that I wasn't going to."

"Then I will. There's nothing wrong with that. Lacey's not going with a date. Nate can come out and pick us up," she announced. "Lacey, you have to let me do your hair and makeup. Have you thought about what you're wearing? Wouldn't it be fun to get something new? We could go—"

"Nothing new for me," Lacey interrupted. "I have a bridesmaid's dress I can wear."

Lacey also wasn't sure that she wanted Cheri to be doing her makeup. On the rare times that her mother, makeup artist to the C-list stars, did her makeup, her mother spent the whole time talking about everything wrong with Lacey's face, the slight asymmetry of her eyes and her overly strong jaw. It wasn't the best way to make a teenage girl feel pretty.

"A bridesmaid's dress?" Cheri didn't like that idea. "But they always look like bridesmaid's dresses. You should get something new. New clothes are always so much fun."

"Not for me, they aren't. Anyway, it's in the hospital cafeteria." She wasn't spending money on a dress she might not wear again, especially because this year, thanks to her brother's wedding, she had something in her closet.

"You don't need anything new either," Pete said to Cheri. "You have lots of dresses at home. Your mom can mail you one."

"Oh, grumpy, grumpy, grumpy." Cheri poked him in the ribs, teasing. "Don't you want me to look pretty?"

He grabbed her hand and pulled her close. "That would be a crazy thing to wish for, you not looking pretty. It couldn't happen. But still, Cheri, you don't need a new dress."

Lacey was not going to get involved in this. Cheri always got home from work before Lacey did; she brought in the mail. She also volunteered to take the recycling into town. But one time Lacey had gone to the recycling bin to retrieve a crossword that she hadn't finished. Rummaging through the newspapers, she noticed two Amazon boxes at the bottom of the bin. They weren't simply broken down by slitting the tape over the seams, but the cardboard had been laboriously cut so the boxes could fit neatly under the papers and bottles. Cheri was trying to hide her deliveries even from Lacey.

* * * *

In the middle of the following week, Lacey got an email from one of the gala organizers asking Lacey if she would again volunteer to run the roulette wheel for an hour. Lacey replied that she would and then raised the issue of the tickets with Valerie.

Valerie sniffed at her. "Since Mrs. Byrd Senior won't need a ride, do you expect the clinic to buy you a ticket?"

Expect? For the last two years, Lacey had felt as if the ticket had been forced on her. "Dr. Bergin's wife already asked if I would do a shift at the roulette table again, so I suppose I will need a ticket, but I can buy my own."

"If that's the way you want it." Valerie sighed as if Lacey had somehow insulted the clinic.

Lacey had once again been outmaneuvered. But why had Valerie even bothered? The issue seemed pointless. The tickets weren't all that expensive. Why did Valerie care whether or not the clinic bought Lacey's ticket? There must be more to this story.

"Who does the clinic buy tickets for?" She had never thought to ask that before.

"Dr. and Mrs. Byrd, of course, Mrs. Byrd Senior, and my husband and myself."

"Why not for the rest of the staff?"

"Oh…oh no. I can't imagine that they would want to come."

Lacey could understand that. The gala was hardly a glamorous event; it was an aging crowd in a faded room. Many of the women wore fancy dresses because they wanted to, but none of the men were in tuxes.

Lacey asked Katie, the young receptionist who was doing such a great job with the new software, if she would want to go if the clinic bought her ticket.

"It's never sounded like all that much fun," Katie replied. "But I have two friends who owe me Saturday night babysits. Is it an open bar?"

"You get tickets for a couple of drinks, but after that it's cash."

"I could live with that."

Later in the day Lacey needed to talk to Bill Byrd about a feline blood pressure medication. She was concerned about the efficacy of one of the generic meds. It was getting harder and harder to have private conversations with him; Valerie, realizing that she had given up too much power when she let Katie be the administrator on the software, wanted to be a part of every conversation the two doctors had. She was concerned that Lacey was going to do something to undermine her…which was exactly what Lacey was planning to do.

Lacey used the medication being a purely medical issue as an excuse to see her boss alone.

It was clear from the family photos displayed around his office that Bill had once had auburn hair. His hair was gray now, and his warm coloring was fading, but he still wore the brown, raisin, and mustard colors that must have looked good on him in his youth. As a result, there was something slightly discordant about his appearance.

He agreed with her that they needed to prescribe the brand-name drug and that he was willing to take a bit of a financial loss so that patients with existing prescriptions wouldn't get hit with the increased cost. He truly did care about the clients and understood their lives in a way that Lacey hoped she would never forget.

That was only part of why she had wanted to meet with him. "I know we have only bought six gala tickets in the past, but is there any reason not to buy more? We could post a sign-up sheet to see who wants to go."

"Valerie has said that no one else would want to go."

"It wouldn't hurt to ask, would it?"

"I don't know..." Dr. Byrd looked uneasy. He hated confrontation. "Valerie usually handles that sort of thing, doesn't she?"

"I thought"—and Lacey had a twinge of guilt for what she was about to say—"that your wife took care of our community relations matters."

"Oh yes." He looked relieved. "I'll ask her."

And the next day the sign-up sheet went up.

Chapter 14

Nate wasn't one for spending a lot of time taking his own emotional temperature, but things were better than he could have ever imagined a life without snowboarding could be. He was energized by the wheeling-and-dealing aspects of what he was doing, negotiating better bids and lower rates. He liked engaging with people on a regular-guy basis. He wasn't a pro rider hurriedly signing autographs or a dude swaggering through the intense bro-culture of the top competitors.

The one thing he would have thought irreplaceable was his tight friendship with Seth and Ben, but it was time to take the *No Girls Allowed* sign off of the treehouse. Seth had gone first, and Nate hoped that he would be next.

Having Lacey let him into her treehouse would require time. For once in his life, he needed to take things slowly. Lacey didn't trust him. He knew that. You didn't win someone's trust overnight. He wasn't going to rush her.

One thing concerned him, and he hoped she understood it. Cheri was a flirt. She was careful around the teenage boys, but with every other male, she flirted—the middle-aged husbands, the old guys, the UPS driver, the produce manager at the grocery store, her own husband, and Nate. She brushed men's arms when she spoke to them; her smiles were coy and quick. She was playful, she was suggestive, she was charming, It was fun. It didn't mean anything.

Nate knew that he almost automatically responded to her in the same light way. It didn't bother Pete. He sure hoped that it didn't bother Lacey.

I'd do a lot more than flirt with you if I could.

It did surprise him when Cheri called one day, asking if she could stop by his apartment after work.

"You can come to the store," he said. The store was two short blocks from the salon. "I'll be there."

"No, let's sit down and have a glass of wine." She named a time that would be too early for Lacey or Pete. Clearly she wanted to see him alone. Why?

Ten minutes before she was to arrive, he carried a bottle of wine outside, setting it and some glasses between the two Adirondack chairs that Mrs. Fischer had put next to the garage. He then shifted the chairs so that they were right in the line of sight from Mrs. Fischer's kitchen window.

It was strange to feel this cautious.

The feeling didn't seem justified. Cheri wasn't flirtatious when he was alone with her. They talked business like two normal people.

She was actually helping him a lot. She had a better feel for business than anyone could have guessed from her girlish manner. From all the gossip in the beauty salon, she had realized that some residents were thinking of the new handicrafts stalls as a place to get rid of their junk.

"Someone slapping together a four-patch out of whatever polyester fabric they had lying around is going to bring down the whole building," she had told him. "You have to assess the quality and have a mix of things. If every stall has the same things, people will leave. You need some repurposed woodworking, some metal, some photography, not just textiles."

She had offered to take on the task of "curating the vendors." She drew up some guidelines and insisted that people needed to take their wares to at least three craft shows over the summer and the fall so that they could understand what sold and at what price.

She had also encouraged him to rethink his "vision" for the variety shop. To the extent that he had a vision, it was about the shop being useful to residents. She wanted it to be "charming and welcoming." She wanted him to keep the old shiplap paneling he had discovered under the wallboard and to display the merchandise in old oak cupboards and pie safes. She wanted him to put in a coffeepot and a few chairs. The men of the town, she said, needed the equivalent of his something-great-grandfather's potbelly stove.

But in all her efforts to talk him into this, she had never insisted that they be alone together. They usually were, but only because it had happened that way.

This intentionally wanting to be alone made him uneasy.

She came walking over from the salon, making it seem as if she were still fifteen and didn't have her driver's license. She had walked to his house that night after he had gotten home from the family trip through the Pacific Northwest. To this day he did not understand why she had had sex with him that night.

He met her halfway down the drive, handing her a glass of wine.

"How lovely," she said softly, her fingers brushing against his as she took the glass.

"I hear the tips are going up in the salon," he said.

"Finally," Cheri sighed. "But it's frustrating. I have worked really hard. The owner's making more money, the stylists are making more money, and I'm not."

"Why don't you ask for a bonus? If you put together some numbers at the end of the quarter, Pete and I can help you figure out a reasonable request."

"The end of next quarter, but that's not until the end of June, is it?"

"Right. That's not a long time, but you know the accounts. You'll be able to do it."

"I'll think about it," she said.

It didn't sound as if she was going to. "Things are working out for you living with Lacey, aren't they?"

"Yes. She's very easy to live with. She's organized, she's predictable, she's always on time, always does what she says she will do."

He had never known her to speak so carefully. "There's not a problem with that, is there?"

"No, oh no. It's just—" She stopped and shrugged. "That education of hers…and I never even got a license to do nails."

Was Cheri asking him to feel sorry for her? This was new. "Don't compare yourself to other people. That's a lose-lose."

She didn't seem to hear. "And I suppose she's also done a super job of handling her money."

"I wouldn't know anything about that." He stopped and looked at her. Something was going on. "What's the deal, Cheri?"

She was rolling the stem of her wineglass between her palms, not looking at him. Oh yes, Nate remembered Pete telling her not to buy a new dress. Was the problem with the fiscal quarter ending in June, that June was too far away?

"What is it? Pete is making great money—"

Her expression froze. He stopped. This was something that Pete didn't know about.

"Is it credit cards?" Nate had gotten too many phone calls from ex-girlfriends not to know where this conversation was headed.

"It's just a little thing," she said, "but they just don't stop calling. They make your life miserable. I thought about changing my cell phone number, but that costs a lot."

"How much do you owe them?"

"Oh, just a couple hundred, it's not that much."

She was lying. Credit card companies didn't torture people for a balance of a couple hundred dollars.

He kept a fair amount of cash in the apartment. When they had been living here, his parents had always tried to have several months' expenses in a lockbox hidden behind his dad's workbench. It was a West Virginia self-reliance thing. You never knew when the bank might lock its doors.

He stood up but waved at her to stay seated. It wasn't that his cash was particularly well-hidden; it was just at the back of his sock drawer, but still...

Why was he thinking like that? Feeling that he couldn't trust her? He went inside, took out five hundred-dollar bills, and then added a few more because he felt bad for her. And a few more because he felt bad for Pete.

He didn't want to just hand her cash. That seemed odd. He would have liked to have put it in an envelope, but apparently, he didn't have any envelopes. He never used the US mail for anything. So he took a sheet of copy paper, folded the cash inside, and fastened it with a paper clip.

He grabbed another bottle of wine. This seemed like a moment for more alcohol.

"Oh, Nate, you are so wonderful." She jumped up as soon as he handed her the little packet. She moved close as if she were going to kiss him, but he managed to use the wine bottle to keep her away. "I'll pay you back, you know I will. But you won't tell Pete, will you? Please, please don't tell him."

Well, shit. Why hadn't he thought this through? Of course, she was going to ask him not to tell Pete, and of course, he was going to have to say that he wouldn't because if he did tell Pete, the whole thing would have been unnecessary. The point of this was not simply to get Cheri's bills paid, but to get them paid without her husband finding out.

What an idiot he had been. She had seemed unhappy, and all he had been able to think about was how he could make her feel better.

And now she was happy again. She was back to being Cheery Cheri again. She poured them each more wine, filling the glasses generously.

"Are you going to be able to drive home?" he asked as they were finishing that glass.

"You can drive me, can't you?"

He shook his head. He'd been drinking too.

"I'll take a little nap on your sofa. Then I'll be fine." She set her glass down, as if she were going to go inside.

No. No. That was a terrible idea. He spoke quickly. "Let's see if Lacey is still at the clinic. You could catch a lift with her." He pulled out his phone, not even waiting for Cheri to respond.

He usually texted Lacey because she didn't take her phone into the examining room, but she wouldn't be with a client this late. He called, and she answered. "Nate, is everything all right?"

"Things are great," he said. "Cheri and I have been enjoying this pleasant evening with a bottle of wine." Then he realized that it would be rude not to invite her. "Are you going to be done soon? Do you want to come over? We're sitting outside my place."

Now that he thought about it, inviting her seemed like a good idea.

"Oh." She was thinking. "That sounds lovely. It really does, but once I got back from lunch, Dr. Byrd was called out on an emergency. I worked both schedules. If I sat down and had a glass of wine, I wouldn't be able to get out of the chair until noon tomorrow."

"We're able to get out of our chairs, but getting into cars is a different story. Could you swing by and give Cheri a ride home with you?"

"Of course. I'm almost out the door."

"Then we will start walking."

The sun hadn't set, but the shadows were long. Cheri tucked her hand in his arm. "Thank you again, Nate, for helping me out," she said softly.

"I hope you will talk to Pete…and that you will use that money for your bills."

"Of course," she said, but she pulled her hand out from his arm.

They hadn't gone more than a few blocks when the Silverado turned up the street. Lacey pulled over to the curb and rolled down her window. The Silverado was high enough that Nate didn't have to twist himself into a pretzel to talk to her.

She must have taken a shower at the clinic. Her hair was wet, and she was wearing a surgical scrub top. When Cheri opened the passenger door, the overhead light came on, and he could see the streaks of damp from Lacey's hair trailing down the faded green fabric of the top.

When the passenger door closed, the light went off, but Nate could smell Lacey's shampoo. It wasn't the orchid one she had used at the clinic earlier in the year. It was more citrusy, less sweet.

Tank squirmed his head up over Lacey's shoulder to greet Nate. The scent of oranges and limes disappeared. The dog had not been freshly shampooed.

Cheri hadn't said anything to Lacey. That wasn't like her. Nate saw Lacey glance across the gear shift at her and then back through the window at him. He knew exactly what she was thinking.

I hope you know what you're doing.

I don't, he let his thoughts answer. *I really don't.*

* * * *

Whether or not Nate himself knew what he was doing, the rest of the town thought he did. People were getting more and more excited about his enterprises. Saturdays, Sundays, and many weekday mornings volunteers were refinishing the oak cabinets in the original building and sorting through the boxes and boxes of old hardware people had unearthed in their garages and barns. They were assembling cast-iron tongs for moving big blocks of ice, miners' carbide lamps, butter molds, and tools for shelling corn, all the things a dry goods store would have sold. Three women had taken their sewing and knitting projects to a craft fair up in the Morgantown area. A couple of men had spent a satisfying Saturday at the burnt-out barn, salvaging boards to repurpose. Nate had had several conversations with the older Mattson son about a business plan for an ice cream–making operation.

Because the resort was on schedule to open in mid-December, the local business owners decided to raise money to update the town's holiday decorations. Residents were no longer bombarded with bake sales and car washes from the high school kids, so the organizations hoped that their fund-raisers would go well.

In the face of this enthusiasm, Fred Kayot had to back off his openly negative editorials in the *Gazette.* He instead pretended to be enthusiastic, professing a hope that Nate would soon turn his energy and resources to opening a business that would provide the kind of steady work that the mines once had.

Kayot was right. Nate couldn't deny that. What people needed were full-time jobs with benefits and pensions. Except for one or two employees at the variety store, Nate's projects weren't going to provide that. You couldn't support a family on hand-quilted place mats and wine racks crafted from copper piping and salvaged lumber. Even the Mattson family viewed their ice cream counter as only a stepping-stone in building a brand that would diversify their business.

Fred Kayot knew all of this. His editorials were deliberate goading. He wanted Nate to fail even if it were by standards that Nate had never aspired to. Nate had no idea what he was supposed to do about it.

Neither did the other three. Cheri cautioned against doing anything that might discourage the town's enthusiasm. Lacey grimaced and offered nonlatex gloves and horse tranquilizers. "They won't solve a thing, but it's all I've got." Pete suggested that Nate call his brother.

"Cooper? Why?"

"Because he has a degree in communications. He knows more about this than any of us."

"You should call him," Lacey exclaimed. "My brother is thrilled that he is going to be able to help me at the end of the summer. You're the one who said that younger sibs like having the roles reversed."

Nate hadn't thought about being pissed at Cooper for a number of weeks, but he wasn't ready to stop thinking of this as a competition. He wasn't prepared to hand Cooper a victory. "I'll think of something."

* * * *

Nate's parents back in Oregon were interested in everything he was doing. They listened to his frustration over the HVAC parts; they wanted to see pictures of the costumes that the living history volunteers were designing for themselves. His mother adored Cheri's ideas about making the variety store a place where people would want to linger, and his father approved of Pete having him hire Greg Hemphill as a manager for the variety store. Greg would be able to help people jerry-rig repairs.

"Pete says that the big box stores tell people to replace, not repair. Apparently this guy can do anything with duct tape and Gorilla Glue. That's going to be our market niche. Duct Tape 'R' Us."

"*Is*." His mother, the former first grade teacher, automatically corrected his grammar. "By the way, have you talked to your brother recently?"

"No. Why?"

"He wants to know what kind of deal you have with the Almost Heaven resort."

"Deal?"

"Are they going to display the town's brochures?" his dad explained. "Are they going to discourage people from leaving their property?"

"Why would they do that?"

"Every minute a guest spends off-site is a minute he is spending money someplace else."

A couple of times Pete had said that the marketing team at Almost Heaven did want to talk to Nate about becoming a professional has-been. That might not have been how they described it, but that was how Nate thought of it. He never returned the calls.

He hung up with his parents and scrolled through his old messages. He found the number Pete had given him and set up a meeting, hoping he was making it clear that he wasn't there to discuss the resort using his name.

Since he had toured the site with Pete in March, Almost Heaven had opened a sales office to market the condos that would cluster around the base of the runs. The condos were being pitched as second homes, not year-round residences, but Stonefield's grocery store was counting on the owners to come into town for their supplies.

The sales office was thickly carpeted and nicely furnished. The condos were being pitched to an upscale crowd. Nate gave his name to the receptionist and then went over to look at the scale model of the resort, which was set up in a glass case in the center of the room.

The model might be to scale, but it was totally wack when it came to climate. The miniature ski lifts climbed up white mountains while the lawns surrounding the timber and stone buildings were emerald green. Unless they were going to put in acres of Astroturf, the place would never have snowy mountains and lush grass at the same time.

He looked at the gray lines of the roadways. There were wider spots in front of the buildings, but they couldn't be more than loading zones.

"Excuse me," he spoke to the receptionist. "Where are the parking lots?"

"We're not showing them." She came over to the case. "But they will be here and here." She pointed to the edges of the model.

"That's quite a walk."

"Oh, we don't expect people to walk. We will valet-park their cars for free, and there will be shuttles operating all the time. See, look at all the stops." She pointed to a tiny blue marker. The resort grounds were studded with them. "Anyone purchasing a condo can arrange to have a convenient space added to their purchase price, but we will offer a contract for grocery deliveries from the big store in the county seat. The goal for the guests is to have a car-free experience. Everything anyone will need will be available on the resort grounds."

Just then the woman Nate was meeting with emerged from one of the back offices. Nate struggled through five minutes of pleasantries—no, he didn't want anything to drink, and yes, the weather had been wonderful, a little cool in the evenings perhaps, but—

After that it took ninety seconds for her to confirm what Nate was dreading. The resort had no interest in having their guests leave the resort grounds. They should buy their ice cream, T-shirts, and souvenirs from the resort shops. So, no, the resort wasn't even going to have a lobby display of brochures from other local attractions.

If the resort had anything to say about it, their guests would never get closer to the town than the bypass road.

Chapter 15

Well, shit, how could he have been such a fucking idiot? *Build it and they will come.* Who did he think he was? Noah? Whatever made him think he was cut out for entrepreneurship? All the planning, contracts, and permits, all the spreadsheets, everything he was so proud of, and the Almost Heaven parking lots had never crossed his mind. Parking in town, that he had thought about, counting the spaces on the streets, calculating how many more they could get by painting white lines in the alley, but where the visitors would park at Almost Heaven? Nope, not a thought… and that was going to be the ruin of everything.

He should have stayed in Oregon and passed out participation certificates. At least he wouldn't have hurt anyone. How much strawberry jam and pickled asparagus had Maddie Everest and her daughter-in-law put up? How many yards of quilt fabric had been in those boxes Mrs. Fischer had been getting? How much time had Tom Leston spent finding usable boards in the burnt-out barn? And the Mattsons. How far along were they in purchasing the new ice cream equipment?

On top of that, he had actually started to have some ideas about how to do what the newspaper was taunting him to do: find a way to get full-time jobs flowing into town. Manufacturing was out of the question; health care was a much better bet. Forrest needed an assisted-living facility, one with activities and social programming. An assisted-living facility didn't need workers who were young and toned with perfect skin and teeth like the resort did. It would need people who were patient and kind, and southeastern West Virginia had plenty of those.

It would be a big undertaking; he would need partners, but who was going to listen to him now? He would be the hotshot who'd come to town and then said, "Whoops, never mind."

This was beyond frustrating. How much could the revenue from ice cream and T-shirts matter to the resort? It would be making money off the rooms, food, booze, lift tickets, and equipment rental. But what a difference the ice cream and T-shirts would make to the town.

He had to do something. He couldn't let Forrest down.

But what? He had no idea. And right now, this was the only thing that mattered.

Call your brother, Pete had said.

How would a degree in communications help? Nate didn't even know what those people studied. But what else was there to do? He couldn't give up. He pulled out his phone and called his brother. He knew that his name would flash up on Cooper's phone. After three rings Cooper answered.

"What can I do ya fer?" Cooper drawled in a very fake backwoods accent.

Nate, usually so physically attuned to himself, hadn't realized that he had been holding his breath. Air gushed out of his lungs; tension eased. Of all the ways his brother could have greeted him, this one made it easier to say the one thing that Cooper might have been waiting his whole life to hear. "I fucked up. I need your help."

Cooper listened to Nate explain how Almost Heaven planned on keeping its guests as prisoners. "That's not really a surprise," Cooper said. "Maybe we can fix it. What's your leverage? What do you have that they want?"

"Nothing."

"That can't be true. Don't they want you?"

Nate sat down for the first time since coming back from the resort. "I suppose they think they do."

"Then that's your bargaining chip. Your contract with Endless Snow is only exclusive west of the Mississippi."

"I have a contract with Endless Snow?" Endless Snow was family. Why did he have a contract with them?

"Of course you do. You might want to read it someday."

He had a point there. "Is there some other way? I really don't want to do that."

"I know you don't. That's why we're developing relationships with the young snowboarders so they can take over and you aren't stuck doing our promos forever, but I don't see any other alternative with Almost Heaven. You've got to do the publicity."

Nate had Cooper and his agent handle the negotiations. Cooper went wide, asking for regular shuttle trips to town and at least one trip a day to pick up and drop off people at any farm or orchard tours.

"Farm tours? Who's giving farm tours?"

"No one yet, but city people like farm tours, let the kids milk a cow and all that."

"And this was your idea?"

"Mom and Dad bought the resort when I was fifteen. I have picked up a thing or two about the hospitality industry."

Almost Heaven was also including the free ice cream coupons in the family package. The town businesses could have brochures and signage in the lobby. The resort gift shop would consider offering some local crafts, and the children's programming director would be open to the museum's costumed interpreters to give campfire talks.

In return, Nate would promote no other resort east of the Mississippi. The only branded clothing he could wear was from Almost Heaven, Endless Snow, Street Boards, and anything associated with businesses in and around Forrest. He would appear at twenty-five welcome parties a year and would distribute trophies and participation certificates at least five times. He would provide childhood pictures of himself snowboarding on these mountains. He would ship out a collection of his medals and old snowboards for a display case. The deal was for three years, with the clock starting when Almost Heaven opened. There were pages and pages of provisions about what would happen if the resort got sold or went bankrupt, if Nate died, if he didn't meet his obligations or got involved in a messy scandal, if the resort failed to meet theirs, et cetera, et cetera.

All the negotiations were kept very quiet, but they didn't take long. When the contracts were ready to be signed, Almost Heaven wanted to make a big deal about his "partnering" with them. Nate felt that he had to agree, and as long as he was being all noble, he asked them to schedule the event on a Thursday afternoon so that Fred Kayot could cover it in the Friday edition of the *Gazette.* He invited the museum volunteers, the Mattson family, and the people hoping to have stalls in the larger building, only telling them that the resort wanted to announce its commitment to the town, something it had never occurred to them to worry about.

He didn't invite Cheri, Pete, or Lacey. He wasn't ready for them to see him being Mr. Celebrity, shaking hands, posing for picture after picture, being anything but a regular guy.

The resort executives spent most of the time bragging about their green construction techniques, which did indeed deserve to be bragged about.

Someone had prepared talking points for Nate, and he described how much the history of the region meant to him personally and how visits to the living history museum would enrich the visitors' enjoyment of the recreational opportunities the mountains provided. Then he signed his name, agreeing to spend another three years not getting traffic tickets.

The local guests enjoyed the cake and champagne. There was one satisfying moment. Fred Kayot had come along with his young photographer, and Nate overheard Fred approach one of the executives to discuss the "opportunities" that the *Gazette* could provide.

"That all sounds great," the executive said. "Let us talk to Nate. He's going to be our liaison with the town."

Kayot couldn't help glancing at Nate. Nate raised his eyebrows and very deliberately looked away.

The most senior executives started to leave, and Nate stayed. The representatives from both the *Gazette* and the county paper left, and Nate stayed. The Mattson family left, and Nate stayed. When the caterers began to pick up the platters, only then did he leave.

He walked out to the cars with the museum volunteers. Some of these people had been his parents' friends; he had, at first, called them "Mr." or "Mrs." Others he talked to three times a week. Now they were all on a first-name basis, and they treated him like a regular guy. But, as he had feared, after all this hoopla the resort had made about him, they were suddenly treating him differently. He was no longer a regular guy.

He drove back to his little apartment and threw his keys on the counter.

Three years of receptions like that. Three years.

By the time this contract was up, he would be giving awards out to preteens who were doing tricks that he wouldn't have a prayer of doing anymore, even if he weren't under medical restrictions. Those kids might not have even heard of him. He would be some random adult getting in the way. It would be different if he were a great instructor like Ben was, but no, he would just be a name, a meaningless has-been.

In three years, all of his records would be broken. That was fine; that was the way a sport should evolve. At least it was fine as long as the asshole who'd held the previous records wasn't pretending that his stats still mattered.

He had to stop feeling sorry for himself. That Aeneas dude had sneaked his family out of their burning city while his comrades were dying around him. He had abandoned his lady friend, Queen Dido, leaving her to commit suicide with his sword. Aeneas probably would have been happy if all he'd had to do was host some happy hours.

Nate had made a choice. He could have hated himself for screwing over the town. Instead he had chosen to hate himself for whoring out his past.

Compared to what the miners had sacrificed for their families, this was nothing. Nothing.

He turned on the TV, then turned it off. He opened the refrigerator and got a beer.

Three years.

He was sitting on the sofa. The leaves of the big oak tree filled the window across from him. They were at the height of their summer glory.

He didn't care.

He heard a car—a big one—turning into the Fischers' driveway, then stop. It must be a repairman.

But the knock was on his door. The Fischers had not installed a peephole. He had to open the door.

It was Lacey.

She was in her work clothes, the slim dark jeans, the white collared shirt tucked into the wide brown belt. The afternoon light, slanting through the oak trees behind her, left her eyes a velvety brown. When the sunlight was directly on her face, her eyes had a circle of green and were flecked with gold.

He wanted to put his arms around her and pull her close, to feel her hands on his shoulders, her breasts against his chest. He wanted to lose himself in the comfort of a woman's body. No, not just *a* woman, but *this* woman. Lacey. His Lacey.

Except she wasn't his. Three months ago, she had made that clear. She didn't respect him. He had joined that club now. He didn't respect himself.

"Lacey." He stepped back, inviting her in. "This is a pleasant surprise." That was always what his dad had said when he didn't know what else to say.

"I came over as soon as I could. Isn't this what you swore you wouldn't do?"

"What are you talking about?" The window was right beyond her shoulder. He looked out at the mass of oak leaves. He couldn't look at her. "These shuttles are a very exciting opportunity for—"

"Oh my God," she interrupted. "That's why you did it."

He wasn't going to pretend, not with her. "No one can know, Lacey. No one. People have to think it's all smooth sailing."

She put her hand on his chest, pushing him toward the sofa. "Sit down. Tell me."

Now the light was on her face, and her eyes had those flecks of gold.

So he told her. About the parking. About how the resort guests wouldn't be coming to town. About how even Cooper couldn't think of anything else to do.

"So you're taking a bullet for everyone else?"

"Don't make me out to be a hero. I screwed up. I fixed it. End of story."

"How much are you going to hate it?" she asked.

"Making the same conversation over and over? Six times per happy hour, twenty-five times a year for three years, that's"—he tried to do the math in his head—"a lot."

"Four hundred and fifty," she murmured.

"Like I said, a lot. A lot of feeling like a fraud."

"A fraud?" She was surprised. "You? Why? How many medals do you have?"

"Not four hundred and fifty. But they are all in the past. By the time we get to Year Three, the kids are going to be like, 'who is this old dude?' They aren't going to wait around to get the autograph of someone they have never heard of. I'm going to end up like one of those guys who wears his gray hair in a ponytail trying to look like he is still cool."

"You're a long way from having gray hair, and the parents will remember you."

"Right, and I know that they are the ones booking the rooms and paying for the lessons, which is what the resort cares about."

"Something's not adding up here," she said. "You like people. You don't mind meeting strangers. You want to encourage kids to get outside more."

"I don't want to be part of a machine that sells the kids a lot of false promises. That's why Ben walked away from everything. Some of the new coaches need a whole bunch of kids in their program to turn out one winner."

"Then be sure that this resort doesn't do that."

She lifted her hand to his face. It smelled of sunlight and wildflowers.

It was so great that she had come. He had never felt as alone as he had this afternoon. He had thought that he couldn't tell anyone about this, that he was going to have to keep it all inside, but he could trust her. She would never tell anyone.

She would help him through this. She would anchor him. She would help him find a mission so that it was about more than the brochures and the shuttle service. He could make sure the resort didn't hire coaches who would lie to the parents. He could motivate the kids, but talk to the parents about the risks and the injuries, make them understand how close he had been to life in a wheelchair.

He put his hand over hers and eased hers down, closing his eyes, burying his lips into her palm. He felt her other hand come to his hair.

Her hands, so knowing, so confident, were unbuttoning his shirt, smoothing over his skin. It was her palms flat against him. This was not a doctor's exploring fingertips; this was the touch of a woman.

He let her do it all, the feathery kiss, the unbuckling, the unzipping. She even rolled the condom down over his erection before straddling him and lowering herself on him, looking into his eyes as she did.

That eye contact felt more intimate than his actually entering her. This was new, this was a different Lacey, lovely, tender, and melting. Afterward he was sorry that they had not stood up and unfolded the bed. He would like to lie next to her, her hair spilling across his chest. He had one arm around her hips and one up higher around her back. He didn't want to let her go, but when she started to shift off of him, he did..

She stood up, reaching for her clothes. "No," he said. "Please stay."

"I'm sorry. I can't. I left Tank at the clinic. I need to go get him."

"I'll go with you, and we can—" He stopped. "Are you regretting this?"

"No, no. I don't know if I am ready to go public yet, that's all."

Why? What was she afraid of? People talking? Of course, people would talk. That's what they did. You couldn't live your life worrying about that.

But he wasn't going to argue with her. He had rushed her once. He wasn't going to make that mistake again.

Chapter 16

She was not going to think of this as a mistake. How could it be? When Nate had moved her hand to his lips, a warm light had flooded through her. Then the warmth had reached out, enveloping him. She had been able to comfort this usually bold, confident man, doing in her personal life what she did in her profession. The animals whose pain she had relieved, the families whose beloved pets she had restored to health, they made her work sacred to her. Now she had brought that gift of ease to a friend.

It didn't matter that they had no future, that she would be leaving in six short weeks. She would always have this memory, a memory of a moment when she had become the person she wanted to be.

* * * *

However reluctantly Nate had signed his contract with Almost Heaven, he was determinedly building an alliance between the town and the resort. Lacey was impressed.

He had gotten the resort to agree to pay for the town's new Christmas decorations and to buy tickets to the hospital gala. Both of those expenses were not much more than a rounding error in the resort's budget. He brought the sales team into town to see what had been accomplished with the museum. He was working with the sports director to steer clear of coaches who wanted to start their own high-intensity training programs.

He had even set up a meeting between the *Gazette* and some key people from the resort.

"Why are you doing that?" Cheri had demanded. "Fred Kayot is the enemy."

Nate shook his head. "A town needs a newspaper."

That was all Nate said, but the next edition featured profiles with the three local boys who were likely to be starters on the county football team in the fall.

"How did you engineer that?" Lacey didn't doubt for a single moment that Nate was responsible for those profiles.

"Are you suggesting that the editorial integrity of the *Gazette* can be bought?"

He acknowledged that Almost Heaven, which had no earthly need to advertise in a local paper, had agreed to take out full-page booster ads, congratulating Forrest kids for their achievements at the high school.

It was good to see him laughing. He was making peace with the bargain he had struck. And he was giving her the credit. "You were right," he kept saying. "It's important to keep snowboarding fun for the kids."

Lacey didn't remember saying anything that resembled that, but she didn't feel called upon to argue about it.

* * * *

The first of the new houses to be completed was being bought by the sales and marketing manager. He invited his associates in for cocktails before the gala. Nate asked Lacey to go with him.

"As your date? Or are you going to ask Cheri too?"

"I wasn't going to ask Cheri."

"Then, no, Nate, no." She wasn't going out in public with him as a couple.

That left him having to explain to Cheri why he wasn't going to drive Lacey and her to the event.

"It wouldn't have made sense anyway," Lacey added quickly. "He shouldn't have to drive all the way out here when he lives in town."

"I don't know why you have to go to that thing, Nate," Cheri said with a pout. "You don't know those people, and you already promised us."

"I need to get to know them," he answered. "I'll be working with them."

"And I don't mind driving," Lacey said. "I have to work on Sunday, so I won't be drinking much."

"I don't want to get all dressed up and then show up in that humongous truck of yours."

"Then you need to drive yourself," Pete said. "You wanted to go. You have a car. You're an adult. Drive yourself."

The theme of the gala was—and had always been—casino night. Because she worked the roulette table, Lacey had, her first year, gone to a thrift store in Charleston and found a black tie, a cummerbund, and a white shirt with a tucked bib. With her one good pair of black pants, she almost looked like a casino employee. She had repeated the outfit the next year, but this year she had her bridesmaid's dress…if you could be a bridesmaid at a wedding that had no bride. Caroline McGuiness, her brother's future mother-in-law, had been delighted to have at least one female in the wedding party. She had insisted on taking Lacey shopping in Chicago and then had paid for the dress. A floor-length strapless sheath made from heavy champagne-colored silk, the dress had a slightly Grecian feel because of the floaty drape that drifted over one shoulder, and then cascaded down the back.

Lacey had felt good in the dress at the wedding. She felt even better in it now. She liked what Cheri had done with her hair and makeup, and she wasn't wearing Spanx.

After she and Caroline had selected the dress, Caroline had asked her if she would feel more comfortable wearing Spanx.

"Ah…maybe." Lacey had no idea. She hardly even owned a dress, much less Spanx. But apparently most women wore Spanx with formal wear. Caroline had bought them, and Lacey had worn them.

Any imperfections in Lacey's butt and thighs came from them being too muscular, something Spanx couldn't do much about. Tonight she left them in the back of her underwear drawer and discovered that while Spanx might make a woman look more attractive, she felt more attractive without them.

And Lacey did feel attractive. She wondered what Nate would think. If he had liked the shirt she had worn to the Mexican restaurant, how would he react to this dress? That was something to look forward to.

"That's a bridesmaid's dress?" Cheri marveled when Lacey came downstairs. "I've certainly been in the wrong weddings. All my bridesmaids' dresses were pastel polyester. But don't you hate wearing a strapless bra?"

"A bra is built into the dress."

"Really? Let me see. Turn around." With her usual lack of boundaries, Cheri tried to turn Lacey around so that Cheri could unzip the dress.

Lacey stepped away. "It's a side zip. Apparently the dress drapes better without a center back seam."

"I wish I weren't so short," Cheri sighed. "I'd love to try it on sometime."

Being petite should not have stopped Cheri from trying the dress on, but Lacey supposed by "try on" Cheri meant "borrow and wear."

Cheri was wearing a very simple black dress, also floor-length. Lacey had thought blondes weren't supposed to look good in black, but Cheri looked as delicate and flawless as a porcelain teacup.

For the past week, the town seemed more excited about the gala than Lacey remembered from previous years. With Dr. Byrd's clinic and the resort buying tickets, the early sales had been strong, and the enthusiasm prompted locals who had stopped coming to buy tickets this year. The organizers had had to bring in ten- and twelve-person tables instead of the usual eight.

Lacey had told the Byrds that she would stop by the nursing home and wheel old Mrs. Byrd over to the event.

"Well, well," the old lady said. "You're going to take the place by storm, are you?"

"I showed you the dress when I got home from the wedding."

"All folded up. It was just a bunch of fabric when I saw it."

"It still is a bunch of fabric. Now, do you need a coat or a wrap?"

"Not me. I'm all covered up. You're the one who might take a chill."

Lacey laughed and leaned forward to release the brake on the wheelchair.

As they were waiting for the elevator, Mrs. Byrd said, "I told my grandsons to be sure that that nice Katie girl from the clinic sits with some young people. She deserves to have fun."

Lacey agreed with that. Living with her son in her aunt's basement, Katie didn't have much of a social life. But Lacey had hopes for her. At the urging of Nate's friend Ben, Katie was taking a series of online computer classes. When Almost Heaven opened, she would be well-qualified for one of their office jobs. Working there, she would meet more people.

The cafeteria was decorated as it always was, with a silver and white theme. The tables were covered with white cloths and the same silvery table toppers that were used every year. The centerpieces were also familiar, big hurricane globes filled with silver balls. But for the first time, little white Christmas lights were strung in a grid over the dance floor, and the room's columns were wreathed with twists of silver fabric. Clearly the decorating committee had scooped up some of the extra money from the increased ticket sales.

Lacey and Mrs. Byrd always sat with Dr. Byrd, his wife, and their friends. "Young" Mrs. Byrd had commandeered a ten-person table, and for the first time her two sisters and their husbands had come in from Roanoke for the event. Lacey had met them once or twice before and was pleased to see them again. She was also happy to see that Katie was indeed sitting at a table with younger people, mostly college students who were home for the summer and whose parents were probably forcing them to come. Cheri was also at that table. Lacey imagined that she was the oldest one there, but she certainly didn't look like it.

One of the twelve-person tables had all the chairs tilted forward, but no sign that anyone was sitting there yet. Whenever someone approached the table, Marjorie Pritchard, the woman Nate had stayed with when he had come in March, waved them off.

Her purpose became clear when the Almost Heaven party arrived. They came in as a group, having all left their cocktail party at the same time. Mrs. Pritchard caught Nate's eye and pointed to the reserved table. He thanked her with a nod and directed the group in that direction.

Cheri immediately popped out of her chair, moving quickly across the room, putting her hand on the dark sleeve of Nate's suit jacket before anyone had sat down. He started introducing her, and Lacey could see Cheri's head darting in a little birdlike movement. She was trying to count the people in the group, checking to see if there were any empty seats. She kept close to the chair next to Nate, but when one man was clearly waiting to seat his wife in that chair, she had no choice but to return to her original table.

Before Nate sat down, he scanned the room. Lacey knew he was looking for her. She was standing on the other side of her table, talking to one of Cassie Byrd's sisters. When Nate saw her, he blinked and his eyebrows went up.

Yes. *Yes.*

She touched the drape at her shoulder, adjusting it slightly, calling attention to her bare skin.

Nate stepped forward. It was almost involuntary. Then someone in the group spoke to him, and he had to turn away.

Her brother's wedding, organized and paid for by Tim's family, had been last fall. Lacey's mother had come expecting to be treated like the Honored Guest, the VIP to end all VIPs, the fairest of them all. But it was Lacey the McGuinesses were thrilled to have join the family.

As a result, her mother had felt slighted, and when she saw Lacey's dress, more elegant and expensive than her own, she sighed and said that Lacey had let her arms get a bit too muscular.

If the social elite of Forrest were offended by Lacey's toned biceps, they did a good job of hiding their distaste. Everyone Lacey spoke to marveled over her dress. The hospital's pharmacist came right over and told Lacey that she would like to introduce Lacey to her nephew as soon as he arrived.

Lacey had an early shift at the roulette table. Being a croupier was more challenging than dealing poker, and worried about making a mistake, she had in the previous years been rather robotic, spinning the wheel and paying out the bets as carefully as if a pit boss and overhead cameras were monitoring her. But one of the men from the resort group immediately came over to help her calculate the pay-outs. He was an older man and was wearing a wedding ring. He wasn't trying to hit on her; he simply liked working with someone he probably thought of as a "pretty girl."

And for the first time in her life, Lacey started acting like a pretty girl, raising her eyebrows teasingly, keeping her smiles quick and seemingly private, leaning just a bit farther forward than she needed to when she raked the chips off the table. What was the point of living with Cheri Willston if you weren't going to pick up a thing or two?

After her shift was over, she let her assistant croupier buy her a drink. He wanted to introduce her to his wife and the others at the resort table. It was tempting. *Why, yes, I am indeed acquainted with Mr. Forrest. In fact, he knows what's inside this dress.* But she needed to get back to her own table. Bill and Cassie Byrd wouldn't feel comfortable dancing if his mother was left sitting by herself.

She sat down next to Mrs. Byrd, and the two of them people-watched. Cheri was working the crowd, selling more of the gambling chips. She was, of course, doing a great job. Katie was dancing with one of the young men from her table. Lacey thought he was the oldest son of the local car dealer.

"That Nate Forrest," Mrs. Byrd said. "He is a treat to look at, isn't he?"

Nate was dancing with one of the women from his table. His movements were graceful and coordinated even though he didn't seem to have any particular knowledge of the dance steps. He was wearing a white shirt and a bronze tie with his dark suit. His hair was neatly combed, and he was freshly shaven.

Yes, that man was a treat to look at, but he wasn't Nate. Nate had rumpled hair and dressed in a snowboarder's careless layers. Nate moved easily through his shoulders. This man's shoulders were formal and frozen. He was on duty.

The people he was with had nothing to do with the recreational side of the resort. Their job wasn't to inspire kids; their job was to sell condos. No wonder Nate was finding the evening difficult. These weren't the people he had anything in common with.

Take me home with you, and I will remind you how to have fun.

A great thought, but not anything that was possible. She had put Tank in his crate before 6 p.m. She couldn't leave him there until morning. She had to go back to the farmhouse. But if Nate came back with her, Cheri would be there, and there would be explanations and Cheri's coy looks, all that.

If you had any guts, you'd make this work.

Who was this person talking to her? It certainly wasn't anyone she knew.

"Lacey, dear," Mrs. Byrd interrupted this dialogue. "Do you mind pushing me a little more? I would like to go speak to Tommy Pearson. If only he weren't sitting with Valerie. I always appreciate it when Cassie manages to keep her from sitting at our table."

Lacey had forgotten. The first year she had come, Valerie and her husband had sat at the Byrds' table. Last year they hadn't. Apparently that had not been an accident.

During the day, Tommy Pearson was on the hospital's custodial staff. At night he helped clean Dr. Byrd's clinic. He was a good worker, but he needed to be supervised as he was cognitively disabled. He had eagerly signed up for the clinic's offer of free tickets, and his mother had come with him. They were happily sitting with the women who bathed patients before surgery. Their warmth and optimism eased people through those anxious moments. The surgeons were grateful, and the ladies received big fruit baskets at Christmas and gala tickets in the summer.

Valerie and her husband were also at that table. Although the hospital ladies were probably delightful dinner companions, even Lacey, who was usually clueless about these things, could tell that this was a low-status table. That would matter to Valerie. She wouldn't be able to have a good time at a low-status table, no matter how lively the conversation was.

Tommy was having a wonderful time, he told Lacey and Mrs. Byrd. He had been thrilled that Katie had asked him to dance with her.

Lacey felt a wince of shame. That would have never occurred to her. Good for Katie. "If your mother will take Mrs. Byrd around to visit the other tables," she said, "I would like to dance with you too."

Tommy was delighted, and his mother was pleased at being elevated to Mrs. Byrd's companion.

In previous years Lacey had tried to avoid dancing. She didn't really know how, but Tim and his father had taken her in hand before the wedding. Now she didn't have to worry about disgracing herself, not that dancing with Tommy required much finesse.

Once she started dancing, she didn't lack for partners. Nate asked her twice, but just as she was about to put her hand in his, an older man had also stepped forward and Nate gave way respectfully.

When were X Game gold medalists expected to be so deferential? Lacey knew how Nate would answer that—*only when they had sold out.*

Eventually the hospital's pharmacist was able to introduce Lacey to her nephew, Brandon Scott. He was light-haired and preppy-looking, having newly graduated from law school. He would be joining a firm in Charleston as soon as he passed the bar.

He reminded Lacey of herself three years ago, new to her profession, unfamiliar with West Virginia, daunted by the size of her debts.

She dropped her pretty-girl flirtatiousness and went back to being herself. He instantly warmed to her compassion. All evening long he had had to pretend to be the glowing success that his aunt had been bragging about. In truth, his record hadn't been stellar. Finding any job had been a struggle. He relaxed as Lacey shared her own experiences and assured him that as the largest city in West Virginia, Charleston was nothing like Forrest.

When the band took a break, they went on talking, standing near one of the silver-draped columns. Brandon had his back to the room, not because he was staking a claim to Lacey—this wasn't romantic for either of them—but because he felt vulnerable, unwilling to let his aunt's friends see his face.

They were still talking when the band started playing again. Even with Brandon blocking her view of the room, she knew immediately that Nate was coming toward her. She gestured to Brandon to turn around.

Nate did look good in formal clothes. Lacey felt the heavy satin of her dress whisper against her as she stepped forward to introduce the two men.

When she had first been with Nate after coming back from treating Big'un, she had been wearing heavy layers. The next day she had been in granny pants, and her breasts had been compressed by the ugly sports bra. When she had gone to his apartment after he had signed the Almost Heaven contract, she had barely taken off her clothes.

But this dress was lined and interlined. The bra was built into the bodice. All she would have to do would be to flip the chiffon drape off her shoulder and reach one hand under her arm. No fumbling for the back zipper. The dress would slide down her body, and there she would be, wearing nothing but her prettiest panties.

No, she would leave the drape over her shoulder. Then, as the dress slipped down her body, the light chiffon would follow, curving over her shoulder, caressing her naked breasts, floating down her thighs.

Why had she been unnerved by her strong sexual response to Nate when he had come back to town? This was fun.

The men were shaking hands. "You will have to excuse me," Nate said, "but I need to borrow Dr. Berryville for a moment."

Dr. Berryville? What was that about?

"Of course," Brandon said politely and then turned to Lacey. "Can I get your number anyway?"

The "anyway" was because he knew that she would be leaving West Virginia just as he was arriving.

He was taking his phone out of his pocket. Lacey was waiting for him to signal that he was ready, but before she could speak, Nate started rattling off her number. Brandon entered the data quickly. Then touching her arm, he said that it had been great to meet her.

"Who was that?" Nate asked sharply.

Don't get crabby with me because you aren't having a good time. "He's a lawyer, about to join a firm in the area." She didn't mention that the firm was actually almost two hours away and that she wasn't likely to ever see him again.

"He seemed to like you."

Nate was jealous. "And I liked him." *Because if there's one thing I know, it is how to be a big sister. Even in this dress, that's what I was to him, a big sister.* "That's not what you needed to talk about."

"Oh, right." It was as if he needed reminding. "Cheri's on track to making a fool of herself. I'm hoping you can take her home."

Lacey looked across the dance floor. Cheri still looked pretty, of course she did, but she didn't look eighteen as she had at the beginning of the evening. She was flushed and disheveled. Her dress had twisted a little, and in the back the top of her bra was showing. She had one of old Mrs. Byrd's grandsons out on the floor with her. Lacey was pretty sure that it was Aaron, the one still in high school. Cheri was trying to show him dance steps, and he looked uncomfortable, as if he were praying to be rescued. A group of men, many of them old enough to be Cheri's father, had turned away from the bar so they could watch her. Lacey saw one of them lean toward another and whisper something. Lacey supposed that it was about Cheri.

"I hate to ask you," Nate continued. "But I can't do it."

Lacey didn't want to leave. She wanted to go on being a pretty girl. She wanted to go on being a sexually aware woman. She wanted to have the courage to do what the voice in her head was telling her to do. "Are you that worried about what people would say?"

"It's not other people. It's— Do I have to spell it out?"

No, he didn't. Cheri had been looking forward to this evening all month; she had wanted it to be special. She was longing for something exciting to happen. If nothing happened at the gala, would the drive home be her last chance? In the car alone with Nate, drunk and happy, would she put her hand on his thigh? Would she start to run her fingers along his inseam?

"I don't think she would actually have sex with you." Lacey found that she wanted to spell it out.

"No. But either I have to reject her, or go along until she can play the outraged wife. Both of those suck, but so does letting her stay here and embarrass herself. Don't you owe it to Pete to get her home?"

The answer to that was easy. Yes. "Let me say good-bye to some people. I'll meet you out front."

Mrs. Byrd had already left, and so it didn't take Lacey long to say her farewells. Cheri and Nate were waiting at the hospital's big glass front door.

Cheri was surprised to see her. "You're leaving too?"

"She's taking you home," Nate said.

"But I thought . . ." Clearly she had assumed that Nate would be doing that. "Then we don't really need to leave. I want to stay. I can call Pete to come get me."

"No." Lacey took her arm firmly. "We're going."

"I'll follow you," Nate said.

"You don't need to. I switched to club soda after one drink. I'm probably more sober than you are."

But in her rearview mirror, all the way home were the bright headlights of Nate's Escalade.

Cheri buckled her seat belt without saying anything, and as they reached the city limits, Lacey glanced across the center console. Cheri had her eyes closed and was leaning against the window. Lacey supposed that the glass felt cool against her flushed face.

She had liked living with Cheri. Cheri enjoyed fussing over people, making them comfortable. Sometimes it felt a little overwhelming— Cheri was always asking her if she wanted a cup of tea, if she wanted the thermostat changed—but mostly it was nice.

Yet this longing to recover the intensity of her youth, the glory of being the homecoming queen, left Lacey uneasy. Why couldn't Cheri appreciate what she had?

At the farmhouse Cheri half-tumbled out of the Silverado even before Lacey had turned off the engine. Lacey had to hike up the narrow skirt of her dress to get out of the truck, and by the time she had resettled her dress, the back door was closing behind Cheri.

Nate was waiting by the side of his car. As she moved toward him, Lacey felt the satin of her dress against her legs again, but this time the fabric was cold.

"Did I tell you how beautiful you look tonight?" he said.

How could he have? They hadn't had a moment alone together. "Cheri did my hair and makeup."

"I could take you back to the party if you would like," he said.

"No." Lacey was not in the party mood anymore. "I don't want to leave Cheri alone."

"I wasn't trying to keep you from having a good time, you know."

She didn't answer. It had felt like it.

"Why not me, Lacey? Why not *me*?"

She looked at him, confused and startled.

"Seeing you with other guys, even the old, married ones, that's all I could think: 'Why not me?'"

It was a clear night, and the moon was three-quarters full, leaving the windmill and the barnyard washed with a pale light.

But it is you, Nate. That's the problem. It's already going to be hard to leave. Don't make it worse.

"You do know," he went on, "that I want it to be me. Every day that I see you, I want it more and more. But I don't know what to do. I'm so afraid of making a mistake again. When are you going to give me a chance to see if we have a future together?"

"A future of four and a half weeks?"

He drew back, puzzled. "Four and a half weeks? What are you talking about?"

"It's the end of June. I'm leaving on August first."

"Wait, wait." His voice was urgent. "You're leav— What are you talking about?"

"My contract with Dr. Byrd is up. I have to leave. You already knew this."

"I do not. This is the first—"

She interrupted him. "Everyone knows. It isn't a secret. And I told you. Back in March, during the snowstorm. You asked if I was getting any of my loans forgiven, and I told you about this, and how Dr. Byrd's next assistant would have to be someone who would buy in to the practice."

"Oh shit." He ran his hand over his face. "That's right. It was over the chili. I forgot. But I hardly knew you then, and you've never mentioned it since, not once."

"I don't like talking about it. I don't like thinking about it, but of course I mentioned it."

"Not to me, you didn't. Are you saying that Cheri and Pete know?"

She nodded. "Pete's always known, and of course Cheri and I have talked about it, since she has to decide if she wants to stay here by herself."

"Then if they knew, how it is possible that no one ever mentioned it to me?"

It suddenly occurred to Lacey that Pete and Cheri never talked about their own future, about any plans to return to Frederick or even to live together. If they weren't talking about their own future, why would they talk about hers?

"When I came back after Seth's wedding," he asked, "did you think I was just interested in some kind of fling?"

"Yes. I knew that I wasn't that kind of person. But, Nate, everything would have ended up exactly the same if you had known. I was not going to get involved with you when I was going to be leaving."

Saying it aloud, saying it to him, suddenly made it sound all wrong. Why hadn't she been willing to enjoy the few months that they would have had together?

Because back then she couldn't. That's all there was to it. She had been scared, scared of a man overwhelming her life, scared of the pain she'd be sure to feel when it was over.

"Do you want to leave?" His voice was urgent. "You must want to stay."

She shook her head. "People like Pete and me...we don't let ourselves want things that we know we can't have."

She must have shivered, because he was suddenly pulling off his suit jacket, draping it around her bare shoulders. She hadn't been conscious of being cold, but the jacket was warmed by his body heat. She pulled it close around her.

"Do you know for sure that you can't?" he asked.

"Dr. Byrd wants to retire in a few years, and he has to sell the practice. He's entitled to get good money for it. To buy any kind of medical practice with the kind of loan I could get, the real estate has to be worth a certain percentage, and with property values around here so low..." She no longer remembered the details, just how touched she had been by Dr. Byrd wanting her to have the practice that his father had started. "Even if I were willing to take on more debt, which I'm not, it isn't possible."

"Then let me do it. Let me lend you the money."

She stepped back, catching the heel of her shoe against the concrete of the windmill platform. Nate reached out to steady her.

"No, Nate, no. I can't take your money."

"But it would be a loan." His voice was urgent. "You would pay me back."

"I can't bear the thought of having more debt, and aren't you talking about using your own money? Didn't your parents ask you to promise not to do that?"

"That doesn't matter," he said impatiently. "This is important. We can make it work."

"I could never take money from a friend."

"But *me*?"

"Especially you."

Her mother had played a little game in which she would try to get other people to pay for things. She would take Lacey and her brother to a bakery and let them each pick out a doughnut. Then, even though Lacey knew that she had dollar bills in a side pocket of her purse, she would count out change, then recount and look distressed when it didn't add up to what she needed. Lacey would try to give her doughnut back, but the clerk would almost always wave them out without having them pay at all. The amounts were always small; it was simply a way of triumphing over other people. Lacey had hated it, hated hated hated it.

She took Nate's jacket off and handed it back to him. "Please don't beat yourself up about forgetting. It wouldn't have made any difference if you had known. At least not to you and me. Even in March I knew it was too late for us. It was always too late for us."

Chapter 17

On top of old Smokey,
All covered with snow,
I lost my true lover
For courtin' too slow.

Since when had anyone ever accused Nate Forrest of acting too slowly?

At least the dude in the song had had the benefit of working up in the snow. Nate was down here in the summer flatlands. How the hell was he supposed to get anything right without some snow to help him along?

Lacey couldn't leave. She couldn't. She loved it here. She belonged here. People loved her, loved the care she gave to the animals.

He had to fix this.

Cheri and Lacey cancelled Sunday night supper the evening after the gala. Lacey had to run out to the dude ranch to check on one of the horses, and Cheri—not surprisingly—had a headache.

What were Sunday evenings going to be like next January? Lacey would be gone, and with the resort open, Pete and Cheri would leave too. There would be pretty ladies coming to the resort, wanting to have a fling with one of the pros, but that's not what he wanted. Not anymore.

After he got Lacey's text cancelling supper, he called Pete. "We've been ditched. Do you want to run over to the Mexican restaurant?"

"I'll pick you up at five."

When Pete arrived, Nate didn't bother with chitchat. "Did you know that Lacey is planning on leaving in August?"

"Sure. It sucks, doesn't it?"

"How long have you known?"

"Forever." Pete looked at him curiously. "You didn't know?"

"She mentioned it once at the beginning, but not since."

Pete nodded. "I imagine the more important something is to her, the less she says about it."

Apparently. "Do you think she would stay if she could, if she could buy the practice?" Nate asked.

"She's not going to be thinking about things that she can't have."

"That was exactly what she said."

Pete looked over at him suspiciously. "You wouldn't be planning to give her the money, would you?"

"It is one obvious solution."

"She'll never take money from you, Nate. Never."

"But there's so much at stake. She loves Dr. Byrd's practice, that he's not out to squeeze every last dime out of the clients, that she gets to do large animals and the pets."

"And she loves West Virginia," Pete agreed. "We know that. But whatever the stakes, you just don't take other people's money."

Your wife did.

"It would be a loan, not a gift."

"My dad told me to ask your parents to cosign college loans for me."

Nate didn't know that. "Did you ask them? What did they say?"

"I didn't ask them. I wouldn't. I was just a kid, but I wasn't about to put them in that position. So, give it up, Nate. Even if Lacey was willing to take on more debt—which she probably isn't—she would never borrow from you, not ever. When it comes to things like this, I understand Lacey better than you ever will."

* * * *

He wanted to discount what Pete had said. Pete was a guy. Guys turned too much into a competition. Look at him and his brother. For one man to have to borrow money from another man was an ultimate admission of testosterone failure. But Lacey was a woman.

The unwillingness to let yourself dream…Nate had had dreams. As a kid he had wanted to be the next Shaun White. Even after he had had to accept that his specialty, Big Air, wasn't in the Olympics at the right time for him, there had been plenty of other dreams, records to break, other medals to earn. He had achieved his dreams because he had worked fanatically hard for each record and each medal.

He got tired of people harping about how privileged he had been, as if he were some kind of trust-fund baby, but he *had* been privileged. His parents hadn't been rolling in cash, but they had been really great parents who wanted to give him every opportunity as long as he was willing to work hard. Even more, they had given him the faith that hard work was rewarded, that it made sense to try as hard as he had. Such optimism was more of a leg up than any trust fund.

If he was ever going to truly understand Lacey, he had to accept that she came from a very different background. She didn't have his comfort when things start to work out. She didn't feel fully safe in her success. Pete was like that too; it was Cheri who had the optimism to encourage him to open his own garage.

He wasn't going to be able to change that about either of his two friends. But that didn't mean that he had to give up.

* * * *

It was easy enough to figure out what Dr. Byrd's building was worth. But Nate had to spend a lot of time on the phone and the Internet to guess what the equipment and the goodwill were worth. Then he talked to loan officers, his personal portfolio manager, his agent, and finally his parents. By Wednesday afternoon he had all the information that he could get without seeing the clinic's actual financial records. He had also learned from Katie that Lacey was staying late on Wednesday night. She had scheduled a video-conference call with some other young veterinarians. They looked at each other's slides, discussed tricky cases they had seen, shared what they had read in the recent research, generally trying to keep up with the advances in veterinary medicine.

Her Silverado was the only vehicle in the clinic's back lot when he walked over a little before seven. He sat down on one of the picnic benches near the fenced dog run, leaning his back against the table, stretching his legs out across the grass. He used to think of himself as one of the most impatient beings on earth. Now he didn't care how long he had to wait.

He got up when the big security lights came on. Once nightfall came, they would wash the parking lot with a white glare, but the summer sun was still over the tree line, and the electric light seemed to be trapped inside the heavy bulbs. The gray steel door opened. Tank's black nose and white muzzle appeared. On seeing Nate, Tank tried to catapult the rest of the way down the concrete steps. Nate was close enough to hear Lacey's gasp of surprise at the jerk of the leash.

In a moment he was reaching over the railing, gripping the leather of Tank's leash to take the strain off her arm.

"Nate, what are you doing here?" In addition to her purse, she was carrying a canvas tote.

"I wanted to talk to you alone, and I guessed Cheri would be at the farmhouse."

"She's out tonight."

Tank, eternal optimist that he was, had slid into a sitting position in front of Nate and was poking his head forward eagerly, trying to sniff at Nate's pockets, hoping for a treat. Nate never had dog treats in his pocket, but Tank never stopped hoping.

At least her dog had aspirational dreams.

"If you don't have to get home," he said, "do you want to go over to the county seat for dinner? There're a couple places with outdoor seating. We could take Tank."

She shook her head. "I have a lot of work to do tonight. Can we talk here?"

"Of course." He gestured toward the picnic table and went to unlatch the dog run for Tank.

They sat facing each other. She folded her hands in front of her. "What is it?" she asked.

She sounded wary. He wanted to reassure her. "I respect that you do not want to take on any more debt."

She closed her eyes for a moment. She was relieved. "Maybe I've been too obsessive about this, but every time I think about buying a new sweater, I wonder if I shouldn't be putting a little more toward the loans. I've been telling myself that I'm leaving here with everything reduced to something manageable, and I can buy new clothes and go to restaurants, that I can let myself breathe."

He loved her. There was no question in his mind about that. The golden-red freckles spilling from the bridge of her nose to scatter across her strong cheekbones, her hazel eyes with the circle of green, their flecks of gold, her rich chestnut hair…he loved her. She was his Colleen.

But he couldn't say that, not now, not yet. "Your plan in your next job is to be an employee again, working for whoever owns the practice?"

She nodded.

"Then work for me."

"What? Work for you? As what?"

"A vet, of course. I will contract to buy out Dr. Byrd's practice. You will go on being a salaried employee. When he retires, you'll be the senior vet, but you won't have any skin in the game. You won't owe me anything."

It seemed perfect to him. How could she say no to this?

And yet she did.

"That's still charity, Nate. It's still taking your money."

"No, it isn't. I could fire you."

"But you wouldn't. We fuss because Dr. Byrd won't fire Valerie. How would this be any different?"

"To start with, Valerie's terrible at her job. You're great at yours."

"How do you know that?"

"What?"

"What do you know about my veterinary skills? We've already established that Bill Byrd can't fire people, so the fact that he's employing me doesn't guarantee anything. How do you know that I am any good?"

"You are, aren't you?"

"Yes. But that's not what I'm asking. I'm asking how you know. Do you even know where I went to school?"

"Wait..." He closed his eyes, trying to remember. "University of California, your diploma's hanging in the clinic, but I never checked which campus, and it wouldn't mean anything to me anyway."

"Would you ever, *ever* recommend that someone buy a business just so his girlfriend could keep her job...and I'm not even your girlfriend."

"This isn't only personal. You're important to the town. The town needs you."

She stood up. "Nate, you are making this a nightmare for me."

"I don't mean to." This was supposed to be a dream, not a nightmare. But he was talking to her back. She was opening the fence for Tank. "You want to stay. This is a way for you—"

"Stop it." She clipped Tank's leash in place and then straightened. "Just stop it. I need to get myself through the next few weeks. I am so incredibly lucky that I have a future, that I have these skills, this degree, that I can support myself with work I love. Do you know how many women's lives would be so different if they had any kind of credentials at all, much less mine? I am focusing on that, on how much I have to be grateful for. I'm not going to give in to some kind of pity party about having to leave."

"Yes, but—"

"There are no buts about it. I have to be realistic. And this unrelenting pressure you're putting me under, Nate, is too much. You're being a bully. And I have plenty of experience scaring schoolyard bullies away from my brother."

"You are not seriously accusing me of being a bully, are you?" He had never bullied anyone in his life. His mom had been the first-grade teacher. How could he have been a bully?

"That's what it feels like from my end, that you are not going to let up until you get your way." She paused, thinking about something. Then she spoke crisply, decisively. "I can't see you. I want you to keep away from me. If Cheri and Pete want to come to the farmhouse, fine, you can come. It's her home too. But remember, I don't want to see you."

What was she saying? He couldn't be hearing her right. It was as if a perfect, unbroken, glittering stretch of snow had suddenly roared and become an avalanche, engulfing him, spinning him.

But you could fight against an avalanche. There were rules—move sideways, create an air pocket. What was he supposed to do now? He had no idea.

He could only do what his father would have done, be a gentleman. He took her bag and Tank's leash, then made a light gesture as if to touch her arm without making actual contact. The Silverado had a keyless remote system. He could reach around her to open the door.

She got in. He closed the door and then took Tank around to the passenger side. She started the engine and looked across the console at him as he put her tote on the floor. "It was UC Davis. I went to UC Davis. It is the second-best vet school in the country. Cornell's better, but I was a California resident, so it was going to cost less."

Chapter 18

On Monday Nate was not at the front of the stores when Lacey walked by at noon. Not on Tuesday either. On Wednesday, he was in the bank when she came in. He nodded politely, but that was it.

Wasn't that what she had asked for?

Friday he made an excuse why he couldn't come to the farmhouse on Sunday.

You didn't want him to go on charging headlong at you. You didn't want him to steamroll you anymore. And he's not. Be happy.

Everything else seemed to be going wrong too. Mrs. Byrd's Medicare supplementary insurance was finally saying that she needed to move to assisted living, and there weren't any good options in Forrest. A few people had gotten their homes licensed, but none had the programming or social activities that Mrs. Byrd had been enjoying at the rehabilitative care unit.

Cheri had strained her back, lifting supplies at the salon. She wouldn't go to the doctor; she was relying on ice packs and evening visits to a massage therapist in the county seat. Lacey spoke up once, saying that because Pete had good insurance through Almost Heaven, going to a doctor and then a physical therapist would be a lot cheaper than paying out-of-pocket for massages. Cheri murmured that of course Lacey was right, but if she did go to the doctor, Lacey didn't know about it.

The Silverado started making a clunking noise. It was under warranty, but the part was on back order.

It had also started to rain; day after day it rained. Other towns along the river were worried about flooding, and Pete sent the construction company's heavy equipment to shore up Forrest's levees. It was still raining on the

Fourth of July. The fields were mud, and the firework displays across the county were all cancelled.

Lacey needed to plan her move. She had so much more stuff than she had come with—not just Tank, but the coats and gloves she hadn't needed in California, the ivy-patterned dishes that Mrs. Byrd wanted to give her. She would need to rent a car big enough for Tank's crate. Would it hold the rest of her things too? How would she know until she actually had the car?

Dr. Byrd had made a slow start in finding a replacement for her. It wasn't easy to find someone who had the interest and resources to buy out a practice in southeastern West Virginia. As a result, he only had two candidates coming in during July.

The first one, Brent Carville, came to visit right after the Fourth. For someone fresh out of school, he seemed to have decent enough skills. He was inclined to run more tests than Dr. Byrd did, but Lacey knew she had been like that when she had started. He was also a little stiff, but Lacey had definitely been like that when she started, too, and now she could put her arm around a client's shoulders and cry along with them when their dear pet took its final breath.

The problem was his mother. Newly divorced, she was planning on moving along with her son. Since she was the one providing the investment capital, she was interested in how the business side of the practice was run, and it didn't take her long to start seeing the problems. Why were so many of the cages taken up by the staff's pets instead of revenue-producing animals? Why did routine prescription refills require so many steps? Why was the office manager involved in that? Why did people calling for test results need to get them from Valerie, not directly from the lab? Why was Valerie leaving some callers on hold for so long? By lunch Mrs. Carville was only looking for problems that involved Valerie.

That made Valerie testy the rest of the week. When the one other candidate, Oliver Hammermill, was coming, Valerie announced that no one could bring in their own pets that day. She wasn't prepared to take herself out of the information flow about prescriptions and test results, but as banning the staff's pets would not inconvenience her or diminish her power, she was suddenly concerned about staff discipline.

There was no doubt that there had been some serious pet creep. Nearly everyone except Dr. Byrd and Valerie was bringing their cat or dog in to work with them. Lacey knew that she had started it. When Mrs. Byrd had been living at the farmhouse, she had taken care of Tank during the day. Like any good farmwife, Mrs. Byrd was vigilant about closing gates that needed to be closed. She would watch Tank dash around the fenced portion of the yard and distract him if he looked like he was about to dig his way to freedom. But once Mrs. Byrd fell, Lacey had had to bring him to work. She was often gone for twelve or fourteen hours. A husky would have gone mad if he'd had to spend that long in a crate. So, Valerie's edict was a problem.

"I'm working a short day," Cheri said. "I won't be going in until nine, and I could be home by three if that helps."

Tank could certainly manage six hours. "That would be a huge help."

"I might not be here when you get back, but don't worry," Cheri assured. "I will definitely be here for a while in the afternoon."

Oliver Hammermill was more poised than Brent Carville, and his skills were better. Lacey was impressed with him for at least thirteen, maybe even fourteen minutes. Then she realized that he was a know-it-all. He clearly thought of himself as the smartest person in the room, a far better doctor than the wise and experienced Bill Byrd. He was going to be in for one big surprise when he realized that Mr. Mattson, a high school graduate, knew more about dairy cattle than he did. Not that it was likely he would ever let himself admit it.

Elite, arrogant, and pompous...Washington, DC, might tolerate people like that, but not West Virginia, not for one blessed moment. By the middle of the morning, all the staff except Valerie were rolling their eyes.

During a break in the afternoon schedule, Lacey checked her phone. Cheri had sent her a short video. It showed Tank romping around the yard, his tail bouncing, him sniffing at something with his black nose. He looked so happy. Lacey watched the video again and then passed her phone to Katie. Over Katie's shoulder Lacey watched the video a third time, even though this was something she saw every single day.

She did love her big, fluffy goofball of a dog.

At the end of the day, she was hustling to get out the door as soon as she could, so she was a little annoyed when Valerie stopped her while she was putting her lab coat in the laundry.

"Dr. Byrd might like your thoughts about our candidates," Valerie said.

Might? Of course, he would want her opinion. Dr. Byrd respected her. He trusted her.

"I assume that you will agree," Valerie continued, "that Dr. Hammermill would be an excellent associate."

Dr. Hammermill was today's good-looking know-it-all. "I'll discuss it with Bill tomorrow."

Valerie hated it when Lacey called Dr. Byrd "Bill," even though that was what he wanted Lacey to call him. "But why don't I just tell him? It would save so much time."

Lacey stopped what she was doing and looked straight at Valerie. "Do not ever speak for me. Ever."

Valerie blinked. "But the other one...that mother...we can't have her around."

Because she would have you fired. "Actually, Katie said that if you just buttered her up a little bit, she wasn't that difficult, and she actually had some good ideas about office procedure."

"I don't know that Katie's opinion counts for anything," Valerie sniffed.

If Valerie were fired, Katie would get her job. Except for the banking, Katie already did most of Valerie's job. And if Valerie weren't fired, Katie would almost certainly leave as soon as the resort opened.

But if Dr. Byrd was going to run his business into the ground because he couldn't let a longtime employee go, there was nothing Lacey could do about it.

* * * *

Cheri's little red car was not in the farmhouse drive, but she had warned Lacey that she might not be home. Lacey anticipated that Tank would start howling as soon as he heard her key in the back door.

But he didn't. Even when the door was completely open, the house was quiet. She hurried through the mudroom, not even putting her keys on the hook. Tank wasn't in his crate. She called out for him. The house stayed quiet.

She glanced at the refrigerator. That's where she and Cheri left notes for each other. There was a new one. *Took Tank with me. Don't worry. He'll be fine.*

Fine? Sometimes Lacey would enter an examining room and know, just know, that there was something terribly wrong with the animal. She would never know what it was—she still had to do the exam and run the tests—but the instinct could guide her to greet the client more gently and to give the pet longer to get used to her smell and touch.

Why did she have this feeling now? What could be wrong? Cheri knew perfectly well that Tank had to be kept on his leash at all times and that if he were left alone in the front yard for too long, he would start to dig.

Where could Cheri have gone? She had no idea. The week after the gala, Cheri had mentioned getting a massage for her back, but she had been out last night too. She wouldn't have gotten massages two nights in a row. Lacy called Cheri's cell phone and got the usually cheery recorded greeting. She left a message and then sent a text.

Then she saw that Cheri had left some dishes in the sink. That wasn't like Cheri, not at all. As breezy as her manner was, Cheri was a meticulous housekeeper.

This was strange. Lacey went online and found that there were only two licensed therapeutic massage centers within twenty miles. Neither one listed evening hours, and both telephone numbers were answered with recordings that said to call back in the morning.

What was going on? Where was Tank?

Pete didn't answer his phone. She sent him a text. *Do you know where Cheri and Tank are? Probably just some miscommunication on our part.*

She turned on the water to rinse the dishes that Cheri had left, but she hadn't even opened the dishwasher when her phone rang. It was Pete.

"Is this message right?" He sounded more agitated than Lacey would have expected. "Cheri's missing?"

"I wouldn't call it 'missing.' You don't always know where she is?"

"No, Pete, of course not. I'm not her mother."

"I'll be right out."

"That's not nec—" But he had already disconnected the call.

Her instinct had been right. Something was wrong.

What would she tell clients to do if their dog was missing? Call the shelters, contact Animal Control.

Except there was no point in calling Animal Control. She *was* Animal Control. The part-time warden was away; the calls were being routed to her. There had been no report of a stray dog, and not just *a* dog, but a beautiful copper-and-white husky with glittering blue eyes—*her* dog.

There probably wasn't much point in calling the shelters either. Her cell phone number was on Tank's collar, so if someone had brought him into the shelter, the shelter would have called her.

But she called the closest shelter anyway, then the other two in the county. None of them had Tank.

What else could she do? Go out and look? She wouldn't know where to start. And wasn't she overreacting? Tank hadn't run away; he was with Cheri. She heard a car pull up in the drive, and she went out to the front porch to meet Pete.

Except it was Nate.

"I'm sorry," he said as soon as he was out of his car. "Pete called and asked me to get out here as soon as I could. He said that Cheri's gone AWOL."

"She's not AWOL." Cheri was a grown woman who had decided to go somewhere. That was totally her right. It was Tank who was vulnerable, Tank who had had a decision made for him. "She doesn't need my permission to do anything. It's none of my business where she goes. But she's taken Tank with her, and I like knowing where he is."

"Doesn't she usually tell you where she's going?"

He had a point. Normally Cheri would tell anyone anything. "She has been a little less chatty since the gala, but she hurt her back. She's been resting more."

"Have you checked her room?"

"No, of course not."

But Nate wanted her to, so Lacey went upstairs. She wasn't sure what she was supposed to be looking for. The room looked normal. Cheri's suitcases were there. Her clothes were there. Her cell phone's charge cord was there. Lacey checked the bathroom. It looked in order, except the wicker shelf across from the sink was empty. Cheri's pink cosmetic case was missing.

Where on earth would someone be going with a dog and a makeup bag?

"It's strange," Lacey told Nate. "Her makeup isn't there."

"Has she done this before? Is there a pattern?"

"I don't know."

But once Lacey thought about it, there was a pattern. In the two weeks since she had hurt her back, she had been out both Thursdays and Tuesday of one week and Wednesday of the next.

"Do you think it's a man?" Lacey suddenly felt uneasy. That might explain the cosmetics bag. "What if it is? And here I went and called Pete."

"But why would she take Tank this time? And when would she have met anyone? Everyone in town knows Pete, as do all the guys working at the resort."

That might not make as big a difference to some men as it would have to Nate. "She does crave masculine attention. She grew up without a father. She was even fascinated by the exotic dancers who—"

"Oh, dear God in heaven."

Lacey stared at him. He wasn't being profane. That was close to a prayer.

He was pulling out his phone. "I think I—you go outside and wait for Pete. Let me make some calls."

He turned his back. When she didn't leave, he moved toward the kitchen. Clearly he wanted this call to be private.

She stood on the front steps waiting for Pete. She was too agitated to sit, but when Pete arrived, she tried to greet him evenly. "I'm sorry," she said to him. "I may have stirred up a fuss over nothing. I was just surprised that she took Tank—"

"I thought you were going to look out for her."

"What?" Look out for her? Cheri was an adult. Why did she need looking after? "I have no idea what you are talking about. She's my friend. I care about her, of course, but I also respect her privacy."

"Oh." He looked startled, as if he expected her to know something that she didn't. "Then nothing. Never mind. Where's Nate? Does he know anything?"

"Apparently. He's inside making some calls, but I don't know to who or why."

"What does he know? Tell me."

"You'll have to ask him. I don't know what he knows. I just told you that."

Pete took the three front steps in a single stride and jerked open the screen door, but he had to step back as Nate was trying to get through the door in the other direction.

"She's fine," Nate said, "and she has Tank with her. Neither of you has to worry about anything."

Lacey exhaled. What a relief. And what an idiot she had been to have worried. Of course, Tank was fine. Cheri wouldn't have let anything happen to him. Lacey should have trusted that.

"Where is she?" Pete didn't sound as relieved. "Did you talk to her?"

"I didn't speak to her directly, but she's fine." Nate sounded casual, but Lacey noticed the set of his shoulders. He was tense and trying to hide it. "I'm going to run over there and pick up Tank so Lacey doesn't have to worry."

That was nice of him, but Lacey wanted to go too. "I appreci—"

Pete interrupted. "Where is she? Where is 'there'?"

"Off I-64 near the Virginia line. She's fine. I can—"

"What the hell is she doing there?" Pete demanded.

"This and that." Nate's voice was very calm. He didn't sound like himself at all. "The two of you sit tight. It's an hour there, an hour back. I'll be back in two hours, maybe three. Everything will be fine."

"No." Pete was angrier than Lacey had ever seen him. "You need to stop this bullshit and tell me where my wife is."

"Can you trust me for two hours? And then let her tell you herself."

"No, you tell me now. And you also tell me why *you* know where she is, and I don't."

Nate was shaking his head. He didn't want to answer. Lacey decided to be the peacemaker. "Let's all go inside for a minute and—"

"The two of you have no idea what you're talking about," Pete snapped. His face was flushed; his chin was jutting forward belligerently. He was glaring at Nate. "And you're going to tell me who you just called, and if you won't, I'm taking your phone."

"Oh, come on, Pete, seriously"—Nate had his hands up as if Pete were pointing a gun at him—"can't you wait and let her tell you herself?"

"You may be strong." Pete took another step toward Nate. "But I have had hand-to-hand combat training, and you haven't. You might as well tell me."

Hand-to-hand combat training? Lacey couldn't believe what she was hearing. Would Pete actually attack Nate? She stepped between them and put her hand on Pete's chest, forcing him back. Then she spoke to Nate. "Whatever it is, Nate, he'll find out. It's either you now or Cheri later. The result is the same."

Nate took a breath. "She's at a strip club. I spoke to the bartender."

"What she's doing at a strip club?" Pete demanded.

"And why did she take Tank?"

"Probably for protection," Nate answered Lacey. "The bartender says that she came in with a dog."

Pete ran a hand over his face. "What is my wife doing at a strip club? Why is she there?"

"Oh crap, Pete." Nate clearly didn't want to be the one to say this. "She had a lot of credit card debt that she didn't want you to know about."

"She's there to make *money*?" Lacey had assumed that Cheri must be bored and curious or something, that she had gone in as a patron. "She's actually on the stage strip—dancing?"

"And how did you know about this?" Pete demanded.

Lacey wanted to protest that she hadn't known, but he was talking to Nate. This was about the three of them, these childhood friends, Nate, Pete, and Cheri, and it was something that had been building for years.

"She came to me. I'm sorry, Pete." Nate clearly regretted what he had done. "She made me promise not to tell you. I knew that it was wrong."

"Did you actually give her money? Behind my back?" Pete sounded as if he couldn't believe it.

"I'm sorry. It was a mistake."

"You're damn right it was." Now Pete sounded disgusted. "Jesus, Nate, that's one thing that's always been square about you. You've never acted like a tool because your family had more money that the rest of us. And I thought that you were still like that... It seemed great that you'd managed to make so much without turning into a shit. I was wrong." Pete reached into his pocket for his keys. "Now you'll have to excuse me," he said with sarcastic formality. "I need to go pick up my wife."

"I'm coming too," Lacey said quickly. "I want to get Tank." She didn't want anyone to forget about her dog. "And if you go alone, you'll have two cars there."

"We'll all go," Nate said firmly. "I'll drive."

Lacey got in the back of the Escalade, sitting behind the passenger seat. No one said anything for the first mile or so. Then Pete spoke, his voice tight. "I should explain something, but I don't want you feeling sorry for me."

"I won't," Nate said immediately.

"Yes, you will. You can't help it. You've felt sorry for me since senior year in high school, when you finally got it through your head that there was no way I could go to college, that I had no options except the military. That's why you always called it the 'military,' never the 'service.' But that's what we did, we served our country."

There was a lot of history between the two of them.

"I know that the Army provided you with good opportunities." Nate was back to using his calm, not-Nate voice.

"Like the opportunity to serve, to do something that I could be proud of. You might be pleased with all those medals you got, but how can you be as proud of anything you've done as I am of my service?"

"I can't be." Nate's answer was brief.

You will be someday, Lacey thought, *all the good you are doing here.* But this was not the time to defend Nate.

"Is this what you wanted to tell us, Pete?" she asked instead.

"Oh no…but remember what I said about not wanting to be pitied. I love my wife, and whatever challenges she has are mine too. I made a vow."

"Okay." Lacey supposed that Nate was as bewildered as she was.

"While I was in Afghanistan," Pete continued, "Cheri got in a couple of car accidents and was spending too much money. Her mother took her to some doctors. It turns out that she has a mental health issue. Borderline personality disorder, it's called. They say it comes from an insecure sense of self-identity. Sometimes she would blame her mom and me for everything. Then two days later she would be terrified that we would abandon her because she wasn't good enough."

Lacey's parents had been narcissists. They had blamed other people for everything, but their vulnerability was buried much deeper than Cheri's. The minute someone hinted at possibly disapproving of them, they instantly dismissed that person as unenlightened.

"It's exhausting to live with," Pete continued. "The books describe it as walking on eggshells all the time because you never know how the person will react. That's part of why her mom came to live with us after she sold the salon, to try to diffuse some of Cheri's extreme reactions to me. And I came out here to get a break. We both needed it."

"Have any treatments helped?" Lacey asked.

Pete nodded. "Meds help with the depression and the impulsivity. And she tries, she really does. And, of course, when she is feeling good, when she thinks she is pleasing people, there is no one else like her."

"She can be the single most charming person I have ever met," Lacey said honestly.

"I was going to tell you guys right away, since the only reason her mom and I thought it would be okay for her to come out here was because Nate was here and there'd be someone else watching out for her. But that first night at dinner, when you two took the dogs out, she begged me not to tell you. She was so impressed with you, Lacey. She couldn't bear you knowing."

"I wouldn't have thought any less of her," Lacey murmured.

It was only sixty miles to the state line, but until they reached I-64, the roads were narrow and dark. The day had been cloudy, so daylight was fading quickly. By the time they reached town, the headlights of the Escalade had clicked on, and the streetlamps, neon signs, and security lights were chasing away any sense of a soft twilight.

The strip club was on the south side of town near the railroad tracks. Its big parking lot was lit with the harsh white of mercury vapor lamps. Dirty pickups and aging cars were in the few rows, and four or five semis were parked along the edge, but the lot was only half full. This was not a nice place.

Lacey undid her seat belt. "I'll go in and get her," she said firmly. "And don't say that you're coming. Cheri won't want it to look like she is being extracted by an angry husband."

"That makes sense," Nate agreed and pulled up to the front door to let Lacey out.

There was a small crowd of men gathered around the door. They were in jeans and camouflage vests, ball caps and work shirts; they had goatees, mustaches, or days-old stubble. A few had tattoos snaking up their necks. Probably attracted by how expensive and gleamingly clean the Escalade was, they were all watching as Lacey opened the back door.

"You sure you're going to be okay?" Nate asked.

"Of course."

She knew how to do this. She knew how to carry herself. She was Dr. Berryville. Even without her embroidered lab coat, people knew that she was not to be messed with. The men stepped aside to let her through, and when someone in the back of the crowd started to catcall, she heard the others telling him to shut up.

The bar was dark and noisy. A very large man was standing inside the door, his arms folded. He was wearing a black T-shirt with *SECURITY* emblazoned in white letters. Next to him was a sign about a cover charge. That's probably why the men were gathered outside. They couldn't afford the cover charge.

The bouncer nodded at Lacey, letting her through without paying.

The bar was dark. Most of the light was shining down on an elevated runway thrust out from beyond the bar. Five or six women were up there dancing, slithering, grinding on top of the bar. No wonder Cheri had been stiff and sore after her first shift.

A woman was suspending herself high above the floor on the one stripper pole. She was using only one arm and the muscles of her thighs. Her skin must have been oiled, as the light gleamed against her muscles. She pulsated to the music, slowly gliding her legs into another unnatural position. Lacey was momentarily mesmerized...as were many of the customers.

But she was here to find Cheri. For a moment she thought that Cheri wasn't onstage, but then she saw her in the center back, partly in the spotlight, wearing only a red sequined thong.

Lacey's heart turned over. Cheri was terrible. No wonder they had put her in the back. Her movements were jerky and hesitant, and even with implants, her breasts looked small compared to the other dancers'. She probably was getting very little in tips. She was failing, and she must know it.

Lacey touched a few camo-clad shoulders to get close to the stage. She caught the attention of the dancer closest to her and signaled that she wanted to talk to Cheri.

When Cheri saw Lacey, she stopped dancing, and despite her glittery high heels and naked breasts, she looked like a small child swaddled in heavy makeup.

Lacey put out her hand, and Cheri stumbled against the dancer next to her, almost falling off the stage. Lacey caught her. "Get Tank and your things. The car is outside."

Cheri nodded and scurried toward a side door.

"No, wait." It was the bartender. "She can't leave."

Cheri was already through the door. "Of course, she can."

"Not without paying."

And Lacey got a quick lesson in the economics of a strip club.

The dancers had to pay a fee to be allowed to dance, hoping to pay the fee out of their tips, but the club took on as many women as could be crammed onstage, dramatically reducing each dancer's tips. Cheri was in the hole; her tips hadn't been enough to even cover what she owed the club.

"This sounds like something the National Board of Labor Relations would be interested in," Lacey said without having a clue whether or not they would be. "So, unless you want a call from them…"

"Okay. Okay, go on." The bartender waved a hand. "She didn't have a chance, you know. Unless you can dance like Maria up there, you've got to trick or do lap dances, and she wasn't doing either."

That was something, Lacey supposed…although if this had gone on much longer, would Cheri have started going back to the private rooms at least for a lap dance?

Beyond the side door was the dancers' dressing room, built for two women, crowded with the belongings of many more. Cheri was already dressed. She picked up a canvas bag, the glitter of her shoes winking from the top.

"Where's Tank?" Lacey asked. She hadn't seen him in the hallway. "Why isn't he here?"

"One of the other girls has a dog allergy so they made me tie him up out front."

"Out front? As in outside? You left him *outside*?"

"He's tied up. You tie him up outside Subway sometimes. And I didn't have any choice. They made me do it."

Lacey whirled and started through the club's main room toward the exit even though the bartender had suggesting leaving through the alley. She had to find Tank. Yes, she did sometimes tie him up for a few minutes on Main Street…in daylight…in a town where everyone knew her and him.

Nate and Pete were standing under one of the big lights. Nate was on the phone. Why hadn't they gotten Tank? Lacey looked up and down the front of the building, hoping to see her dog. Cheri brushed by her and started running toward Pete. He stepped forward and held out his arms, pulling her close to him, bending his head over her hair. In the light from the big security lamps, his hands looked strong against her fragile back.

That was loyalty, that was "for better or for worse," that was love.

What would it be like to have that? To feel that safe because there was someone who, whatever you had done, would open his arms?

But where was Tank? Why hadn't Nate and Pete seen him while they were waiting? Pete and Cheri were already walking toward her car, Pete's arm around her, keeping her close.

Nate was still on the phone. Who could he be talking to? Then he extended his free hand. He was holding Tank's leash. Dangling from the end was Tank's collar. She didn't understand. Why would—

The collar was cut. Someone had cut Tank's collar.

Chapter 19

Her hand was at her throat. "Oh my God..."

"It's not good. We asked around. It happened almost three hours ago. Some crazy drunk thought it would be funny. A few guys tried to catch Tank, but he took off."

Tank was loose. Tank had run away. Lacey looked over Nate's shoulders at the road, seeing the lines of headlights whipping by, hearing the grind of the heavy semi as it turned into the lot. What chance would an innocent, goofy, beautiful dog have?

She felt sick. Tank. *Tank.*

"I need you to focus." It was Nate's voice. "How far could he have gone?"

"I don't know. I don't know." Focus. *Focus.* "He's not conditioned like a racing dog, but still, without a load he could probably go fifteen or twenty miles an hour for quite a while. Maybe more. I've never timed him."

"He could be almost home."

She shook her head. "That's not what huskies do."

"Still we need someone to be there. Do you have the Mattsons' number?"

"No. Why would I?"

"Because you can access the clinic database through your phone."

That was right. Katie had logged in a lot of overtime, entering the clients' contact info. Lacey had no idea why Nate wanted to call them, but she fumbled through her purse, looking for her phone. When she found it, she couldn't seem to figure out what to do. She handed it to Nate.

Why would anyone think it fun to take a knife, lean down, and cut a dog's collar? How could this be happening? Just this afternoon she had been watching a video of Tank playing in the front yard.

"Tyler, the high school kid, said that he would go over and wait in case Tank comes home." Nate handed her back the phone a minute later. "He'll stay until we get there."

"But we're going to go look for him, aren't we?" She felt frantic. "We have to."

"Of course, we will. But let's try to be as smart about this as we can." Nate touched her back, guiding her toward the Escalade, opening the passenger door for her. Once he was behind the wheel, he spoke again. "Is Pete right that whatever chip Tank has doesn't have a tracking device?"

She nodded. "It's just for identifying a dog, not for finding one."

"Do you have any sense of what direction he might go?"

"No. It would be completely random. He will want to run. It's not that he's running away. Huskies just love to run. It's what they are bred to do. He won't be going anywhere. He will just be going."

"The roads, fields, neighborhoods, the train tracks?"

"The train tracks?" That was a horrifying thought.

"There wasn't a train today," Nate assured her. "It only comes through three days a week. Two guys came in on ATVs, and they said they would go search along the railroad right-of-way."

"That's not legal," she said automatically, "riding along the railroad tracks."

"Why do you think they were so eager to do it? Now, can you give us any sense about where else to look?"

"I guess he is less likely to run through a neighborhood...although he certainly could. I've tried and tried to train him about moving cars, so he might avoid the highway and busy streets. If I would have to bet, I would say the country roads or the snowmobile trails."

But would he remember her training? Or would the joy of running send him charging down the interstate?

Nate turned on the car, pulled out of the parking lot, and then started making calls. He was using the speakerphone integrated with the Escalade so Lacey could hear. It was clear that this was someone he had already talked to. He wasn't having to explain anything, but he was immediately talking about posting on blogs and putting up signs. "We're not that far from the Greenbrier." The Greenbrier was a grand old resort in the Alleghenies. "Will you call them? My name might do some good... Thanks, Justin, thanks. I'll keep in touch."

"Who was that?" Lacey asked.

"Believe it or not, the photographer at the *Gazette.* He maintains their website, such as it is. He's already reached out to the bloggers around here and up in Pocahontas."

Greenbrier County, Pocahontas County... That was so much space. How would they ever find him?

They took the back roads home, knowing that Pete and Cheri would be watching out on the interstate. Lacey peered out the window into the darkness, foolishly, desperately hoping that she would see a flash of copper and white. Any time there was an open gas station, Nate stopped and left his card.

But no one had seen him.

Ten miles after they crossed the county line, a big SUV with a roof-mounted light bar, all the lamps glaring, came crawling up the road. The light was blinding; Nate had to pull over to the shoulder until it passed.

"That's not legal either," Lacey murmured. "Those lights are only for off-road."

"Yes, but he's probably looking for Tank."

"Really? He's looking for *my* dog? Who is he?"

"I don't know. It could be anybody."

"Yes, but... I mean... How did he find out?"

"I told you. It's been on the websites and the blogs for more than an hour. The Scout troops and at least two of the churches have alerted their members. People around here care about you, Lacey."

Driving on the back roads and stopping at each open gas station meant that they didn't get home until well after ten. All the gates at the farmhouse were open. Lacey knew what that meant. Tyler Mattson was a farm kid, and farm kids knew gates. If Tank had come home and run into the yard, Tyler would have slammed the gates shut.

Three teenage boys were lounging on the front porch. Tyler introduced his friends. The boys all said how sorry they were. "My older brother and his girl are out on their motorcycles," one of them said. "They said they'd stay out all night, and when they have to go to work, we can use their bikes to keep looking."

Lacey murmured her thanks. This desperate clawing anxiety, the helplessness, and then this bewildering sense of gratitude... It was too much.

"It's great," the boy continued happily. "He's never let me use his bike before."

Once again it was strange to go into such a quiet house. Cheri's note was still on the refrigerator. *Don't worry,* it read. *He'll be fine.*

How could Cheri have written that and then left him tied up in front of a seedy strip club?

"Where do you think Pete and Cheri went?" she asked.

"My place. I called Mrs. Fischer and asked her to let them in."

"Good. I mean, thank you. I'm not quite ready to see her."

"No. She would spend a lot of time trying to persuade you that she hadn't done anything wrong."

"But she did. You know that, don't you?" Lacey wanted him to agree. Surely, he wouldn't dare defend Cheri.

"Indeed, she did. I'm still trying to wrap my mind around her having this mental disorder, but I called her mother, and—"

"You called her mother? Why did you do that?"

"You heard Pete. Paula's a part of this, trying to help Cheri manage her situation."

Lacey shook her head. She was not used to mothers being part of the solution. In her experience, mothers created the problems. She didn't know what to say, so she changed the subject. "How did you know about the strip club?"

"Because Cheri asked me about them twice, whether I'd ever been in one. Now, I'm going to start some coffee. Do you want any?"

"We're going back out, aren't we?" She hadn't thought this through. They should have asked Tyler or one of his friends to spend the night at the house.

"No, we aren't," he said flatly. "You're in no shape to do anything except get yourself in a car accident, and frankly I am a lot more useful coordinating things here."

"Coordinating? The people on the motorcycles and all?"

"I called Ben. He's setting up an interactive map so people can trace what roads and trails they've searched. As soon as he has it done, Justin will post it on the *Gazette*'s website."

Ben? Justin? Oh right. His snowboarding friend and the *Gazette* photographer. "I don't believe this. I didn't know people would do this much even for a missing child?"

"They'd do more for a child. You'd get helicopters for a kid. And the sheriff and the police department. The authorities can't spend tax dollars on a dog, so it's all just people wanting to help."

"Does Fred Kayot mind us using his website this way?"

"I'm not sure that Justin cares. The website will get more traffic tonight than it does in a month. Now, Lacey, I know that this is tough advice, but is there any way you could sit down and relax?"

"No."

"What about just sitting down? Can you manage that? And no, not here, where you can look over my shoulder, but in the big chair in the living room?"

"I can manage that."

But she couldn't. Five minutes later she was back on her feet, in the kitchen. "I have to do something, Nate."

"Then help me think. If Tank does have the sense to keep away from moving cars, then we need to search in the open fields. How are we going to do that? With all this rain we've had, the ATVs are going to get stuck, and tractors are too slow. Do we have any other options?"

Lacey pictured Tank running joyfully through a field, his tail up, his legs stretching out, his spine gliding smoothly. "Horses," she said suddenly; they were the other animals she could picture running through a field like that.

"Okay, good. Where can we find horses by tomorrow morning?"

"There's a dude ranch an hour north of here, but this is their peak season. They aren't going to have any horses or riders to spare."

"Do they know you?"

"Actually, yes. I take care of their horses."

"Okay, then. Let me call them."

"But asking people for favors like this, that makes me uncomfortable." It was one thing to put out an appeal on the Internet; people could ignore that. But a one-on-one request... Didn't that put people on the spot too much?

"You want Tank back, don't you?" Nate asked.

Yes, she did. She sat down across from Nate, her hands folded on the table in front of her.

The owner of the ranch, used to making himself heard over barn noises, had a loud voice. Lacey could hear both sides of the conversation. His wife had already told him about Dr. B's dog being missing; they were wondering what they could do.

Nate outlined the situation while Lacey frantically whispered that he should say that she knew that this was peak season and that—

The owner dismissed the concern. "An actual emergency will thrill some of our guests. They love the idea that we truly do need to put them to work."

He went on to say that he would load the horses into vans first thing in the morning, but at some point, he would need more precise directions. "I don't mind trespassing for a good cause, but not on a wild-goose chase."

"As soon as I have anything, I will let you know," Nate promised.

"But what if we don't hear anything?" Lacey asked as he ended the call.

He reached out and covered her hand with his. "You can't think that way, Lacey. You just can't."

But how could she help it?

"If you're going to go to work in the morning," he continued, "you need to get some sleep."

She shook her head. "I can't leave. What if Tank comes home?"

"Someone will be here. If not me, someone."

She supposed that she needed to set an example. The world didn't end because a dog had run away. She could still do her job.

Except right now it did feel as if her world were ending.

She slept a little, but not much. When she came down in the morning, Nate was still at the kitchen table, but he was asleep, his head down on his crossed arms, the overhead light gleaming against his rumpled hair. At the sound of her footsteps, he jerked awake, rubbed his hand across his face, and pressed a key on his computer, then another one. He shook his head. No news.

She made coffee and went upstairs to shower and dress. There was still no news when she came back down. She went to the refrigerator to get something to eat, but the sight of Cheri's note made her stomach churn.

It was strange not to have Tank to feed, Tank to let out, Tank to shove into the rear of the Silverado's cab. He always wanted to sit in the front... and not just in front, but in her lap. She could have barely reached around him to the steering wheel if he had crawled onto her side of the truck. She certainly couldn't have seen over him. But he wouldn't have cared about that.

Don't you miss me? Don't you wish you were home?

She was a mile outside town when her phone rang. It was Nate.

He started speaking right away. "Someone saw him an hour ago."

"He's alive?" Last night she had known in her heart that if someone did find Tank in the dark, it would have been his body. But he was alive. Someone had seen him alive.

Just after dawn a farmer had heard a noise out by his garbage cans. When he had looked out his window to check, he saw a white and reddish dog that ran off the instant he opened his back door. The man's lands were along the border between Greenbrier and Pocahontas Counties just outside the Monongahela National Forest. Tank must have run north up the Greenbrier River Trail.

"He's going to be hungry," she said, "running all that way. Maybe if a couple of people would put out some food..."

Tank had never gone without food, even though he had often acted as if she had tried to starve him to death. He had never had to forage. How would he be able to take care of himself?

And how could she ever think of moving to Illinois while he was still in West Virginia?

Most of the stories of dogs walking five hundred miles to return to their owners were Internet fairy tales, embellished and sentimentalized. And they were never about huskies. Lacey knew that. But...but...what if he came back to the farmhouse and she wasn't there?

* * * *

Her first client brought her a loaf of banana bread.

Lacey was almost speechless. "Thank you." The bread was wrapped in plastic wrap and tied with blue curly ribbon.

"I wish we could do more to help you find your dog. We can barely trust our cars to get into town. But I wanted to do something."

"This is nice of you, I appreciate it."

She had told Katie that unless someone caught Tank—which would be very hard since he wasn't wearing a collar —she didn't want any updates on the search. She needed to be able to focus on her work.

But the clients kept telling her. The dude ranch had loaded up their horses and were sending them toward Pocahontas. Two men from one of the construction crews had spotted him from their ATVs. They had given chase and tried to corner him along a hog wire fence—which, if Tank had been a more aggressive dog, might have been a terrible idea—but the ever-cheerful Tank had thought it was a game, and of course he won, darting away.

That was going to be the issue, actually catching him. Someone could have their hand on him, but there would be nothing to grab on to. Even if you managed to get your arms around him, he was strong and would have momentum on his side. He would be able to squirm free from almost any grip.

Katie told her that Mrs. Byrd had called. This was one call Lacey had to return. Tank had been her dog too.

"I can't believe how nice everyone is being," Lacey said after they had commiserated.

"That's how Forrest used to be. People like getting excited. When we got the levees, it took all the fun out of a rainstorm. We used to fuss endlessly about being flooded. And the high school football season was all anybody talked about. Your Nate Forrest has been trying, but people need something to rally around. And the construction workers are involved looking for Tank. That's nice, them caring."

Yes, it was, but Lacey was surprised at Mrs. Byrd's reference to Nate. "He's not 'my' Nate Forrest," she protested. "He's a friend, that's all."

"And you're telling me he hasn't noticed how pretty you are? Oh, but I know you. You don't want to talk about it."

That was certainly true.

Lacey had a few minutes before her next appointment. Most of the messages on her phone were good wishes from people who had heard about Tank. There was one from Nate. The volunteers from the living history museum were taking over sitting at the house. He, too, was heading over to Pocahontas.

Then there was a message from Pete. *We've got Cheri's stuff cleared out of the farmhouse. Heading back to Frederick now. Dan P. will take over the kennel. We're praying for Tank. Wish I could have said good-bye.*

Cheri was leaving. And Pete too. He was leaving his job with all its benefits and authority, walking away from a huge end-of-job bonus, to do what was right for his wife...because if it were right for her, it was right for him too.

Lacey was putting her phone back in her pocket when another call came through. It was Nate. "I suppose there's no news," she sighed, not even greeting him.

"No. I've got him, right here—"

"What?" She sat up. "You have him? Tank? Where? How? Are you kidding?"

"Of course, I am not kidding. He's dirty, smelly, and sound asleep, but he seems okay. I can hold the phone up if you want to hear him breathe."

"No, no. But really? You have him? You found him?"

"It was a group effort. I'll tell you all about it later. Where shall I go? Farmhouse or the clinic?"

"Farmhouse. I want him there. I want him home."

Home. The farmhouse was home.

Katie and Stephanie were at the door to the break room. They had heard. They knew.

"Go home," Katie said. "We'll make it work. Everyone will understand."

Lacey started pulling her lab coat off. "Will you call Mrs. Byrd?"

Tank was coming home. Tank was coming home.

As she passed the cemetery, an oncoming car started honking and flashing its lights. The passenger shouted happily at her as she passed. It must be one of the museum volunteers, leaving the farmhouse. The news must already be up on the website.

Nate wasn't there yet. She went in through the back door as usual.

An unfamiliar Crock-Pot was sitting on the kitchen counter; three flat pans covered in foil were next to it. A piece of masking tape across the glass lid of the Crock-Pot read *MATTSON*. Lacey lifted the lid, and the vinegar tang of a barbecue sauce rose upward. She peeked under the foil that covered the pans. There was a chocolate cake, lasagna, and some kind of green bean dish, each from a different family. She opened the refrigerator. There were two disposable plastic containers that hadn't been there this morning.

People had brought her food. She would never, ever be able to eat this much, especially as she was leaving in three weeks, but the idea was so... so heartwarming. She couldn't think of another word for it.

Several times Mrs. Byrd had asked her to get out the heavy old Mixmaster so that Mrs. Byrd could make a buttermilk cake for someone. Lacey was going to find that recipe and take it with her. In her next job, she was going to be the sort of person who took other people buttermilk cakes.

Nate would be coming from the east, and the house faced west. Lacey put an extra dog collar by the front door and went upstairs to the back bedroom. She looked out the window down the straight county road, waiting. A blue sedan. A white minivan. Then nothing for a moment, and finally a smudge of black cresting the hill. She flew downstairs and grabbed the extra collar. She was already through the gate when Nate pulled up. She cupped her hands to peer through the back window. Tank was fast asleep. Not even the car stopping had woken him up.

She opened the door and took hold of the bungee cord that was looped around his neck. That woke him up. When he saw her, he tried to scramble to his feet. His tail started wagging madly, slamming into the seat of the car; he thrust his muzzle into her neck. He was happy to see her.

"Oh, you horrible, horrible dog." She struggled to fasten the collar around his neck. "Do you have any idea what you put me through? You should feel so guilty."

But he didn't. He had enjoyed his day of running, and now he was home and happy to see her. She would feed him, she would scratch his belly and play with his ears, then she would let him go back to sleep. After that she would feed him again. Who wouldn't be happy?

Nate had the gate open. She marched Tank through, her hand on his collar and her thigh against his flank. As soon as Nate closed the gate, she let go of the collar, but Tank stayed beside her as if he were the most faithful Saint Bernard, determined to escort her safely through a mountain pass. What a hypocrite he was.

She took him to the front steps and ran her hands over him, checking for swellings and cuts, feeling the steady beat of his heart. She looked at his pads. They were going to need some attention. And he was remarkably dirty, thanks to last week's rain. Mud had dried and crusted, acting like hair gel to leave parts of his coat clumped into stiff spikes.

He tried to squirrel himself onto her lap. She pushed him away. Flecks of dried mud sprinkled her shirt and her jeans. He stretched his muzzle out across her thighs and twisted his body around her like a mud-caked pretzel.

Nate was standing on the walk, watching. He was still wearing the khakis and blue shirt he had been wearing last night, but now the khakis were filthy, all along the front and especially inside the thighs, along the inseam. At some point he must have had Tank clamped between his legs. He would have used the strength of his arms and legs, the power of his entire body. Once Nate had Tank, he would have never, not ever, let her dog go. She knew that with all her heart.

"I may be furious with this beast," she said, feeling Tank's heavy breathing against her, "but I can't thank you enough. Who found him? How did it happen?"

"There were a couple of us. It was a group effort. You once said he liked to run through windbreaks."

"I did? When would I have said that?" She had no idea whether Tank liked windbreaks or not.

"When you were talking about taking him out on the sled. You said that he liked the windbreaks."

"I had forgotten about that."

"After we circulated that idea, some riders from the ranch saw him running broken field patterns through a stand of trees. I was nearby, and they were able to keep near him until I got there."

"But how did you catch him? Did he come to you because he knew you?"

"That helped, but I didn't catch him. He caught me. I decided that everyone chasing him had probably seemed like a game. So I got his attention and started running the other way. He came after me."

"So you stopped trying to catch him? That's so—"

"So out of character? Yes, my dad would say that it goes against all my warrior instincts. But it gets better. After running away like a total coward, I pretended to fall down, and I lay there like a completely worthless human being. He came up to see what was going on, and for once, I actually did have treats in my pocket. He came close enough for me to grab him. But

I was using my arms and my legs to hold him. I couldn't have gotten off the ground and secured him without help from the riders."

Who else could have done this? Who else would have remembered about the windbreaks? And what man, strong enough to hold on to a squirming mass of dense canine muscle, would have thought to become so passive? Physically powerful men couldn't do that; they were too used to relying on their strength.

And perhaps last March, Nate Forrest couldn't have done that either. Last March he would have trusted his body, his speed, his muscle, more than any other part of himself. Now he knew that he could calculate and plan.

You do have the person who will open his arms whenever you need him. She had told him that she didn't want to see him again, and yet he had stepped forward do the one thing that no other person could have done.

And she was thinking of leaving him?

"I don't know what to say." She knew that sounded lame, but it was the truth. "Your remembering about the windbreaks. I would have never thought about that."

"The night after the gala I went back home and swore I was going to think back and remember everything you had ever said to me. I wasn't going to forget again."

Lacey's breath caught, but before she could speak, he went on, getting out his phone as he spoke. "You aren't going to love this, but we should post a picture of you and Tank, just to let everyone know how grateful you are."

She was grateful, there was no doubt about that. So she prodded Tank and tried to get him to pose on the steps, thinking to go for the classic dog-person head shot with the person having both arms around the dog's neck so that the two faces were nearly level.

It was a spectacular failure, and Nate took pictures the whole time. There were pictures of Tank blocking her face, of her twisting away as he tried to lick her on the ear, of her with one arm out trying to get her balance while he was squirming over her. They were very happy, very unflattering pictures.

"Oh, go ahead and post them all," she said. "I hope you'll stay for dinner, but I need to take him around to the hose. There's no way I'm letting him into the house like this."

"I'm not much cleaner than he is."

"You know where the shower is. You know where the sweats are."

But he stayed outside and helped her with Tank, holding one of Tank's paws off the ground while she shampooed him. That kept Tank off-balance enough that he couldn't shake his coat and spray them with water. But they both still managed to get wet.

Half an hour later, they were clean and sitting at the kitchen table just as they had been last March. He was wearing the same sweatshirt that he had taken off to make love to her.

Had it been making love? Maybe not quite, but there had been warmth and affection. It had been more than "having sex."

They were both tired and at first didn't say much, but eating gave them enough energy to talk about Pete and Cheri. Pete had called Nate on his way out of town.

"I knew them leaving had to happen," Nate said, "just not so soon."

"It was the right thing, at least for them."

"Are you worried about me? I'll be okay. It won't be as much fun as when the three of you were here, but I have ideas, things that will keep me busy after the stores and museums are up and running. I'll be fine."

"But I won't be."

He drew back. "What are you talking about? Why won't you be okay? I thought being a survivor was what you did."

How well he knew her. "But I've never lost as much as I would be losing now—the clinic, the way everyone helped to find Tank, and you. I've never lost anything like you before."

"Me?"

"This morning I felt like I couldn't leave West Virginia because my dog might still be here. So how could I think about leaving without ever having given us the kind of chance you wanted us to have? I want to believe that someday I can do for you all that you have just done for me."

"Oh Lacey…" He shut his eyes, then pressed his fingertips to his forehead, tenting his hands over his face, hiding his emotion. "You already have." His voice was muffled by his hands. "You already have."

"By turning you away last spring? I didn't do that to help you."

He uncovered his face. "But that's what happened. Everything I have been doing has been in hopes of getting you to respect me."

That was almost certainly an exaggeration, but Lacey wasn't going to quibble. "I want to work for you when Dr. Byrd is ready to sell the clinic. It will be hard—"

"No, it won't." He sat up, his voice eager. "Why would it be? Are you worried about me bullying you? I won't do that. I promise. You believe that, don't you?"

"Not for a second," she said mildly. "You come on strong, Nate Forrest. That's who you are. But I'm not scared of that anymore. You push me, I'll push back. I have the tools to stand up for myself."

"Tools? You are not talking about that bronzini thing, are you? The one you rip off a cow's nuts with?"

He was talking about the Burdizzo. "No, stupid. Bronzino is a fish. I was talking about emotional tools and emotional resources."

"I don't know what those are either," he said, masculine to the core. "But I want to be clear about something. Is this only about Dr. Byrd's practice and West Virginia being 'almost heaven'? Or I am part of the equation too?"

"You are. I don't know what the equation adds up to. I don't even know what variables we are solving for, but there is an equation with both of us in it."

"You do know that you're better at math than me, don't you?"

"I can calculate in my head better, but you understand finance a lot more than I do. And speaking of that—"

She was concerned about his parents. He had promised them that he would not use his own money for any of the ventures in Forrest, but if he was going to buy out Dr. Byrd, he would probably have to guarantee the loans with his own assets.

"I talked to them before I mentioned it to you. They thought it might not be the best investment, but they could see how it was good for the town. My dad was concerned that if you decided to move on, I'd have to hire another vet, but my mom wasn't worried about that."

"She wasn't? Why not? It seems like a valid concern to me."

"She figured we'd get married sooner or later."

"*Married?* Wait, Nate, no. That's so far ahead of everything. I just said I'd give our relationship a chance, that I'd go to cocktail parties with you. Marriage. No. Why would she ever say that?"

"Ben said something to his mom, and she read a whole bunch between the lines. Then Ben's mom said something to my mom, and she read even more into it. That's what happens in normal families, Lacey."

She didn't know enough about normal families, about mothers who cared. "No, seriously, Nate, we are so far from thinking about marriage. Really."

* * * *

But whatever Dr. Lacey Berryville was or was not willing to think about, the town of Forrest was soon talking as if everything was settled.

Old Mrs. Byrd was the first to offer to pay for Lacey's wedding dress.

"I don't want to seem disrespectful or ungrateful," Lacey said, "but we aren't talking about getting married. We aren't engaged or anything like that."

"That's only because he doesn't have a ring yet," Mrs. Byrd said briskly. "And you need to tell him to get one that is bezel set. Then you won't have to take it off at work because the stone is set down and it won't snag on things."

Lacey wasn't sure what to say. She had no idea what a bezel was. It sounded like something from Harry Potter. "I didn't realize you knew that much about jewelry."

"Oh, I don't know a thing. Another one of the ladies here, her daughter was visiting from Charlottesville. And they know about those things there."

Another resident...a daughter in Charlottesville... Lacey did not want to know how the subject of her possible engagement ring had come up.

When Nate suggested that she take a Sunday off so they could go spend the day at the Greenbrier Resort, a jeweler was waiting for them at one of the little shops. His tray did indeed contain a number of rings with sleek, contemporary bezel settings...even though Nate said that he was frightened of words that started with *b* and had a *z* in them.

"Like 'blintz'?" Lacey asked. "My seventy-four-point Scrabble word?"

She called her brother that night, and the next day he and Tim were trying to rearrange their schedules to come to West Virginia and meet Nate. They also wanted to buy her dress, an offer they had to soon rescind. When she heard about the engagement, Tim's mother said—not for the first time—that Lacey was the closest thing to a daughter that she would ever have. She would consider it a privilege to buy the dress. She could come to West Virginia or Lacey could come to Chicago so they could shop together.

Lacey, still a little too risk-averse for a woman about to marry Nate Forrest, went with the sure thing, Tim's mother.

The wedding couldn't be elaborate, as Lacey and Nate decided to have it on Columbus Day weekend. No one had time to fret about matching the votive candles to the save-the-date cards. Valerie, the clinic's soon-to-be former office manager, was so terrified that she wouldn't be invited to the wedding that as soon as she learned the date, she announced to anyone and everyone that she and her husband were planning a big trip. She didn't want their absence at the festivities to be a mark of great social shame. It turned out that she did receive one of the heavy cream envelopes, but it was too late. She and her husband were stuck going on a vacation that they didn't want and couldn't afford.

Nate asked his brother to be his best man. Pete and his two snowboarding friends were the other groomsmen. Lacey's brother walked her down the aisle, and Nate's little nieces, ecstatic in their fluffy white dresses, were the flower girls. She had three bridesmaids: Nate's sister, Katie, and—despite her fussing and fussing—the secretly delighted Mrs. Byrd, wheelchair and all. Lacey's honor attendant, looking exquisite in a dress that Tim's mother had bought, was Cheri.

West Virginia can be beautiful in October—the cool mountain air, the trees glowing on the hillsides, the crisp apples. But it isn't always. So what happened on Lacey and Nate's wedding day?

It snowed. A lot. Lacey had to tromp from the car to Nate's childhood church with snow boots under her wedding gown. Out-of-town guests arrived so late that they had to come straight to the church, taking their seats in whatever they had happened to have worn on the plane. The beautiful wedding cake didn't make it across the mountains from Charlottesville; the church ladies made sheet cakes.

But the snow boots were more comfortable than the strappy little shoes Lacey changed into, and the sheet cakes were fresher than the bakery one would have been. Why should a little snow worry anyone? There was one thing about snow. It was going to melt.

Don't miss the next book in the Standing Tall series

by

Kathleen Gilles Seidel,

due out in November 2019.

Autumn's Child

Turn the page and enjoy a peek at an excerpt of

Ben and Colleen's romance!

Available at your favorite e-retailer!

Chapter 1

Mrs. Norton W. Ridge IV could name every bride in town who had given birth to a "premature" baby seven months after the wedding. She never forgot who had fallen in arrears on their country club dues. And the young man who had come to tee off in baggy cargo shorts...wouldn't his grandfather be rolling in his grave right now, just *rolling*? Mrs. Ridge, the former Miss Eleanor Alexandria Burchell, was a good old-fashioned Southern...ah...difficult woman with exacting standards and an unforgiving spirit.

"Why are people so afraid of her?" a granddaughter's boyfriend had asked.

"She's lonely," the granddaughter had answered, trying to explain what she wasn't willing to say, that her grandmother was a sharp-tongued, rich old lady who had chosen being powerful over being loved.

Mrs. Ridge had spent her married life in Carlsville, Georgia, a once well-mannered town north of Atlanta. Like many small towns in the South, Carlsville had faded. The young people moved to Atlanta. The country club first opened its restaurant to nonmembers, then the golf course, and finally it had to shut its doors altogether. Miss Dessy's Shop for Ladies closed. The Ridges were the only one of the old families who had held on to their money. Eleanor Ridge had accepted the impoverishment of her town, the declining affluence of her friends, and her own aging with matriarchal grace. Wasn't decay the natural course of things in the South?

What Mrs. Ridge had proved unable to endure was the reverse, the sudden improvement in the town's economy. A massive pork-processing plant had gone up on the grounds of the country club, running two shifts a day, providing many, many jobs. New people came to town; new stores opened; all the rental properties were taken. There was money in town. Homeowners were getting ahead of their own bills by leasing out rooms in their basements. The high school football team had new uniforms; the public library had money to buy new books.

But it wasn't elegant money. The country club was not reopening; Miss Dessy's Shop for Ladies remained shuttered.

The new people were immigrants, speaking languages that Mrs. Ridge did not understand. The new grocery store stocked foods she had never seen. She could not pronounce the names of the people serving on the school board and the town council. The town had better suited her when it was fading, when the paint on the white porches weathered and peeled, when the wisteria vines grew thick and heavy and the honeysuckle toppled the fences.

But the rusty cars with loud mufflers, the plywood skateboard ramps, the Catholics renting space in the Baptist church for their ever-growing Sunday school offended her. Her friends were moving to the city to live with their grown children, but Mrs. Ridge had more resources and options than they did. She announced that she would start living year-round at her summer home in the Blue Ridge Mountains of Virginia. She was still invited to bridge luncheons up there. The historic inn in the nearby village still had white tablecloths in the dining room, and its parking valet always retrieved her car first, even if other people were waiting in line. Up there she was still treated as she expected to be.

Her daughter and her older son had objected to the expense involved. The house would have to be winterized, a first-floor bath installed. Mrs. Ridge had replied that she was not accountable to them for how she spent her money. They had fretted about how many valuables she would be leaving in the vacant Georgia house. She responded by taking everything with her. Two interstate moving vans carried boxes of china figurines and chests of sterling silver flatware. Rugs were rolled and swaddled in plastic. Artwork was boxed in custom-built wood crates. Less than half of this would ever get unpacked.

Her lawyers, Timothy Healy and his son Ryan, had wanted to do an inventory of those valuables while they were being packed. Mrs. Ridge's will had a years-old, pages-long attachment listing individual family heirlooms. The Healys wanted to be sure that the items on the list could be matched up with the actual possessions. Mrs. Healy announced that that was nonsense. Surely everything was still there—why would anyone in the family have ever sold anything?—and as for knowing what was what, who couldn't tell a Dresden Rose fruit bowl from a Les Cinq Fleurs vegetable dish?

She had arrived at the lake in late December and quickly realized that the ladies she had played bridge with weren't there. They were summer residents, just as she used to be. She had no one to lunch with, no one to complain about, no one to bully. By March, out of isolation she would never admit to, she announced to the Healys that she was agreeable to an inventory. But no, they couldn't hire someone local. How could she be expected to have a stranger in the house? They needed to send someone she knew, someone she could sit down to dinner with.

She had spent more than eighty years making sure that she got her way. She wasn't going to stop now.

* * * *

Of Mrs. Ridge's three children and six grandchildren, only one, her younger son's daughter Colleen, had any sympathy for her.

"Try to understand," Colleen said to the two friends she had invited to spend spring break with her at her grandmother's lake house. "She will criticize you for violating rules of etiquette that you never knew existed, but it will make her happy."

"I don't like the sound of this," Colleen's fellow teacher Amanda said from the front seat of the car. "I'm from Missouri. We have character, not manners."

Amanda's boyfriend, Jason, was driving. "You two teach in a private school." Jason worked in the fund-raising office of the University of Virginia. "What could be worse than private school parents?"

"My grandmother can be."

"And we teach in a parochial school," Amanda corrected. "Our families are nice. At least most of them."

* * * *

Ben Healy looked out his window on Friday afternoon. Mrs. Ridge had assigned him a room at the front of the house, and he could see the driveway that curved down to the fortress of spruce, white birch, and aspen trees that protected the property from the stares of passing motorists. He would be able to see the car drive up.

This was some kind of crap-ass joke.

Ben had been a professional snowboarder, having had sponsors since he was a young teen. He'd had a great run, he and his two closest friends training together as kids, sharing a chalet at a resort in Oregon while competing as adults. But he was realistic enough to know when he had peaked. Having always been analytical and interested in details and systems, and being one of the few snowboarders with a college degree, he had done a "boot camp" in software engineering and was now working on a master's degree in cybersecurity.

The program was mostly online; he had a lot of flexibility about timing and location. The faculty did take a spring break, so he decided to take a week off as well. He had offered to go down to Georgia and help his family for a week. He had assumed that he might be cleaning out the garage, scanning old files at the law firm, or taking the nieces and nephews into Atlanta to go to the zoo. But his mom had said that her garage was clean. His dad and brother said that if he truly wanted to help, he could supervise the inventory of an elderly client's valuables. She wanted someone from the family to come. Ben said that he could do that.

Oh, and she was now living in her summer place in southwestern Virginia.

That was okay. Ben had nothing against southwestern Virginia.

And the client was Mrs. Ridge.

Mrs. Ridge was a piece of work, but if they needed him, he would go.

Then his father said, "And there's no reason to think that Colleen would be there."

Wait. What? "Why would Colleen be there?"

"I just said that there was no reason that she would be."

"Yes, but you said it. If there really was no reason to think she would be there, if she were off in the Peace Corps or manning a mission to Mars, you wouldn't have said anything at all."

"She lives in Charlottesville. She teaches French at a high school there."

Charlottesville was about ninety minutes from Mrs. Ridge's new home. There were suddenly all kinds of reasons why she might be there.

Snowboarders need to be fearless; it helps if they are insanely so. Apparently, leaving the pro circuit had robbed Ben of his manly courage. He checked Charlottesville's public school calendar. Their spring break was a week after Mrs. Ridge was commanding his presence. If Colleen was coming, it would be after he had left. Mrs. Ridge probably wanted to spread out her visitors.

When he arrived, he had been greeted at the door by an elegant woman who introduced herself as Leilah; she was Mrs. Ridge's "house manager." Ben had no idea what a house manager did. He had never heard of such a job. Mrs. Ridge was resting, Leilah said. She would show Ben to his room. She waved him toward the wide front staircase, but she didn't offer to take his suitcase. Apparently house managers weren't footmen.

"We're expecting the other houseguests to arrive shortly," she said as they reached the landing. "Mrs. Ridge's granddaughter is bringing two friends with her."

Granddaughter? Ben forced himself to take a breath. There were two granddaughters, weren't there? Colleen had a female cousin. Ben couldn't remember her name. Maybe it was her.

No, it wasn't her, whatever her name was. Colleen was the only one of her generation who ever paid Mrs. Ridge any attention. But what about the school calendar? Spring break wasn't supposed to start until a week from Monday.

For the public schools. He hadn't thought about checking the private school calendars. She could be teaching at a private school or a parochial one. The Ridges in Georgia had been Episcopal for generations, but Colleen and her brothers had been raised in Chicago as Catholics. She could be teaching in a Catholic school with a different schedule.

So she was coming. He was a big boy, wasn't he? He could handle it. What was the big deal? They had only had a summer fling four years ago. It hadn't lasted. End of story.

Except Ben's friends, especially the two guys he had grown up training with, hadn't let it go. Everyone had adored Colleen. And not just Seth and Nate, but all three families too. His family had known Colleen her whole life. Nate's parents, Mr. and Mrs. Forrest, had been employing her at their resort that summer, and they thought she was just as marvelous as Ben's own family did. Seth's family, the Streets, had never met her, so you might think that they wouldn't have a strong opinion, but the three moms talked to each other way too much, and so the Streets also thought that Colleen was the torch on the top of the Statue of Liberty.

When you were with a woman like that, after a while you started to wonder what she was doing with you. Why would Colleen Ridge, glowing and vibrant, gifted at languages, stick around with a guy like him?

He must be fooling her, he finally concluded. She must not realize that he wasn't as good of a snowboarder as Seth and Nate. He didn't have Seth's style or Nate's muscle. He had as many medals as they did because he was consistent. On his own, he could earn bronze medal after bronze medal; silver and gold came only when someone else screwed up. He had as many sponsors as anyone, but only because the sponsors liked the way he looked in their clothes, not because little kids wanted to grow up and be Ben Healy. His green eyes and Irish cheekbones were more valuable than his McTwists.

Surely Colleen would dump him the minute she saw the real him.

It had been easier to be a jerk.

Once the summer had ended and he was back on the pro circuit and she was on the East Coast, he had become the Disappearing Boyfriend from Hell. He would return her phone calls with a text. He would wait two days before answering her texts. He would discourage her from coming to events, saying that all the spectators would be drunk. He would answer all of her questions with monosyllables, and when she would push, trying to recapture the magic of the summer, he would say even less. Then he would lie and say that everything was fine, that nothing had changed. Of course, she had eventually broken up with him. He hadn't given her much choice.

He cringed at the memory of how badly he had behaved. He tried not to think about that time. It wasn't Colleen he dreaded meeting, but the person he had been to her, the self-defeating, self-sabotaging moron. Of all the things that good Catholic boys had to feel guilty about, Colleen Ridge was what brought him the most guilt.

Don't miss the next Stand Tall novel

by

Kathleen Gilles Seidel

in

November 2019!

AUTUMN'S CHILD

will be available at your favorite

retailers and e-retailers.

Don't miss Ben and Colleen's story!

Printed in Great Britain
by Amazon